SHADOWS

OVER

HEMLOCK

E.A. Copen

Grim Cat Press LLC

Grim Cat Press LLC
Bowling Green, Kentucky

This is a work of fiction. Names, persons, places, and incidents are all used fictitiously and are the imagination of the author. Any resemblance to persons living or dead, events or locales, is coincidental and non-intentional, unless otherwise specifically noted.

© E.A. Copen 2020

First Edition

Cover design: Covers by Christian

Edited by: Edited AF

SHADOWS OVER HEMLOCK

Book 1 of FELIX CROSS

ISBN: 978-1-7353290-0-0

Shadows Over Hemlock

For tomorrow's children. May they grow up to be better than us.

"...We do not wrestle against flesh and blood, but against the rulers, against the authorities, against the cosmic powers over this present darkness, against the spiritual forces of evil in the heavenly places."

Ephesians 6:12

Every year, hundreds of exorcisms are held in private homes all over the world. While church attendance has declined significantly in recent years, requests for exorcisms have increased. In response to the flood of calls, The Vatican trains roughly 250 new exorcists per year.

As of 2020, there is still a worldwide shortage of exorcists.

CHAPTER ONE

Whoever said that possession was nine-tenths of the law probably didn't mean demonic possession, but that didn't make him any less right.

Judge Turney wiped sweat from his bright red forehead as he bent over one of his marble countertops across from me. They called him "The Bulldog" in legal circles. At first, I'd assumed that had to do with his no-nonsense demeanor. He had a hell of a reputation in the courtroom. After watching him piss himself during a simple exorcism, and afterward pull out his checkbook with a trembling hand, I decided the nickname had come from the way his jowls hung. The whole "tough on crime" act was a façade.

The judge clicked the end of his ballpoint pen and put it to the carbon paper in front of him. "How much did you say?"

"Two-fifty."

He looked up from the checkbook. "For a prayer and a little water smeared on her forehead?"

"No, that was the first hundred," I clarified. "The

other one-fifty keeps it out of the papers."

"What a scam," he mumbled, turning back to his checkbook.

It wasn't like he couldn't afford it. His Lincoln Park home was worth a cool half-million easy, even in the current economy. With all the bribes he took, the backroom deals made, his investments, and his salary, two hundred and fifty measly bucks was nothing. He just didn't like the idea of giving it to me. The cheap bastard was lucky I didn't slap a fifty-dollar asshole tax on the back of it.

"Cash," I added, sticking my hands into the pockets of my oversized coat. "Unless the L ticket machines are suddenly taking checks."

Judge Turney glanced up from the check he'd been about to write, staring at me as if he doubted I was serious. When he finally figured out I was, he grunted, pulled a wallet from his back pocket, and carefully counted out the sum.

I grabbed the fistful of twenties and carefully folded them over, jamming them into my jeans pocket. "Thanks."

He said nothing but walked me to the back door and held it open for me. I guess I couldn't be seen coming and going through the front. What would the neighbors think of a grubby, unshaven stranger in a long coat coming and going in the middle of the night? I was probably bringing down the property value just by being there. Maybe that was a good thing. The median rent in Chicago was a bit high if you asked me. Not that I wasted my money on housing. There were plenty of places to sleep in a city of almost three million.

Icy wind brushed against the skin under my eyes,

stinging like salt on a fresh wound. I made my way down the concrete steps. The wrought iron gate's hinges groaned as I pushed it open and stepped out onto the sidewalk. Darkened windows loomed like eyes in brick faces, peering down from behind the sleeping buds of buckthorn and green ash trees. Gray clung to scaly tree trunks, providing cracks for little green lines to crawl through. One day soon, those green threads would become vines and Bissel Street would come alive, green and welcoming. In late March, the budding trees did little more than cast lumpy shadows in the moonlight. Patches of dark ice clung to the shadows where it stayed just cold enough to keep them from melting. Smoke rose like dragon breath from dryer vents, car exhaust, and both my nostrils.

My lungs seized with the first truly cold breath I took in the shadows. Breath exploded in a desperate cough that left me doubled over and dizzy. My lower back throbbed, reminding me I'd broken it in two places once before. Surgery had saved my legs, but the old scars hated the cold, and so did the bones. I spat onto the pavement and watched the dark spot spread as I wiped my chin clean. Dammit, I needed to spend winter and spring somewhere warmer.

It was a fifteen-minute walk to Fullerton Station, and I spent every step cursing my stupid decision to take the judge's case. If I hadn't been so desperate for cash, I wouldn't have answered when I got the call. I knew I should've charged him more, but I was always worried if I asked for too much, they'd report me to the Church. I wasn't technically authorized to perform exorcisms, but then a real exorcist couldn't do the job for less than three grand, let alone three hundred. If they showed up to do the work.

Two-fifty would buy me a few trips on the subway, a warm meal, and a bus ticket out of Chicago. Maybe I'd go south to Birmingham. It was warm in the South.

Before I hit the subway, I ducked into a convenience store where I bought two packs of Marlboros, a candy bar, and a newspaper.

The kid behind the counter stood on his tiptoes to reach the cigarettes on the high shelf behind him. "You should switch to vaping. It's better for you."

I tossed a lighter into the mix and slapped a twenty onto the counter. "I don't smoke because I care about my health, kid."

Fullerton Station was closest, but I felt like a walk so I skipped it in favor of wandering the streets. Walking after a job was a habit, almost as addictive as the nicotine I inhaled as I did it. I had to do something to clear my head. Every case was different but difficult. Even the judge's wife hadn't been an easy one. Every demon I cast out was one less of the Devil's soldiers on Earth, but I didn't do it because I was altruistic. I didn't even do it for the money, though I'd take what I could get. I supposed it was my penance for the one soul I couldn't save all those years ago.

I stopped on the side of a bridge with cars rushing by behind me. A steel cage stood between me and the option of a fifty-foot drop into traffic. I took the stub of a cigarette from between my teeth and shoved it through the grate, watching as it crashed into the pavement only to be crushed by blind progress. After two cars, there wasn't much at all left of the once bright red spot. My fingers curled through the holes and I leaned against it, pondering the fall. Suicide was a cardinal sin. I wondered if that was the only reason I hadn't considered it lately.

"Jesus, I really have hit rock bottom, haven't I?" I sighed and pushed myself away from the grate, limping to the nearby stairs. They led to a small area beside the highway, a walking tunnel covered in graffiti.

Noise echoed through the tunnel, the muffled sound of a struggle. I looked up. Three guys were pulling on a woman, mocking her with kissing gestures, groping her while she struggled to get away.

"I said stop it, Chris!" She yanked her arm free from one of them and managed to get a few steps before another stuck his foot out and tripped her.

All three laughed.

Walk away, Felix. I closed my eyes and turned my head. Don't get involved. It's not your problem. It's her fault for hanging out with assholes like that.

The weight of an invisible hand settled on my shoulder. "Do not withhold good from those who deserve it when it's in your power to help, Felix. Proverbs."

Dammit, Sean. Ten years gone and still lecturing me.

"Stop it!" the woman shouted.

I sighed and turned back, fingers curling into fists. "Hey, assholes."

The three guys froze. Apparently, they hadn't noticed me before. One of the many gifts I'd honed over the years was being virtually invisible if I didn't want to be noticed, but now they were looking right at me.

"Leave the lady alone," I said.

One guy grinned. "We were just having some fun, weren't we, sweetheart?"

She leaned away.

"Doesn't look like she agrees with you."

The biggest of the three broke away from the pack to scowl down at me. "She ain't your concern. Move on, asshole, before I teach you a lesson."

His guys circled me.

I met the woman's eyes. She shook her head and mouthed, "Just go."

Too late for that. "She said to leave her alone."

The first punch hit me in the back, just above the lowest scar. Red and white lightning flickered behind my eyes and I folded, paralyzed by the flash of pain. Tiny pebbles and wet newspaper that stunk of cat piss lined the bottom of the tunnel. I curled myself up against it, hugging my ribs with one hand and shielding my face with the other. Tennis shoes crashed into my shoulder, ground against my cheek, and snapped against my legs. Fists struck my fingers, the back of my head. Every blow blurred together, becoming a rhythm of pain. Hands yanked my shoes away, dove inside my pockets, turning out everything I owned onto the pavement.

The worst part wasn't the beating. It was the sympathetic look on the girl's face as they did it. She knew what it was like to be where I was, and she'd know that feeling again. For all my trouble, I hadn't made one bit of difference in how her life was going to turn out. I was as helpless as she was when all was said and done.

They beat me, robbed me, and left me lying in that cat piss tunnel without ever having uttered more than an expletive or two. The big guy grabbed her by the arm and hauled her away with a warning to shut her mouth and walk faster or else. I thought it was all over until she yanked free and ran back to me.

She fell to her knees, lifted my chin so she could

look me in the eyes. "Thank you. I'm sorry. I'm really sorry." She pulled away, letting my head fall.

It wasn't until she left that I realized she'd pressed one of the crumpled twenties back into my palm. I stared at the money, watching little red dots appear.

"You're bleeding," Sean's ghost whispered. "Get up."

My body moved on its own, staggering up on two legs. Somehow, I limped out of the tunnel, but that was as far as I got before the dizziness made me fall on the side of the road.

I don't know how long I lay there before a car pulled to a stop next to me. I expected some good Samaritan. Instead, a man in black leaned over me.

"Well," said the man in black, "you're a fine mess, Felix Cross."

I closed my eyes. "Go away, Xavier."

"It's Bishop Xavier, or Your Excellency, and not this time. Get in the car, Felix."

I sat up, my head swimming. The coppery taste of blood filled my mouth. I spat it away from the bishop.

"Come on now." He hooked his hands under my arms and half dragged me back to a waiting limousine, shoving me in the back. We were moving before I could even process what was going on. Bishop Xavier held out a white handkerchief. "Pinch your nose and lean forward. You're getting blood on the upholstery."

I did as he instructed.

Xavier sighed and crossed his arms. Like most clergy, Xavier had a grandfatherly look to him. His neatly trimmed white hair sat beneath a red cap and his black frock bore the red trim of his office. A large cross hung around his neck and a big, brass ring adorned his finger. He looked like a helpless old man, but I knew him to be as shrewd and ruthless as they came. "What happened, Felix? Who did you pick a fight with this time?"

"No one. Not that you'll believe me." I shifted my grip on the handkerchief.

"Keep squeezing."

"I am, Goddammit!"

The bishop shook his head. "Don't do that here, Felix. You won't take His name in vain, not while I'm here."

I closed my eyes and took a few breaths through my mouth. The air still held a coppery taste. "How'd you find me?"

"The Lord works in mysterious ways, doesn't He?" Xavier smirked.

"It was the judge, wasn't it?" I loosened my grip on the handkerchief and chanced raising my head.

Xavier shrugged. "I did speak with Judge Turney an hour or so ago. I believe the word 'extortionist' was used in the same sentence as your name."

"I charged him two-fifty. You tell me the Church could've done it cheaper." I balled up the handkerchief in my fist.

"Absolutely not," said the bishop. "Nor would the Church have gotten involved at all. The Turneys are Protestant. It just so happens that the judge and I are golfing partners."

"Figures." I crossed my arms and leaned back against the seat.

Xavier and I weren't friends, but I knew him from my seminary days. He used to teach courses like Advanced Demonology and Angelic Interpretation. Sean and I had been his star pupils ten years ago, before Sean went to Hell and I let my life fall apart. Since then, the Church and I maintained an uneasy peace. They didn't bother me and, in return, I didn't expose the conspiracies and lies for what they were.

The bishop opened a small compartment in the car next to him and offered me a cigarette and a lighter. It wasn't my brand—I could tell that much by how it looked—but he'd gone through all the trouble of securing a peace offering. I wasn't going to refuse it. I seized the cigarette with shaky fingers and bent over, lighting it. The first rush of nicotine was always the best, better than sex.

I caught him staring at me with that smug smile on his face and sighed. "What do you want, Xavier? You wouldn't have picked me up if you didn't want something."

"I have a case that might interest you."

I shook my head and flicked the ash into the divot in the door handle. "I don't work for you, the Church, or any organized religion. I thought I made that clear when the Jesuits approached me."

"I'm not offering to hire you as an official liaison for the Church. Simply as an independent contractor, which you have already been for almost a decade now. You can bill me hourly if you want." He tugged a manila folder from where it'd been tucked next to his seat and held it out to me.

I turned away without taking it. "Sorry, not interested."

"But you haven't even read the case file yet."

"I don't need to. I know what's in it. Some bullshit the Church wants to cover up and lie to the public about, or some problem you can't deal with openly. That's why you're offering it to me instead of one of your exorcists. You can't do anything about this officially, whatever it is. Giving the case to me gives you plausible deniability."

Xavier frowned. "I've been keeping tabs on you, Felix. Berlin, Dubai, Bombay, Shanghai, Tokyo. You've been around the world, studying under some of the world's most respected philosophers and theologians in a variety of religions. You've sought out every demonologist or expert on Hell from here to Siberia. That makes you the world's most foremost expert on demons. Yet you have no permanent address. You drift from place to place, sleeping in gutters, grifting your way to your next meal regularly."

I shrugged. "So?"

"I know what you're after, Felix. You want to bring him back."

I took a long drag on the cigarette and let the smoke out slowly, staring out the window at the passing lights, saying nothing.

Xavier put a hand on my shoulder. "Sean is gone, Felix. I know how it feels to lose someone you care so deeply about."

"After all this time...after what you did, you want to bring him up now and pretend you care?" I turned my head, glaring at his hand on my shoulder. "I've dealt with enough demons to know when I'm being emotionally manipulated. No offense, Your Excellency, but fuck you."

The bishop withdrew his hand to flip open the file. "Does the name Raina Hemlock ring any bells?"

"No, should it?" I thought a moment, realizing the name seemed familiar somehow. "Wait a minute. She was that rich girl who disappeared. They thought the parents killed her but could never prove it. The investigation should've ruined the father's career in politics, but somehow wound up catapulting him up in the polls."

"Well, she's no longer missing." He turned a page, pretending to examine the papers in the folder. "A young woman about the right age turned up about two years ago at the Hemlock estate, claiming to be Raina."

"The Anastasia grift," I said. It was one of the oldest in the book, and one of the most difficult to pull off in the modern day thanks to DNA and dental records. It was named for the supposedly unaccounted for Princess Anastasia of Russia. Several girls were put forward with people pretending to have housed the escaped princess. If they'd pulled off the scam, they stood to inherit wealth, fame, and a royal title. Sadly, the real Anastasia was dead, and Raina Hemlock likely was too.

"That doesn't seem to be the case. DNA confirms a match." He held the file out to me again.

This time, I took it, flipping through the notes. "What does this have to do with demons?"

"Well, Raina seems to have lost her memory. They put her through some controversial therapies in an attempt to help her recover those lost memories, all of which are detailed in there. Long story short though, while in an altered state, Raina claimed she'd gone to and subsequently returned from Hell."

I found the page in the file holding a drawing Raina had made while in her allegedly altered state and lifted it into the passing streetlights. "Do you know what this is?"

Xavier shrugged. "I couldn't make anything of it."

"It's an inverted map of Hell. The sulfur lake, the fiery pits. It's all there. It's just a mirror image." I turned the page around, marveling at the level of detail.

It was a crude drawing, but there was no mistaking it. She'd even labeled the locations of interest, and in ancient Aramaic no less. Backward. Short of scouring some of the world's most ancient and sacred texts as I had, there was no way this Raina girl could have reproduced the map. I flipped the file closed and lowered it into my lap. "Where?"

"Where what?" He raised an eyebrow.

"Where is she?"

Xavier sprouted one of his smug grins. "First thing's first. Let's get you cleaned up and dressed in something that doesn't reek of cat urine."

CHAPTER TWO

The bishop took me to the downtown Hyatt and put me in a room for the night. He had a full staff follow me to my room. They shuffled through the door, bringing in luggage I didn't own, placing it in a pile on the floor near the simple closet. He told me I could have anything in those bags without any obligation, but that I'd have to sign some paperwork before I took the job officially.

I sat at the table across from Bishop Xavier and a chubby Church lawyer with glasses too small for his face, only half-listening to his legalese. Whatever they shoved at me, I signed it. It didn't matter what sort of gag order the job came with. The pay didn't even matter to me, and neither did the benefits, though I'm sure whatever cookie Xavier offered was generous.

For the first time in ten long years, I had a lead that might bring Sean back. It could be a false lead and it was still more than I'd ever had. All those years, trekking the globe in search of knowledge and secrets had brought me no closer to freeing Sean from Hell than I had been the day I lost him, but this girl might hold the key. If not, if everything she said turned out to be a lie, I wanted to be the one to expose her. I hadn't even met Raina yet and already I both loved and hated her for opening a wound she alone could close again.

So, I signed away the life I had and accepted the one offered by the bishop. All it took was a signature, three initials, and two handshakes. Ten long years of work culminated in an hour of bureaucratic bullshit. The lawyer, the bishop, and all their staff members picked up their documents and left me alone in a strange room with a stranger's luggage.

I stood in the center of a pyramid of black bags, numb and exhausted. It was too much to deal with so late, so I dragged myself to the shower instead. In the pristine bathroom, I carefully stripped off my coat, folded it, and laid it over the back of the toilet before standing in front of the mirror.

The face that stared back at me was thin and withered with a splotchy, unkempt beard and messy ashen hair. Blood had crusted in both nostrils and stained my cheeks. I had swollen, dark eyes, but not from the beating. That was from lack of sleep. The shirt I wore had been white once, but it was a sweat and bloodstained rusty yellow now. I glanced over at the coat. I'd been so careful with my things. The coat was a treasure on the street, and so were decent shoes. Few people had warm clothes, so I felt lucky.

Now that I was safely behind walls in the relative comfort of a hotel room, I could see the coat was torn in places, missing buttons, and stained up. It was a revolting second-hand bit of clothing. How could I ever have thought I was lucky to have it?

How could I have ever let myself fall so low?

"Fuck this," I snarled and gripped the shirt by the collar. It tore off my body in scraps that I let fall to the floor. My disgusting socks went in the trash along with the torn jeans and the underwear I'd had as far back as I could remember.

I'd had the money to dress better, to eat better, to live better, but I'd squandered it on other things. On drink, on bus tickets, on cigarettes and junk food, on back-alley blowjobs and horse races and cockfights. Anything and everything that would distract me, make me feel less alone.

At first, after losing Sean, I poured myself into my work. That was the part everyone knew about, my travel days. I clung to the hope that knowledge would be my salvation, but all it brought was more misery, the aching, damnable need to learn more. I was always one book away from the answers I needed. The missing piece was out there, I was sure of it.

Until I wasn't. I turned my back on theology, philosophy, science, and hope, grasping for anything and everything as I fell. I'd spent the last two years flirting with one addiction after another, but I had yet to find a drug that could replace Sean.

In the bathroom of that hotel, I stripped, shaved, clipped and scrubbed it all away, rinsing the last of that version of Felix Cross down the drain.

What remained was still thin and haggard, but less broken. I was too world-weary to get back the hopeful glint I'd once had in my eyes, but I could put forward the image of a man with a future at least. A man who wanted answers and wouldn't let mundane things like life, death, and eternal souls get in the way. That part of me couldn't die. I needed that part of the man I'd become as sure as I needed breath in my lungs.

In a few short hours, I shed my skin and left the bathroom to stand naked in my hotel room with my luggage and my case file. The first suitcase I opened held a black button-up shirt, the same sort that priests wore. I'd worn the same shirt for years during seminary and had once hoped to add a standard white-tabbed collar to it. Despite what I'd once believed, the boring life of a priest had never truly suited me, but the black did. I put on the shirt and the familiar black slacks that went with it.

Tucked into the front of the suitcase, I found another gift from the bishop: a pair of black leather driving gloves. I ran my hands over the material with a frown. Xavier was one of the few people who knew about my gift. Or curse, depending on how you looked at it. Gloves went a long way to shutting parts of it down, but not all. Still, it was a thoughtful addition, one I appreciated more than anything else.

Like riding a bike, I mused, standing in front of the mirror.

Dressed the part, I finally took the Hemlock girl's case file and laid all the pages out on the bed before stepping back. The way I'd arranged the pages, it was impossible to read through it and make sense of anything, though the images were still easily visible. I picked up the picture of eight-year-old Raina. In the school photo, she looked like every other little girl her age, dressed up in her white button-down shirt and dark green pleated skirt. She'd worn a sweater for picture day. It was the same color as her skirt but bore the monogrammed letters RH. The curls and fat cheeks of early childhood had faded, leaving her thin-faced and dark-haired, but that wasn't what caught my eye; it was the smile. You can tell a lot about a kid from the way they smile—or don't. Raina wore hers like a frequent burden as if she'd been practicing that smile for weeks on end. It could be like every other false smile for every other school photo, or it could mean something deeply troubling. Children were natural smilers. That it should be such a chore for Raina might mean she'd had a sadder childhood than most.

I put the photo down and picked up another, this one of the woman who claimed to be Raina. The resemblance was there in the sad eyes, the dark hair, and the curve of her nose, but this Raina wasn't smiling. She glared at the camera as if she could set it on fire with her gaze. Her hair fell limply over her shoulders, pooling on a pale and bony chest. She was thin as a matchstick and wore a dress of faded pink, which only seemed to make her look paler.

I remembered her case from the news. To remember a news story after fifteen years might've seemed like I paid a lot of attention to it, but I hadn't. Reporters droned on about the Hemlock family all summer, and tabloids dogged them for years. What happened to Raina Mae? You couldn't stand in a grocery checkout line without seeing that headline for years afterward.

Shady publications came up with many stories about what'd happened to the wealthy senator's disappeared daughter, turning her into a Satanic sacrifice during the Satanic Panic days, or claiming she'd been kidnapped by aliens when Ancient Aliens were all the rage. As long as Raina Mae sold, they'd milk every buck they could. The bored masses loved nothing more than a good scandal.

Facts in the case of Raina's disappearance, however,

were few and far between, as I found in her case file. The mother, Laura, put Raina to bed at eight the night before and went to a campaign fundraiser with her husband. The girl was left with her nanny, who verified Raina was safe and in bed as late as midnight. By the time the parents came back at two, Raina was gone. No signs of a struggle, no signs of a break-in. It was as if she'd simply gotten up and walked out. Search parties combed the Kentucky woods near the senator's summer residence for two weeks before they gave up. All they ever found was a single ballet flat caked in mud, size one. It might've been Raina's but DNA was inconclusive.

I rearranged the pages, closed my eyes, and ran my fingers over them. Words lifted from the pages, floating in the air like whispers. They were nonsensical, meaningless sound to my ears, crashing against me like waves of smoke. I flinched with each strike but didn't waver. It wasn't the words I needed from the file. Anyone could glean clues and facts from files. If Father X wanted just another detective, they wouldn't have sought me out.

One whispered word grew louder, rising like a drumbeat from where it was buried deep inside the file: *Eglobelam*. The word meant nothing in the languages I'd studied. Not Latin, Aramaic, Arabic, Hebrew, or Greek. Not anything. Yet the word rose so loud, pounding at the inside of my head, it had to mean *something*.

My fingers closed around a page and my eyes snapped open. I lifted the page I'd grabbed and frowned at another sketch. This one was yet another map of Hell, but based on Dante Alighieri's *Inferno*. Dante's work had been largely allegorical for the political climate of his day, calling out powerful people in politics and the Church he didn't like. His accounting of the geography of Hell wasn't at all accurate, but it still had its place in the study.

Raina's depiction, like her other map, had been drawn flipped, all the writing and images backward so that it'd only be readable in a mirror. I took the map to the bathroom mirror and held it up.

There you are, you little devil. Malebolge. The word that had jumped out at me had simply been a reverse of Dante's label for the eighth level of Hell. Roughly translated from Dante's original Italian, Malebolge meant "evil trenches". These were the places where sinners were punished in the inferno, deep trenches. The eighth such trench was reserved for deceivers and liars who gained from the lies and misery they spread to others.

But why had that word resonated so strongly? What did it mean to Raina? The only way to know would be to speak to her directly, which I'd get to do sometime late tomorrow. For now, I had my first clue. I'd spend the plane ride down to Louisville refreshing my read of Dante's work, and checking to see if there were any new scholarly articles to do with it. Raina had developed an intimate knowledge of the text. I was looking forward to quizzing her on it, and anything else she knew.

I returned to the bed and placed the page carefully in the empty spot. It was only by chance that I glanced at the page above it, but I was glad I did. I snatched it up and skimmed what looked to be a transcript of an interview with the mother.

Laura: She isn't herself. Don't get me wrong; she is

E.A. Copen

my daughter. Of that, I have no doubt. But the therapies have brought out some part of Raina we can't deal with. Although you never know what you'll get with her. One morning, she might be pleasant and well-behaved. By evening, she could be spewing curses at us in who knows what language? She hit the housekeeper. Did I tell you that already? Anyway, it's nonstop nightmares. She doesn't eat. Sits alone in her room in the dark making those awful drawings. Even when my girl shines through whatever darkness has fallen on her, it's as if she's been somewhere else. She doesn't remember all the awful things she's done.

Laura, Raina's mother, described the various therapies they'd tried to help their daughter with. Raina had a strict regimen of medications. Anti-psychotics, anti-depressants, sedatives...the girl should've been so doped up she didn't know what day it was, not speaking Aramaic and Italian backward and drawing detailed maps of Hell. If this was a possession, it was an advanced case.

Why didn't you call someone sooner? I wondered as I gathered up the pages, stacking them neatly back in the file folder. *I know why.* Getting openly involved would be bad press. The girl's famous and her father's a prominent political figure. Imagine a priest showing up to perform an exorcism on little lost Raina Mae. The family would never escape the tabloids again, and neither would the poor exorcist who performed the rite. The Church wasn't willing to touch the case with a ten-foot pole, no matter how much money Senator Hemlock put in the offering plate.

But no one knew me, and I didn't have a distinctive white collar. I was this girl's last and only hope, but I was also a viable scapegoat for a distressed Church. Fine by me. If this Raina girl had even a shred of useful information that would get me closer to Sean, it was time well spent.

I closed the file and placed it back on the table where I'd found it. The hour was late, and it'd been a long time since I'd slept in a proper bed. I looked at the neatly made king-sized bed in the middle of the room. How many other people had slept there? I had no doubts they'd changed the sheets, sanitized everything, but how do you sanitize a space of emotions? Would it be enough?

My fingers curled around the hem of the bedspread, pulling it back. A white sheet lay on the bed underneath. I placed my palms against the cool, soft surface. My mind immediately flooded with the euphoric sensation of skin on skin, panting, desperate breaths strangled by flashes of pleasure, and the cooling sticky touch of sweaty palms.

I pulled away and staggered back a step, gasping as if I'd just come up from a deep dive. With a sigh, I raised my trembling hands to run them through my hair. Clean or not, mankind had yet to figure out a way to sanitize emotion from a place. The bed wasn't safe for someone like me, not if I wanted my dreams to be my own. So I pulled down the duvet, rolled up a spare sheet I found tucked in the closet, and curled up on the floor next to the table to sleep.

CHAPTER THREE

THEN

"Think of exorcism like a pipe." Bishop Xavier stood at the front of the lecture hall in the dark, the light from his PowerPoint presentation reflecting on his bifocals. The only spot besides his glasses that shone in the darkness was the tiny strip of white he wore at his collar. Nevertheless, the bishop waved his arms as if the people in the back could see him gesticulate. "Demons enter the body. The afflicted often describe this as occurring through physical openings such as the mouth, though it isn't uncommon for victims of possession to describe sexual intercourse as the inciting event."

Felix stifled a yawn next to me.

I looked at him and hated him all over again because he never had to brush his hair to make it look good. The jerk could just roll out of bed and throw anything on too, as long as it was black. He swayed as if he were about to fall asleep.

I elbowed him and whispered, "Did you get your

passport yet?"

"No," he whispered back.

"Felix, you know those take forever to get mailed to you."

He shrugged. Typical Felix, always waiting until the last minute to do anything. I was starting to wonder if he really wanted to go to Mexico with me. We only had this one chance to travel and see something great before we took our vows. After that, we'd be sent out into the world to serve, probably at parishes too far away from each other to maintain any friendship. Sure, we'd write and call at first, but that would drop off. Distance and the business of the job would separate us forever. It should have made me excited. Instead, I dreaded it more with each passing day. I had an appointment next week to talk with my seminary advisor. Maybe I should tell him I wasn't going to go forward with the vows.

"I'll get it done," Felix promised. "Tomorrow."

"That's what you said last Tuesday."

Xavier clicked to the next slide. "Once inside, the possessed may begin to show signs such as suddenly gaining knowledge of a previously unknown language, self-harm, personality changes." He clicked to the next slide. "The goal of exorcism is to irritate the demonic and coax them into exiting through the same orifice through which they entered. As I said, like a pipe." New slide. "The afflicted may become violent in an attempt to get the exorcist to cease the rite, but that is a rare occurrence. Most exorcisms are short, benign, and easily performed inside thirty minutes or less."

Felix elbowed me, sending my pen streaking over the page. "Hey, I've got an idea. We can become drive-thru exorcists. Exorcisms in thirty minutes or less."

Even as irritated as I was, I had to admit that was a funny idea. One only Felix would come up with. I let out an involuntary snicker and had to cover my mouth to keep from bursting into laughter.

"Something to add, Mr. Cross?" Xavier crossed his arms and frowned at the two of us sitting in the front row.

Felix cleared his throat and stood. "Yeah. The things you're describing—personality changes, violent outbursts, strange speech—can't those also be attributed to mental health conditions? How is anyone supposed to know the difference?"

Xavier's eyes slid to me. "Mr. Yeats, care to enlighten your friend?"

I sat up straighter and lowered my pen. "It's usually already ruled out by the time any certified exorcist arrives. Mental health treatment is always preferable to the religious rite of exorcism."

"That's right," beamed Xavier. "Because when you go forth to perform an exorcism, you become wholly responsible for the afflicted person's physical, mental, and spiritual wellbeing. It is therefore not a contract that should be entered into lightly. You may sit, Mr. Cross."

Felix sank into his seat and muttered, "Suck up," to me.

"No, I just read the material."

"Nerd."

I smiled to myself. "Slacker," I said and went back to scribbling more notes without looking up.

The lecture ended shortly after and I stood, slinging my backpack over my shoulder as I did.

"Mr. Cross and Mr. Yeats." Xavier's voice boomed through the room. "I'd like to speak to the two of you."

Felix and I exchanged a worried look but stepped out of the slanted seating area and onto the wide lecture floor. The other students gave us curious glances but knew better than to hang around. Xavier would chew them out if they tried. He might've been a man of God, but he had a vicious tongue when he wanted, and a lot of pull in the department.

Felix closed on Xavier without missing a beat. "Your Excellency, I know I did bad on the quiz last week—"

The bishop held up a hand. "This isn't about the quiz. In fact, it isn't about grades at all. To be honest with you, I don't care about your grades, Felix. Either of you. I know potential when I see it, and I know when it's being squandered." He adjusted his bifocals, staring down his nose at me. "This is an introductory level course. Why are you in it?"

"We needed one more elective this semester and we wanted to take one together." I shrugged. "This was the only one with space left."

Xavier's nostrils flared. "I see. And you, Mr. Cross? Is it the same with you?"

Felix nodded. "Yeah, pretty much."

He scrutinized us each for a moment. "You're bright lads at the top of your class. I've seen your course loads. Hebrew, Aramaic, and Greek, Felix? Advanced courses in all? Why?"

"I'm good with languages." Felix shrugged again.

"And yet you're barely capable of pulling a passing grade here." Xavier crossed his arms.

Felix's lip twitched. "I thought you didn't care about grades."

Xavier ignored him, turning to me. "And you, Mr. Yeats. I read your paper on the ethics of exorcisms.

You're very well informed. Too well for an introductory course."

I scratched the back of my neck and eyed the door. I'd rather be anywhere other than standing there under his gaze. "Honestly, I just picked that topic because it seemed easy to defend."

"I see." The bishop raised his chin and snapped closed the attendance book in his hands. "I want both of you to meet me this evening at the east gate. Seven o'clock sharp."

"But—" Felix started to cut in but the bishop interrupted him.

"Be there, Felix, or we're going to have to start talking about your grades. And you, Mr. Yeats…" He sized me up quickly. "Just be there."

The bishop shuffled out of the lecture hall, leaving me alone with Felix. The space suddenly felt too large without him in it, too empty.

Felix jammed his hands lazily into his pockets. "You picked it because it was easy to defend? I thought you were interested in ethics."

I turned my back to Felix with another shrug and went to collect the last of my belongings from the desk in the front row. "Ethics, yes. Exorcisms…I mean, maybe. As much as anyone else, I suppose. It's a curiosity. But did you know the official text, drafted in the sixteen hundreds, went unrevised until 1999? The new text is still largely the same. You have priests performing the rite of exorcism the same way people did at the time of Rembrandt. In my opinion, the modernization done in the late nineties wasn't nearly enough."

Felix clapped me on the back and flashed one of his goofy, boyish smiles. "See? You are into it."

"I'm surprised you're not more interested." I tucked my pen behind my ear and we began the slow climb to the rear of the lecture hall.

"Why would I be?" Felix shook his head.

"Oh, come on, Felix! You might not be the most bookish student at seminary, but you're no pushover when it comes to stepping in to do the right thing. People still talk about that time you hit Sister Matilda with her own ruler back in fifth grade."

A stripe of red burned across Felix's cheeks. He turned his head away. "Well, what was I supposed to do? Just stand there and let her beat the crap out of Ned? The kid was already getting smacked around at home. I imagine if he'd gone back with bruised knuckles, he'd have gotten worse from his dad. Who still hits kids in school anyway? It's not right, hitting someone who can't hit back."

"See what I mean? You have an intuitive sense of justice. Possession is the ultimate event of the powerful exerting control over the powerless. That's totally your thing."

Felix grunted. "Yeah, if it's real."

I stopped him just short of the exit. "What do you mean if it's real? You don't believe in it?"

His shoulders slumped with a heavy sigh and he glanced at the door. "I believe in a lot of things, Sean. I believe there's a God in Heaven and angels who attend to him. But Hell…" He shook his head. "I don't know. Maybe we make our own Hells here on Earth. I mean, if Hell is literally a place where man lives separated from God, aren't we already there?"

"Not exactly what they teach here." I pulled open the door and held it for him.

"One could argue the goal of education is to teach

the student to think for himself and not simply to spout what he's been taught." Felix ducked through the door.

It was an October afternoon in New York, about four o'clock. Somewhere behind the gray, cloud-filled sky, the sun sank toward the horizon. It'd be dark soon. I'd been in classes all day, since before the sun came up, and Felix had been at it almost as long. He had an early study session on Tuesdays.

There were certain benefits to the off-campus housing arrangement we'd shared since our second year at seminary, but the walk back in the chilly October evening wasn't one of them. At least, not when I had to do it alone. On Tuesdays, however, we both had our last class together, which meant we walked back together. It'd become the one thing during the week I looked forward to. Something about the quiet of the evening, the slow stroll on the street before it got packed, walking shoulder to shoulder…it felt more natural than any other part of my week, like that was the one thing I knew I was supposed to be doing.

I wished I could be as sure about seminary. Everyone around me claimed to have heard a call, as if God somehow spoke directly to them. I'd never had that. I'd only gone to seminary school because that was what my father wanted for me. It was that or medical or law school, and my interests didn't align with those.

When I announced I'd be heading to the New York Theological School, it was the one time my father seemed happy with my decisions. It seemed even more right when Felix said he was considering the same. I didn't want to be a priest, but I didn't know what other avenues might still be open to me.

I glanced over at Felix next to me. He had his doubts too. We'd stayed up late so many nights, talking about our worries, fears, the things we disagreed with about Church doctrine. What if the place and the courses were not right, but being with each other was?

He smirked at me. "What? Something on my face?"

"Nothing." I fixed my gaze forward. "Just thinking about after."

"Still having doubts?"

I lifted my shoulders and let them fall, focusing on kicking the tiny pebble along the sidewalk. "Father Micah said doubts are natural at this stage."

"That's why you want to go to Mexico, huh?" He sped up, turning around to walk backward a few steps once he got ahead. "We've had our heads in books too long. We need to go out and see the world before we take vows. It'll be good for us both, I think."

"What if we just went and didn't come back?"

He stopped so abruptly I almost ran into him. "Run away? And do what?"

"I don't know. Anything we want? There has to be something you've always wanted to try your hand at and never had the chance."

"Maybe," Felix said, then shook his head. "But now I've got student loans and family expecting me to become a priest. I think it's probably too late to change course now."

I lowered my head and pushed past him. "Sometimes I just don't feel like I belong. Like this isn't me. Like I'm meant for something else. Something…better. Father Micah said that was pride talking and gave me a whole litany of prayers to recite. Do you think it's pride?"

"I think Father Micah is so old, he forgets what it's like to be young and have doubts." Felix gripped my shoulder. The gesture was meant to be reassuring, but it only stirred more doubt in the pit of my stomach.

We went back to the tiny apartment we shared where I had enough time for a nap and a quick dinner before Felix woke me with a knock. He leaned against my door, the sleeves rolled up on that black shirt he had six copies of. "We'd better leave now if we're going to be on time to meet Bishop X."

I almost rolled back over and went to sleep. Felix might need the extra credit, but I didn't. I was acing the class without even trying. Besides, I had an eight o'clock class the next morning and a midterm to study for. I thought up every excuse I could, but my curiosity won out.

I should have remembered what curiosity did to the cat.

The evening was darker than usual, probably due to the heavy cloud cover. It was supposed to be a full moon night, but the only light on campus came from the windows and occasional streetlamp.

The eastern campus gate was more of a stone archway with a Bible verse engraved over the stones: The fear of the Lord is the beginning of knowledge; fools despise wisdom and instruction. It was from Proverbs, an often quoted but rarely understood book. I stood beneath the arch, considering the words and their implications when it came to school. Was I a fool? I didn't hate learning. My mother said I was just bored. She was probably right. I couldn't remember the last time I'd been challenged in a class. Everything was too easy, too predictable. Life was just one day after another, going through the motions. All that stood out were those Tuesday afternoon walks. Once I lost that, what would I have?

"I knew I should've worn my warmer coat." Felix

30

hugged himself and paced back and forth. "Where is he? He said seven sharp, right?"

"Yep." I glanced at my watch. It was two after seven. Felix never was any good at being patient.

"Do either of you boys smoke?"

I spun around, surprised to find the question had come from Bishop Xavier. He'd put on a long coat, and dressed in his official church garb, a black cassock with red trim and a bright red skull cap. It did a good job covering his bald spot.

Felix finally stopped pacing and stepped up to where I stood, frowning. "I'm pretty sure nicotine is addictive, and addiction is supposed to be a sin, isn't it?"

The bishop put a cigarette between his lips and lit it, letting out a slow, relieved mouthful of smoke after. "Probably. I'm sure they teach you boys that here, but when you go out there, in the real world, and you see the things I've seen…let's just say God gave us coping mechanisms for a reason."

"Whatever happened to prayer and fasting being the only acceptable coping mechanisms?" I asked.

Bishop X tucked his cigarettes and lighter away. "After tonight, you might change your position on that, Mr. Yeats. Come. This way." He stepped through the archway toward the street, smoking like the exhaust on a car in January.

Felix and I exchanged a single nervous look and rushed to catch up.

"What's this all about?" I asked, falling into step with the bishop.

"When was your last confession?"

Felix's nose wrinkled in confusion at Bishop X's question. "What?"

"Your last confession." Bishop X rolled his hand and quickened his march down the street. "You'll need to be absolved before we begin. You know what, never mind." He stopped, turned, and made the sign of the cross over Felix. "*Ego te absolvō a peccātīs tuīs in nōmine Patris, et Filiī, et Spīritūs Sānctī.*" Then he turned and did the same for me, giving the traditional sacrament for absolution, though we'd confessed nothing. That done, he grunted in satisfaction and returned to his hurried walk.

"Does that even count?" Felix asked me, shaking his head.

I shrugged. "He said *ego te absolvō*. That's the important part, right?" I huffed out a breath and we rushed after the bishop. "What's the hurry, Your Excellency?"

We arrived in one of the school's parking lots and the bishop ushered us to a white Kia sitting in a space reserved for clergy and professors. "One never dallies when there's a soul on the line. Not when it's within your power to save someone. Always act. Remember that."

We slid into the back of X's car, crammed too close together, and breathing each other's air. The stale, burnt air filtering through the car's heater made the inside of my nose dry and irritated the mounting headache I'd been fighting ever since I woke up.

After we got out of the parking lot, X reached over to turn down the heat slightly so he wouldn't have to raise his voice to talk over the roar of it. "Three weeks ago, I was called to perform an exorcism for a local woman. I didn't think much of it. Only about one in three thousand cases is truly demonic possession, but this one…" He shook his head and gripped the steering wheel tighter. "I have seen the face of evil, gentlemen, and it wears the mask of a child whose soul lies on the edge of damnation. For three long weeks, I have worked to help her. It's been a process, but I can no longer do it on my own. I need help and you two…were available."

Felix leaned forward. "But we're not trained exorcists. Don't you have to be certified or sanctioned or…something?"

"Speaking as a bishop of the Church? Yes. As a man of God and true believer, I know all one needs is faith in the divine and a good strong back. I have the former. You two will be the latter for me tonight." He took a sharp turn down a narrow, one-way residential street lined with middle-class homes smashed up against each other.

Bishop Xavier parked his car in front of a little white two-story bungalow with neatly trimmed bushes outside. Every light in the house burned through open blinds and tied back curtains, casting the world beyond in an off-color electric yellow. Every light save one in the very top bedroom where darkness still reigned supreme.

He shut the car off and twisted around in his seat. "Are you ready?"

"I don't know the first thing about performing an exorcism," I said.

"It's easy," replied the bishop. "Just do as I say and hold your ground. The demon's goal is to shock and distract you, to make you feel fear, doubt, and guilt. You mustn't let it get to you, Mr. Yeats. Stand fast in your faith, and let God be your strength. And whatever you do, do not give the demon your full name. Understand?"

I nodded emphatically.

"Good." The bishop grunted and exited the car.

I stayed in the back seat a moment, staring at the house as he stood in a pool of dirty light, gripping a bag and looking up at the darkened window. Faith in God and a strong back. I had that much, didn't I?

CHAPTER FOUR

NOW

I jerked awake to the seatbelt ding and a nauseating drop in the hollow of my gut. The stranger next to me bent over to place their tablet in the bright red purse waiting on the floor. I turned my head and watched the barren city landscape of Louisville, Kentucky tilt. The plane had begun its descent. Within minutes, we'd touch down at the Louisville airport where I'd meet the Hemlock liaison.

I put a fist to my aching forehead and let out a deep breath. I must've fallen asleep. I hated dreams like that, the ones that were half memory, half nightmare. Every time I closed my eyes, it seemed like I was stuck reliving that awful night. I couldn't escape it, no matter how much time passed.

"You should try chewing gum."

"Huh?" I looked up.

The woman next to me offered me a foil-wrapped piece of gum with a smile. "The headache. It helps."

I grumbled my thanks and took the gum. The

sudden descent wasn't so much the cause of my headache as the first signs of nicotine withdrawal and dehydration, neither of which the gum would help with. Yet it would help me wake up, and maybe shake some of the darkness my nightmare had left behind. It was like standing in the cool of an invisible shadow. I could feel the effects weighing me down, even if I couldn't see it.

The plane rolled into the airport and I disembarked just like I had a thousand other times in a thousand other cities. The jetlagged shuffle down the narrow aisles, escalators, and moving sidewalks was so familiar to me now it was second nature. I found my way down to the luggage platform and watched bag after bag snake by, chewing my gum.

A homeless man in a ragged coat walked along the line of waiting passengers, hand out, begging for change, cigarettes, anything they were willing to give. The woman who'd been sitting next to me grabbed her bag and hurried away from him without ever acknowledging the man.

That was me, I thought, watching the man work the line of passengers. If I'd been dressed the way I was just a day earlier, she wouldn't have given me the time of day. The woman passenger shuffled by me, not paying one bit of attention to the stranger in black she'd been so kind as to offer him gum in his time of need. Her bright red purse hung off her sleeve while she fought to juggle her wheeled luggage and the phone on her ear.

In a flash of movement, I slid my hand into her purse and brought out her wallet. With my back turned to her, I hunched over slightly and opened it. *Credit cards, a couple of ticket stubs. Ah, here we are. Cash.* I took two twenties from the fat wad tucked in the wallet and pocketed them.

The man shuffled up to me. His rank smell hit me long before he was ever close enough for me to hear him ask in a raspy voice: "Got any change, Mister?"

I passed the man both twenties I'd lifted from the woman's wallet.

The man lit up with a toothy smile. "Bless you, sir. God bless ya!"

"Not lately." I picked up my bag and took a few steps away from the platform. The woman was still chatting away on her phone, completely unaware she'd been robbed.

"Felix…" Sean's voice was chastising in my ear, as if he were standing right behind me, ready to scold me.

"She doesn't deserve the kindness," I grumbled.

"It's not really up to you though, is it?"

I closed my eyes and sighed. "Fine. But only because I don't need it." I stepped up to the woman and tapped her on the shoulder. "Excuse me, ma'am," I said, holding out the wallet. "I believe you dropped this."

"Oh! Oh, my! Thank you so much, young man! Oh, my trip would've been ruined! You're so kind. Here, take a little something for your trouble." She started to open her wallet.

I held up my hands. "No thanks needed. Just…be kind. Pass it on."

"Of course! Always!" She flashed a big smile, and promised she would, though we both knew she wouldn't.

"Fucking hypocrite," I muttered under my breath.

"You did good," Sean said.

I swear, if I didn't turn my head, I could see him

walking along beside me in the corner of my eye.

"Felix Cross?"

The voice caught me off guard. I hesitated, my first thought that it might be airport security. Did they know what I'd done? Yet when I turned, I found a man in a suit far too nice to have been bought on a security guard's salary. He was tall, broad-shouldered, with a bass voice to match.

When I took his hand, it was like shaking hands with a mountain. "That's me. You're the Hemlock liaison?" I nodded to the whiteboard with my name on it.

"Yes, sir. I'm Mister Hemlock's driver. He sent me to fetch you." He lowered the whiteboard and reached for my bag.

"I've got it," I said. "I was expecting to meet with someone from the family directly. Guess that was too much to ask for huh?"

"Mister Hemlock's in Washington, sir. Mrs. Hemlock's tending to Raina and the staff. Afraid I'm all that's available."

"That's not how I meant that to come out." I put a palm to my forehead. "Sorry, man. I just got off the plane. Haven't had a cigarette since this morning. They don't let you smoke at the airport anymore. My head's killing me."

"That's all right. I understand. Car's this way, sir." He ushered me toward the nearest door.

"Just Felix is fine. I spent too many years calling my father sir. I don't like it."

He nodded. "I understand that. My name's Jacob then. Welcome to Louisville, Felix."

"I've been here before, though it's been a while." I looked around the airport at all the tired faces, the shifty glances, the quick looks away as I passed by. I'd almost forgotten what the South was really like. A lot of people thought Kentucky was just north enough not to count as the true South, but ask any Kentuckian and they'll tell you different. The division lines between North and South were drawn back during the Civil War, which put Kentucky firmly in the South.

The last time I'd been in the Bluegrass State, Muhammad Ali had just died. His funeral had been all over the news. That was what? Four? Five years ago? That was a lifetime for me, but it was nothing for most. In such a short time, you wouldn't expect much to change, but the world was a different place now. Political divides had widened into uncrossable canyons. Old wounds had been opened on the national political stage, those cuts seeping into the local economy and infrastructure to form a unique sort of disparity for Kentucky. The air was different. It felt rougher in my lungs. Stained.

Wherever there was turmoil and division, demons found the opportunity to thrive.

Jacob brought me to a limousine waiting outside and opened the back so I could put my suitcase inside. The black bag seemed so lonely in that gaping space. I almost wanted to crawl into the trunk with it. Instead, I got into the back, which was uncomfortably large as well. I should have worn something nicer, something like Jacob's suit. Instead, I'd worn what was comfortable: black slacks, the same black button-down, and a black suit jacket that I'd since shed. I'd been hauling it around over my shoulder since I got off the plane. In the back of the limo, I rolled it the same way I'd rolled up my makeshift pillow the night before and set it in the seat next to me.

The limo moved out of the short-term parking space as smooth as warm butter on fresh bread.

"So how long have you worked for the Hemlocks, Jacob?" I asked.

He bobbed his head. "Three years. Drove another senator before that, but I like Mr. Hemlock much better."

"Why's that?"

"Personality, I reckon. The other senator wasn't so talkative, but Mr. Hemlock, he treats me like family. He's good to me and mine. A good man, Mr. Hemlock." Jacob glanced at me in the rearview with the last line, the truth of his words reflecting in his eyes.

I fidgeted with the pack of cigarettes under my thumb, tucked neatly in the folds of the black jacket. "Don't suppose Mr. Hemlock's a smoker when he's in the car, is he?"

"No, sir. I mean, Felix. But I can pull over once we get out of this traffic if you like. We're in no hurry."

"One never dallies when there's a soul on the line," I muttered.

"What's that?"

"Nothing. Don't worry about stopping. I should quit anyway."

He shrugged. "Whatever you say. You're the boss."

We hit I-65, driving south toward Shepherdsville. Cracked pavement and rusty guardrails marked the passage of the city. Squat trees leaned over concrete barriers, threatening to reclaim their land. Tractor-trailers belched out great black clouds of exhaust, their dirty chrome lines shivering and shuddering along next to minivans and rusty trucks flying their Confederate flags. We passed a truck with one of those "don't tread on me" bumper stickers and I wondered if the redneck who'd slapped that on his tailgate actually knew the history of that phrase.

"Only in Kentucky," I grumbled, shaking my head.

"Better here than Mississippi," said Jacob. "But then, anywhere's better than Mississippi. It's ranked fiftieth in the nation for just about everything except the rate of incarcerated youth."

"You from Mississippi, Jacob?"

"I'm from everywhere." He gestured to the road in front of him. "I grew up an army brat. Born on a base in Germany, or so they tell me. My dad was stationed just about everywhere though, at one point or another. Working for the Hemlocks is probably the longest I've stayed in one place all my life, truth be told. You strike me as a traveling man. You been around?"

"I have," I admitted with a nod. "Just about everywhere a man can go. I'll be honest. Kentucky's not my favorite."

"It's got a certain charm to it though, don't it?" He smiled, big and wide and genuine.

We sped past the truck with the bumper sticker. "Maybe I just haven't seen enough of it yet." I turned my attention forward. "What do you know about Raina?"

He said he'd been employed for three years, which meant he worked for the Hemlocks when she showed up. As an employee of the family, he had a unique perspective on the situation I wouldn't get from the family proper.

"You mean do I think she's legit?" He shrugged. "Not my place. But they say the DNA and dental records match, so it must be true. I mean, you can't fake DNA, can you?"

There were ways, but it was difficult. It'd be more

difficult to pull off a grift lasting years. The beauty of a good con was how quickly they moved. Keep the mark looking at the left hand so they can't see what the right's doing. Even the best conman couldn't keep that up for two years. The more I thought about it, the more Raina seemed real.

"What about this whole demonic possession angle?" I asked. "Do you think that's real?"

"I'm a God-fearing Christian man, Felix. Same as the Hemlocks. I don't see how a man can live in the world today and not believe in the Devil." He paused as he eased the car into an exit lane. "Now, if he can possess a person, that's a different story. Before I saw Raina last week, I'd have told you I didn't believe in that, but the things I saw…" He shook his head again. "Mrs. Hemlock says that girl's got the Devil in her, and I believe it."

"I hope so. I'd hate to have come all this way for nothing."

His brown eyes flashed in the rearview mirror, unsure. "They told me you were coming to help her. That true?"

I sighed and fidgeted in the back seat for a moment before unrolling the jacket and shrugging it back on. "To tell you the truth, Jacob, I don't know if I'm here for her or me, but either way I'm not leaving until we both have some answers." I pointed to the fast food place just up the road on the exit we'd taken. "Pull over there for a bit, would you? Just long enough for me to smoke one."

"Yes, sir," said Jacob with an accommodating nod. "You're the boss."

***

Jacob drove me down a long, winding road that coiled into a tight circle in front of an antebellum home. Four great white columns stretched from the front porch to hold up the second story. Two additions had been made to the original central structure, each folding back like the tired wings of a dragonfly. Willows and hemlocks leaned into the space around the house, crowding it with shadow. It was still too early in the year for the willow tree to have sprouted, leaving naked fingers to scrape against the windows on the side of the house.

We stopped in front of the stairs leading to a wide front door. I reached to open my door, but Jacob practically threw himself out of the car in such a hurry, I didn't have time before he opened it for me.

"Thanks," I said.

"No problem." Jacob swung the door closed. His eyes traveled up the front stairs to the door, widening with worry. "Felix, I feel there's something else I ought to tell you before you go on in there. I know it isn't my place since I'm just an employee and all, but…well, be careful. Not everything around here is as straightforward as I've been."

"I'll keep that in mind." I tugged off the glove on my right hand and offered it to Jacob.

He took it with an iron grip.

For Jacob, it was just a handshake, but for me, it was a window into a stranger's life. The strongest emotion bled through at first as uneasiness, but that quickly subsided as we shook hands, replaced by guilt. He felt he'd done me wrong, bringing me to Hemlock House, but why?

I didn't have time to look deeper. That would've made the handshake awkward, so I took my hand back, pulled the glove back on, and went to collect my suitcase from the trunk.

A sudden scream startled us both away from the car. Jacob hesitated, but I took off for the front door, certain what I'd heard had been one of the Hemlock women under attack. I found the front door unlocked and threw it open.

A set of stairs ascended to the next floor almost immediately on my left, a red runner tacked down over polished hardwood. Down the stairs stalked a female lion. She paused at the sight of me and hunched her shoulders, limbs coiled like springs. In a flash of movement, fur, and claws, the lion leaped from the stairs straight toward me.

CHAPTER FIVE

I lifted my arm in front of my face. Better to lose an arm than my head.

The cat's jaws, however, didn't bite into the meat of my forearm. It fell just a few feet short of where I stood at the bottom stair and let out an ear-splitting scream, an encore to the one I'd heard earlier.

When she was done, I cracked open an eye to find the big cat panting and staring at me with wide, intelligent eyes.

"Emily! Sit!" The woman who'd spoken stood at the top of the stairs, well out of reach to stop the lion from eating me if it chose. She stood roughly five and a half feet tall and dressed as if she were expecting a dinner party, not a house guest. She wore a dress the color of crushed strawberries with sleeves that hung low, leaving her neck and shoulders bare. Sparkling gemstones dripped from everywhere they could be: ears, neck, wrist, ankle. A different colored band circled each one. It was hard to tell just by looking at her if she was closing in on thirty or fifty, but I suspected the latter. Thirty would be too young to be Mrs. Hemlock.

I gave the lion another pensive glance. She wasn't as big as I initially thought, nor as lion-like. At least, not an African lion. Judging by her size, she couldn't be full-grown, but that didn't make her less dangerous.

The woman put her hand on the banister and descended slowly. "Don't mind her. She's just throwing a bit of a temper tantrum. I'm afraid I haven't been able to spend as much time with Emmy and her brother since I've taken over tending to Raina directly." She reached the bottom stair and smiled as she scratched the big cat's ears and chin, absently flicking ash brown hair over her shoulder. "I'm sorry. Here I am going on and on and I haven't even introduced myself yet. I'm Laura. Laura Hemlock." Laura put her hand out, but not like she expected a handshake. More like she expected me to kiss her knuckles.

I shook her hand just as I had Jacob, except I didn't take my gloves off for her. "Felix Cross."

"Yes, Father Biggs told us to expect you. What he didn't mention was how cute you were."

Oh boy. Two minutes through the door and I'd already been attacked by two cougars. I put on my best boyish smile and tried to seem at ease, though I didn't know which predator to fear more: Mrs. Hemlock or the lion. "Well, I'd be worried if Father Biggs had an opinion on that."

She laughed. It was forced, but she almost fooled me. She was good, Laura Hemlock. A born socialite.

"Sorry for busting in like that," I continued. "Your driver didn't mention you had exotic cats on the property. I thought it might be you or Raina screaming."

Laura stroked the cat's fur. "*Puma concolor*, they call it in Latin, more commonly known as a mountain lion. They don't make for very good pets, but they are protective. You have to be firm with them. They respect power like any beast."

"I didn't realize it was legal to let big cats roam around on the loose in Kentucky."

"Oh, legality." She waved a hand at the idea, a wicked glint in one eye. "Let the old men worry about the laws. Anyone who tries to separate me from my fur babies is in for one hell of a rough time. We have very good lawyers, Mr. Cross, which is part of why you are here. My lawyers advised me not to bring in an exorcist. I'm not the kind of woman who likes to follow the rules. Besides, Emmy's never hurt anyone. She and her brother are good babies, isn't that right?"

"Just Felix."

She nodded. "Then you must call me Laura."

The door behind me shifted as Jacob slipped through it and placed my bag on the floor next to it. I hadn't meant for him to bring it in, but I'd gotten busy talking to Laura. She didn't even acknowledge him except to shoo him away when she saw him. Jacob gave the mountain lion a quick glance and backed out the front door, closing it behind him.

Standing there in the entryway, alone with Laura and her mountain lion, I couldn't help but feel like meat in a butcher shop. Sliced, weighed, analyzed by some hungry prospective customer…Laura's gaze was unrelenting and uncomfortable, but I didn't dare look away. She was smart and had too much experience with wild animals which needed to be tamed with a dominant gaze. If Laura expected me to cow under the same pressure, she had another thing coming.

The corner of her mouth quirked up into a satisfied smirk. It would take more than a big cat and a sultry glare to make me break into a sweat.

Another pale, thin figure in a long gown shifted in the shadow of the doorway at the top of the stairs. "Momma?" A woman spoke, but the tone belonged to a scared child, one that had just woken from a nightmare and asked to crawl into bed with her mother.

Laura gripped the bottom hem of her dress and hiked it up slightly, spinning to march back up the stairs. Her heels made a loud clip-clop sound with each step, like a horse stamping impatiently. "What're you doing out of bed, Raina? I told you to stay in bed!"

The cat followed her up, right on her heels.

The Raina that shuffled out of the darkness was not the same one from the photograph. She'd lost even more weight, and the bruises around her eyes had expanded, darkening into a deep purple. Her lips were dry and cracked bad enough that she had fresh scabs. Her cheekbones looked sharp enough to cut glass, skin pale enough to be nearly translucent. Every little knob of each joint poked through the skin as if it might pierce it. A rainbow of colors stained her fingers and spread in dry streaks through her hair and over her yellow dress.

"But I ran out of cyan," said Raina, swaying slightly. Her voice was flat now, emotionless. "I can't finish it without cyan."

Laura reached her daughter and lifted Raina's arm. It hung limply in Laura's grasp.

"Laura!" I took two steps forward gripping the banister.

Laura looked down at me. Was that color in her cheeks embarrassment? She'd probably meant to clean Raina up before I got to see her, but I couldn't risk that. I needed to see the girl as she was.

"Do you mind if we have a quick chat? The three of us?"

Laura frowned at Raina, then back at me with a huff. "I don't know what good conversation Raina will be. When she gets like this, all she does is paint and hum."

"I'd like to see, if you don't mind."

"I suppose that is why you're here, isn't it? Very well then." Laura shifted her grip on Raina. "Come along, dear. Let's get you some more cyan."

I took the stairs up two at a time, leaving my bag at the door without a second thought. Just as I made it to the top of the stairs, Laura guided Raina into a room on the left. I followed.

The first thing that hit me was the smell. Advanced cases of possession often left behind a sulfuric stink that soaked into a space. It came on so gradually that sometimes it passed unnoticed to those living with the possessed. They might pick up on it at first, but as time passed, their noses grew used to it and their brains stopped picking it up. The human mind was like any other computer: great when it worked, but it shut down background processes when overwhelmed. The scent of rotten eggs was so thick in Raina's room it stung my eyes.

The room had been a bedroom at some point, judging by the rumpled bed, but was now primarily Raina's studio. Dozens of canvases laced the room. Some held detailed watercolor paintings of dark landscapes where shadow and fire crawled from every crevasse. Others had simple charcoal drawings of people. One caught my eye almost as soon as I was in the room.

I went straight for it, picking it up from where it lay in the corner, half-buried by empty paint cans. It was a charcoal portrait of a man in profile. Familiar eyes stared back at me, dark and sunken. Three days' worth of beard crawled up the cheekbones. The faded hood of a beaten and torn jacket hung off the shoulders while smoke crawled up from a half-smoked cigarette.

I stared at my face from the day before, immortalized in streaks of gray on a pristine white canvas. "When'd she do this one?" I held it up for Laura to see.

Her eyes widened. She touched her fingers to her bottom lip in surprise. "I don't know. She does so many."

"Tuesday, January fourteenth," Raina recited, her voice flat. She picked up her brush and dabbed it gently against the canvas before her. "Proverbs three, verse twenty-seven."

I nearly dropped the canvas.

Laura frowned. "Does that mean something to you?"

I didn't tell Laura, but that was the verse Sean had quoted in my ear just before I stepped in to help the woman in the tunnel. The verse that'd gotten me beat near unconscious. I'd met more than one clairvoyant in my day, but never one that could hear ghosts that weren't really there.

I put the profile image down and turned to move around the room, studying the others she'd done. There weren't any other faces I recognized, nor any connection I could find between the people and places she was drawing. Some smiled in euphoria while others lay face down with bottles all around them.

It could be chance, I told myself. I didn't have the most distinctive face in the world. It could be I was seeing similarities that weren't there, or I was staring one of the clearest signs of demonic possession straight in the eyes.

Raina murmured in a sing-song voice as she worked. I leaned in, listening closely.

Laura crossed her arms and shook her head. "You can listen all day and it still won't make a lick of sense. She's talking nonsense."

"She's singing backward." It wasn't an impossible trick to pull off, but singing in reverse was a lot more difficult than speaking it. To verify what I was hearing, I dug my cell phone out and held it close to her, recording her words. After a minute or two, I ended the recording and put it in another app to play for Laura. "Recognize the song?"

Her eyes widened. "It's a hymn from church. *Power in the Blood*, I think it is."

I nodded. "That's the one."

"I don't understand. Why backward?"

I tucked my phone away, frowning at the back of Raina's head as she continued through the song, working her way toward the first verse. "Same reason for the inverted cross and the same reason every demon in Hell is fluent in Latin. They get off on mocking the divine."

Laura leaned in, nose wrinkled. "So, it's true then. She's possessed by some demon?"

"Maybe. There's really only one way to know for sure." I shrugged off my jacket and handed it to Laura, who seemed surprised to have it tossed to her. The gloves came off next, tugged free one finger at a time. "Raina Hemlock?"

The paintbrush froze, but she made no move to answer.

"All right, the hard way it is." I clamped a bare hand on her stick-thin wrist.

Before I could get a clear read, she spun around and sucker-punched me so hard I went flying back, crashing through several paintings. The paintbrush dropped to the floor with a click. Her head twitched to the side, and she let out a barking, guttural growl.

I sat up and drew a sleeve across the corner of my mouth, leaving a streak of crimson behind. "You just made a mistake, asshole."

Raina grinned while a strange clicking sound emanated from her throat.

I pushed to my feet and unbuttoned the cuffs of my shirt, rolling up my sleeves. "My name's Felix Cross. That's Cross with two S's at the end."

Her head twitched to the side twice unnaturally fast. "I see you've heard of me."

She smiled and lunged for me awkwardly, fist balled as if to strike. I readied to take another hit, but whatever had control over Raina's body let go at the last second. She collapsed and I caught her.

"Oh my God!" Laura covered her mouth. "Is she all right?"

She started toward us, but I held out a hand, keeping her back. Now that the entity had temporarily released its hold on Raina, if only for a moment, I could get a proper reading. I placed a hand over Raina's forehead.

Nothing happened. No visions. No flood of emotion. It was like trying to get a reading on a black hole.

Raina's body suddenly stiffened, back arching. Her eyes rolled back and spit spilled down the side of her mouth. Her mouth moved as she gasped for air. Like a rubber band, she snapped back the other way, shooting upright with a rough intake of air. "Mommy! Mommy, please!" Her voice broke as she screamed at the top of her lungs, body stiff and frozen like a corpse with rigor mortis.

Laura pushed away from the wall and threw herself to her daughter's side. "Mommy's here, darling! I'm right here!" She took Raina's hand and tried to force her daughter's fingers closed around her own, but Raina's joints had locked up completely.

She screamed bloody murder for a good sixty seconds before suddenly going limp and falling over into my lap, panting with exhaustion. Thin, shaky fingers gripped my shirt. "Please," Raina whispered, her voice hoarse. "Please make it stop."

Laura rubbed Raina's back. "We will," she promised. "We're here to help you."

I wished I was so sure. Without my gift, I didn't even know where to begin.

CHAPTER SIX

THEN

Marci Reed seemed like a normal nineteen-year-old girl in photos. Her parents lined the walls in the living room and hallway with pictures of a smiling teenager posing with friends, with a soccer ball, in a prom dress.

Bishop X didn't tell Felix or me anything about her or the family. He introduced us with a whisper to the worried mother as she dried her hands on the hem of a red apron. She nodded and the three of us made our way up a set of narrow, creaky stairs.

Felix paused on the top step, blocking my advance. He put his hand over his mouth and nose. "That stench!"

It wafted down the stairs to hit me next. I turned my head away so I wouldn't gag. "What is that?"

X took his hand off the wall where he'd steadied himself and turned around to address us. "The demon will do anything to stop us from completing the rite. It will assault all your senses. Show no weakness, Mr.

54

Yeats."

X entered the room to the right. Felix and I followed him, doing our best not to react to the increasingly foul smells burning our eyes and the insides of our noses. The room was unnaturally dark, as if all the light had been sucked up and spat out from the place. Three layers of newspaper coated the window. The light switch didn't work when X tried it either. The only furniture was a threadbare mattress on the floor to which the girl was tied. In the darkness, I could only barely make out the outline of a small face and bony limbs, but I'll never forget the sound coming out of her. Like toilet water bubbling up out of the world's oldest, angriest septic tank.

Bishop X put his bag down near the door and crossed the room to rip the newspaper away from the window. Pale moonlight flooded the room, pooling on the girl who couldn't have weighed more than seventy-five pounds. She hissed and twisted, turning away from the light. All her writhing in the light exposed bright red sores covering the girl's body.

The shock of seeing how sickly she looked finally gave me a reason to lower my hand. "She needs a doctor."

"Her mother is a pediatrician." X cast the wadded newspaper aside. He didn't sound the least bit bothered by the girl's state. "Though for our purposes, we won't be following the rite of exorcism so strictly."

I frowned. "I don't understand."

X bent over his bag, opened it, and drew out his purple stole. He kissed it and draped it carefully around his neck. "I want you to take everything you think you know about exorcism and demonic possession. Wad it up into a little ball just as I did with the newspaper.

Now throw it away. Forget every last bit of it because it won't help you here."

"But in your lecture you said—"

"Forget it, Mr. Yeats!" X drew himself up in front of me, face hovering inches from mine. His voice shook the walls and made the possessed girl tilt her head back and laugh.

I swallowed and lowered my head.

X gave me a heavy look as if to drive the point home, then went back to digging in his bag. A moment later, he emerged with a vial of holy water to sprinkle a few drops on the girl's forehead. She growled and twisted away as he began the invocation. When she turned back, three distinct blisters had formed on her forehead exactly where the water had touched.

I stepped forward, leaning over the girl who didn't look much like a nineteen-year-old girl at all now. The girl's head snapped up as Bishop Xavier dove deeper into his liturgical prayer. X spoke his lines, calling upon God, and Felix answered in echo on automatic.

My lips, however, stayed still, eyes fixed on the girl's.

Demons were supposed to have red eyes, or yellow, or some other unnatural color. I'd heard story after story detailing black eyes, or cloudy eyes, or eyes with no pupils, but Marci's eyes weren't like that at all. Hers were a light golden brown, the color of warm honey. In the center sat pupils like black suns, dark flames bleeding into brown like the grain in mahogany wood. These weren't the eyes of evil. They couldn't be. The Devil and his legions could never mimic such human eyes.

I see you, boy! The voice came scratching at the inside of my skull, a whisper and a scream all in one.

I blinked. It felt like drawing sandpaper over my eyes. When I opened my eyes again, the room was different, full of darker, deeper shadow. Father X stood aside, dabbing sweat from his red neck with a handkerchief. How long had I been standing there?

Felix nudged me with an elbow. "You hanging in there?"

"Yeah." I put a palm to my forehead, massaging the ache between my eyes. "Just tired. What time is it?"

"Just after three," Felix answered before turning to the bishop. "How long are we going to be here?"

X sighed. "As long as it takes. Once the rite has begun, it can't end. Not until it's complete."

I glanced over at the girl. Her eyes were closed now and she was snoring gently. She seemed relaxed, as if she were unaware she was rotting from the inside out, tied to a bed in a filthy room. "I thought you said most exorcisms are quick."

"Most, yes. But this girl has been afflicted for some time. It's a very advanced incident. In any case, all the prayers and rituals must be concluded." He tucked his handkerchief away.

I wanted to ask him what he would do if they didn't work. Was there some more advanced form of exorcism he might resort to? Some additional prayer or ritual that wasn't widely known? Or would he simply declare defeat and let the demon take its prize? I didn't dare ask in front of Marci though. X would get mad at me and send me away, and I didn't want to walk home in the dark by myself.

I put a hand on the bishop's shoulder, jerking my head toward the door to indicate I wanted to talk to him alone.

He nodded. "Felix, keep praying. I need to step out

a moment."

"Me?" His eyes widened and he looked around. "What should I pray?"

"Whatever you want, but if you're unsure, start with a few Hail Marys and work your way from that." He pulled open the door, waited for me to go through it, and then shut it behind him when he exited. "What is it, Mr. Yeats?"

"What if it doesn't work?"

His left eye twitched. "Pardon?"

"The exorcism. What do you do if it doesn't work?" When he didn't answer, I went on. "You said this was an advanced incident and that she'd been afflicted for a while now. Seems like this isn't your first visit to the house either. So, you've tried this before and it doesn't seem to have worked in the past. Is your plan to just keep banging your head against a wall, hoping for a different result?"

"Of course not!" said the bishop. "That's why I brought you and Felix along."

"What difference is our presence going to make? Felix is clearly out of his element and I don't even think we should be doing this. Look at the girl. Those sores are infected. She's underweight and malnourished. Possessed or not, she needs a hospital, Your Excellency, not an exorcist."

X's eyebrows went up. "So, we're only to perform the rite for the perfectly healthy? I assure you, Mr. Yeats, if that's the case you're waiting for, you'll never find it. No one who's feeling well calls for help. Call it stubbornness, call it idiocy, call it a sin, but the one rule that always holds about the afflicted: they will wait until it's too late to ask for assistance."

"And if the girl dies of a septic infection because

you'd rather pray over her than let real medicine help her?" I gestured to the door behind him.

He put a hand on my shoulder and squeezed. "What you're calling real medicine would only treat the symptom, not the underlying cause. The results would be the same. Remember, Mr. Yeats, we aren't fighting for Marci's life. This is a battle for her immortal soul." X let me go and straightened, adjusting the purple stole. "If you have doubts, you may leave at any time. I won't force you to participate in something you'd rather not take part in. I had hoped your presence would help, but…"

"But what?"

X sighed, his whole body deflating with the escape of air. "Maybe I was wrong about you."

Even then, I saw it for what it was. An all too familiar manipulation tactic, a ploy. For a moment, all I could hear was my father's voice in my head, calling me weak, pathetic, stupid, useless.

I closed my fingers into a fist and swallowed the burning coals of anger. "I'm here because you asked me."

Bishop X stopped, his hand on the doorknob.

"My back is still strong," I continued, "and I have plenty of faith. If we're doing this exorcism, then let's do it and get it over with." I pushed past him, jerked open the door and strode back into the room.

Marci's eyes were open, and though her mouth wasn't smiling, the eyes were.

Bishop Xavier entered the room and gently closed the door behind him. "Gentlemen," he said with an air of gravity, "Please restrain Ms. Reed and hold her still while I continue the rite."

He prayed throughout the night, sometimes asking

us to join in, sometimes anointing Marci with holy water or oil. Marci resisted, as anyone would, sane or otherwise. She shouted obscenities at us in English, Latin, and a few other languages, but none were impossible for her to have learned on the internet.

The longer the rite droned on, the more I became convinced that what we were doing wasn't in Marci's best interests. I felt her tiny, weakened bones resist my hold and cringed at the bruises my hands left behind holding her down. Looking at the gray and red rings on her wrists and ankles left me feeling sick at my stomach.

At dawn, Marci's mother came, and we helped her force-feed her daughter sedatives. It took twenty minutes for them to kick in. When Marci was finally still and out, X said one final prayer and closed the session.

Felix and I walked the eighteen blocks home in that morning twilight, not saying a word. It differed from all the other long walks full of laughter, jokes, and hopeful talk of what we'd do once we got back. A shadow hung over us, every step leaden. Felix walked with his head down, watching the sidewalk pass under his feet. We were inches apart, but he felt miles away, lost in his own world.

I wanted more than anything to ask what he was thinking about, but I feared the answer. He was thinking about that girl, Marci. About helping her, about saving her. I wished we'd never agreed to go with Bishop X.

By the time we made it back to the tiny two-bedroom unit we rented on the second floor of the same student housing nearly every student at the seminary lived in, my feet and back ached. The first thing I did was run for the bathroom and vomit. Whether it was nerves, the smell lingering in my nose, or the stress, I didn't know. I hung there over the toilet for a long minute before I was able to stand.

I caught sight of my reflection in the mirror and froze. When had I started to look so much like my father?

No, I growled inwardly and pulled off my clothes. *I can't be like him.*

Even as I stood in the shower under the painfully hot water, I didn't know what else to do to change. I couldn't quit seminary. Quitting would make him right. I'd be useless, nothing but a financial burden. Nothing but the son he wished he'd never had. A disappointment in every way. I'd have nowhere to go but crawling back to him. I could just imagine his satisfied smirk as I sat at the kitchen table, begging for him to give me a place to stay until I got my life back together. I closed my eyes and turned the hot water up.

I didn't put the shirt back on afterward, wandering out into the living room to stare bleary-eyed into the welcoming light of the refrigerator. My stomach growled, reminding me it'd been almost twelve hours since I'd eaten. The only things we had in the fridge were leftover chicken wings, eggs, and a block of Colby cheese. The idea of eating any of it made my stomach turn.

The thin neck of a clear bottle with a red label stuck up in the back. I pushed aside the cheese and gripped it. The glass felt cool against my palm. Vodka. When had we even bought this? Neither Felix nor I were much for drinking. I shook the full bottle, watching the contents slosh back and forth. That's right. We'd gotten invited to that party and almost went until I got cold feet and decided we shouldn't. Felix had bought the biggest, cheapest bottle he could find at the drugstore down the street, and it'd sat in the back of the fridge for almost four months.

I closed the fridge and grabbed plastic cups from the stack next to the sink before going to sit on the sofa next to Felix.

"What's this?" he asked as I poured two inches of the stinging drink in each cup.

I picked one cup up and held it out to him. "Drink."

Felix frowned at the cup.

I tried to focus more on the burning alcoholic smell wafting from it than the scent of Felix's sweat. If I thought too much about it, I'd start to wonder if he tasted as good as he smelled.

"Why?" Felix asked.

"Because I'm getting drunk and I don't want to do it alone." I picked up his hand and forced the cup into it. "Now drink."

"Don't you have class in an hour?"

I tipped the cup's contents into my mouth, cringing at the sting before I swallowed. I'd never drunk rubbing alcohol, but if I did, I imagined that's what it'd taste like. Burned like fire all the way down and kept burning while it churned in my gut. "I just spent the night helping an exorcist try to force a demon out of a girl only a few years younger than us, Felix. I'm not sure I care about the ethics of Church administration at the moment." I refilled my cup. "Drink, Felix."

Felix moved the cup toward his lips but paused, lips parted. He considered the cup as if it were a live scorpion, tail curled and ready to strike, and moved his tongue along his bottom lip, a nervous habit. If he knew about me, about what I thought about every time he did that, what would he do?

I closed my eyes. *Then stop thinking about it.* If only it were that easy. "Dammit, Felix." I slammed the bottle down and snapped my eyes open. "I'm twenty-five years old. I feel like I haven't lived. That's all I could think about last night, you know? All the things I haven't done."

"Like what?" Felix finally took a taste, cringed, and moved the drink away from his face.

"Never been drunk, for one," I said. "Never left the country. Never seen a kangaroo."

"There aren't any vows that say you have to give up those things."

I took another sip. The second one wasn't quite as bad. "Well, except maybe getting drunk. That counts as a sin."

"Look at you." Felix raised his cup. "The choir boy's not so innocent after all, eh?"

"I'm not a choir boy." I sighed and melted into the cushion behind me. "Well, I've missed out on a lot of sins too. Never worshipped another god, for one. Not that I think any are worth my time, honestly. Never murdered, stolen, committed adultery…"

Felix downed more of his drink and stifled a cough. He sighed and tossed the empty cup onto the table, leaning back into the sofa. "You tell me. How did all that make you feel?"

I glanced over at him, the lazy way his hand draped over his arm behind his head. Part of me hated him for being so comfortable, so easy to look at. If only I'd gotten another roommate, I told myself. If only he wasn't so kind, and funny, and sweet when the moment called for it. Felix had his flaws, but he had a sort of raw goodness at his core that was difficult not to like.

I turned away and considered the clear liquid remaining in my cup before answering. "Alone. Small. Helpless. All I wanted was to get out of there and take her with me. She needs a hospital, not an exorcism."

"Maybe," Felix agreed from behind half-lidded eyes. He stretched. It pulled his shirt up just enough to show his stomach. "I don't want to think about it anymore."

"But we're going to have to go back, Felix. You know that." I shifted on the sofa to put my drink on the table. "It's not done. X is going to ask us to come back and keep coming back until either we beat that thing, or she dies. Those are the only two ways this can end."

"Do you want to tell X we're done?"

"No, I want to help her. I can't stop imagining how awful she must feel. Think about it. How bad we felt. It must be so much worse for her. When I was in the room with that thing, it was like something cold and icy had coiled up inside of me and eaten every connection I had. You were right there, and yet you seemed miles away. I just need to feel something between now and then that isn't so damn empty." I stretched and pushed myself sideways, suddenly sprawling over Felix's lap.

The muscles in his thighs contracted, and he froze momentarily, unsure of how to react. His face went blank and his eyes glazed over. He looked so shocked, I couldn't contain myself.

I put my hands on my face and laughed into them. "You look funny from this angle. Did you know that?"

Felix chuckled and relaxed slightly. "Probably not my most flattering angle, huh?"

I lay there looking up at him, unsure of what to do

next. Was it the drink that made my stomach feel as if I'd swallowed a thousand furious butterflies? Or was that something else? Maybe I could blame the vodka for the strange tingling warmth spreading through my limbs, but deep down I knew it was more than that.

It was wrong on so many levels, what I was feeling. All my studies, all the doctrine and the sermons told me so. It was right there in Leviticus in black and white, that damnable verse: You shall not lie with a man as you do a woman; it is an abomination. I told myself the same thing I always did, the same excuse. It wasn't like we were having sex. Attraction wasn't sex, and what I felt for Felix was too deep to be simple lust. We'd lived together for two years, studied together, laughed and cried together. How could it be a sin to love someone?

If you have any balls, you'll bring it up in confession, I always told myself. But I didn't. I was a coward, a liar, and a pretender. I knew if the confessor found out he'd tell my seminary advisor and I'd never be allowed to finish. I'd have to go back to my father, head hung low. Only this time, it'd be worse. I'd have to tell him the most disappointing thing of all, that I was me and I'd never be the me he wanted me to be.

"You've got a strong chin," I said. "And handsome, kind eyes, if that means anything." The words tumbled out on their own. "And comfortable thighs, although I'm not sure that's appropriate to say. I can't not say it. Everything's just kind of falling out, isn't it? Oh well. Would it be awful if I took a nap right here? Just until this wears off."

Felix put a hand on my chest and shifted, leaning back. "I think the vodka was a bad idea."

I smiled and pinched the skin between my fingers to keep from reaching up to touch his face.

"Probably."

We were quiet for a long time, just sitting there. I kept glancing at the front door, which we'd left unlocked. Strange. We always locked it. What if Bishop X or someone else from seminary came in and saw us like this? The best thing to do would be to get up and go to bed where I couldn't do any more damage, but I couldn't will myself to move. All I wanted after a night of horrors was to sit tucked against the one person in the world I knew I could trust, drinking in his warmth.

"It's okay, Sean," Felix muttered, half asleep. "We're going to be okay."

I drew my knuckles against the side of his cheek. "I hope so."

CHAPTER SEVEN

NOW

L aura and I sat down in the dining room. It had one of those long wooden tables, the kind not fit for a regular home. I always imagined people only bought those tables because they wanted to sit impossibly far away from the rest of their family. Laura, however, pulled her chair uncomfortably close. Her lioness stalked to a big kitty bed in the corner, turned a circle and lay down, watching me lazily.

"So when will you begin the exorcism?" Laura asked, folding her hands on the tabletop.

I cleared my throat and scooted an inch to the left. "Well, a typical exorcism is fairly simple. It involves repeated prayer, anointing, and the ritualistic use of sacred objects. In Raina's case, I don't think she'll benefit from that sort of exorcism."

Laura blinked rapidly and sat back. "Well, what other sort of exorcism is there?"

"There are hundreds of different rituals aside from the one used by the Catholic Church. Exorcism is as old as humanity's belief in demons, stretching back as far as we have written records. Every culture, every religion, every people has a ritual for the banishment of unclean or evil spirits." I licked my thumb and opened the little notebook in front of me, flipping to the first blank page. With a click of the pen, I got to writing. "They all have one thing in common, and that's the belief that the possessed person plays an important role in expelling the spirits. Raina must participate."

"But I don't understand. How can she if she's…well, you saw her."

I nodded but didn't stop writing. "What's the most difficult thing you've ever done, Laura?"

She pulled her hands away, absently touching her chin and staring at the lioness curled in the corner. "I suppose it was giving birth to Raina. It wasn't an easy birth."

"I imagine at some point, you thought you couldn't do it."

She nodded slowly. "I was so afraid."

"What changed your mind?" I put one elbow on the table and used it to prop up my head.

"What choice did I have? Raina was coming whether I was ready or not. A mother does what she must." She smiled at me, but it felt forced.

"Raina is scared," I explained. "All day, every day, there's something in her head, telling her she's weak, she's a victim. The demon wins when she buys that completely. The first step is going to be convincing Raina she's not some helpless victim. We need her to fight." I turned to the page and finished writing before ripping it out and holding it out to Laura.

"Thank you." Her fingers closed around the paper,

but I held onto it until she met my eyes.

"Don't thank me, Laura. Not yet. Before this is over, you're going to question me. You'll disagree with my methods, say I'm being too harsh and expecting too much. It won't be easy to watch. I'm going to hurt your daughter, Mrs. Hemlock. She's going to cry out in desperate pain and beg for you to stop me. Every instinct you have is going to want you to save your daughter from what I'm about to do because that's what a mother should do. I want to be very clear. You cannot save your daughter. I can't save her. Not even God can save Raina. Raina must fight to save herself. I will do whatever is necessary to convince her to do so. It won't be easy to watch, so look away if you must." I released my hold on the paper.

Laura remained frozen, thin fingers grasping the page while it trembled in the air. She swallowed and lowered the page to the table. "But if her life is in danger—"

"Her life *is* in danger, Laura."

"You can't exorcise a corpse. Surely you're obligated to keep her alive at all costs." She stared at me, expecting an answer I couldn't give.

I folded my hands slowly and leaned forward. "How far do you want me to go? How much pain can she take? How much suffering is too much? Whatever you think the answer is, multiply it tenfold. I've seen the possessed laugh while breaking their arms. Do I stop then? Do I let the demon win? What about when she breaks her restraints and bashes her head against the wall until she's bloody and brain-damaged? Maybe we call it quits then?"

"Stop it." Laura turned her face away. "Stop it, I don't want to hear it." She started to rise.

I forced her back into the chair. "You need to hear it because it could happen. Anything could happen and you need to be prepared for that possibility."

"Let me go!" She pulled away from me.

Her cat suddenly leaped up onto the table with a feral scream, panting, eyes wide. I stared into the creature's reflective green eyes, seeing myself. I may have changed my clothes and shaved my face, but I still had that glint of madness in my eye.

Sean stepped into the reflection behind me, hands in his pockets. He gave a subtle shake of his head. "Too far, Felix."

I released Laura and ran my fingers through my hair, tugging it up. "As long as Raina is screaming, she's alive. Remember that, Laura. We lose when she stops breathing, or when we stop trying. Every other ending is a victory." I picked up the paper she'd left behind and held it out to her. "You forgot your list."

Laura hesitated before snatching the page out of my hand and eying it for the first time. "One three-inch mattress pad," she read. "Two digital thermometers. Unused blanket and pillow, still in packaging. Two packs of Marlboro cigarettes to be delivered daily." She lowered the page. "What the hell is this?"

"It's a shopping list. I don't imagine you've seen many of those since you probably don't do your own shopping."

She inhaled a deep breath through her nose before she wadded up the paper and threw it at me. "I'm not your personal shopper!"

I let the paper ball hit me in the face. It bounced off and rolled to a stop at my feet. "Those are all the things I require if you want me to do this. If you're not willing to do your part, I'm happy to go." I wasn't, not really.

Raina had answers I needed if I was ever going to free Sean, but I knew the mother would cave. They always did. "I also need unrestricted access, day and night, to Raina's bedroom, her studio, and one full bathroom."

"This is insane!"

I stood calmly and bent over to collect the list, smoothing it out gently on the tabletop as I spoke. "The definition of insanity is doing the same thing over and over again and expecting different results. You've tried everything else to help Raina and it didn't work. Now, we try it my way." I held the paper out to her again.

Laura eyed it, incredulous, but took it from me a second time. "I'll have Jacob bring you what you need."

"Thank you," I said. It never hurts to be polite.

She summoned another member of her staff—this one a thirty-something with a tight black bun, a ruffled white apron, and a black lace choker—to escort me to the guest room. The décor looked like it hadn't been updated since the Victorian days. Ugly, brown splotchy wallpaper stood behind a decorative headboard. Pillows stacked one on another in a great pile at the top of the bed, all of which I'd have to remove. The maid pulled back the long white lace curtains, revealing a huge window that let in the evening sun. Light bounced off the embellished standing mirror and fell on the opposite wall in a shimmering puddle. Art adorned the walls, but it was all boring landscapes featuring trees, fields, and streams snaking through an endless expanse of dead grass.

I walked over to the writing desk tucked in the corner where I dropped off my notebook and pulled out the velvet-cushioned chair.

"You a military man?" asked the maid. She'd taken to fluffing up the pillows I'd never use.

"What makes you ask that?" I eased into the chair and stretched out my left leg to rest the aching joint.

"My father walked like that on cold days." She nodded to my outstretched leg. "He got hurt in a parachuting accident. Broke his back. Gave him a limp and left him with a cane and aches for the rest of his life."

"No, not as such. I fought a war of a different sort." I lifted my foot and used the other to pull off my shoe. It clattered to the floor loudly, drawing her disapproving eye. "Sorry. Didn't catch your name."

"It's Willa. Willa Meechum."

"How long have you worked for the Hemlocks, Willa?"

"Oh, quite some time," Willa answered, smoothing her hands over the blanket I had no intention of using. "Since before Raina's disappearance. I was her nanny."

I looked her up and down. "A little young to have been working here fifteen years ago."

"I'm older than I look." She adjusted the curtains.

"So you were the last one to see her before…whatever happened." I rubbed my chin. "What's your take on all this?"

She raised an eyebrow. "My take?"

"Your story. What happened that night?"

Willa interlaced her fingers and let them droop in front of her. "I've told my story a hundred times since then, sir. I'm sure if you're curious you can find a tabloid or a newspaper somewhere that has everything you want to know."

"Felix," I corrected, "and I'd like to hear it straight from you. Even the most unbiased reporter can't help but put a spin on the stories they tell."

She frowned. "I'm afraid it's not all that exciting. Mrs. Hemlock put Raina to bed and left for a fundraiser. I checked on the girl every hour, on the hour, with my last check at midnight before I turned in. The girl was sound asleep and comfortable, the doors and windows locked. Shortly after two, Mrs. Hemlock's sobs woke me and I ran to the kitchen from the guest quarters to hear Raina was missing."

"That's it?"

She spread her arms and shrugged. "That's it."

I didn't buy it. Her story was too well-practiced, too devoid of details. Even after fifteen years had passed, she should've recalled more details from such a traumatic event, even if they were invented.

I tugged my cigarettes from my shirt pocket and lit one, considering the nanny-maid as I did. On the surface, the Hemlock household seemed like just another family under siege, but what sort of rot would I find once I scraped away that first layer? What lies and secrets lay beneath, waiting in quivering darkness to be exposed to the light? Someone somewhere was lying about what'd happened fifteen years ago, and feeding me half-truths about the situation now. I was sure of it. I couldn't trust Laura or Willa any more than I could Raina.

"Nice collar," I said, nodding to her. On closer inspection, it wasn't just a normal collar. It looked like lace from a distance, but it was just an ornamental leather piece with some dull pearls.

Willa touched her collar. "Thank you. It was a gift."

I grunted. "I bet. Do you always sleep in the guest room?"

Her head snapped up, nostrils flaring. I'd touched a

nerve, but Willa was a trained professional. She knew better than to argue with her employer's guests. She'd keep quiet for now, which was fine by me. Unlocking a family's secrets took time, and the more she stewed and squirmed, the juicier the reveal would be.

Willa folded her hands in front of her again. "Will there be anything else, sir?"

I snorted and turned around in the chair to face the desk. "I never asked you to do anything for me in the first place."

The door squeaked open, then banged closed. Feet shuffled away from the door toward the stairs.

I waited until she was too far away for me to hear anymore before I opened the notebook and began my notes.

Dear Sean,

It's been 3,786 days since you left and finally, I have a lead. It's come through an old friend, or maybe an enemy. I'm not sure how you'd think of X if you were still here. I'm not sure how I think of him, actually. He seemed genuine, but I think that's only because he needs me. He'll gladly toss me into the ditch he found me crawling out of if I get to be too much trouble.

He's sent me to Kentucky where I'm supposed to help Raina Hemlock. Yes, that Raina Hemlock. Her family suspects she's possessed by some devil, but I think there's a deeper problem, one that's affecting the whole family. I felt it as soon as I was on the property, the dark shadow looming over the family. Although I agree that most of the activity seems to be centered around Raina, I can't deny that something strange is going on with Mrs. Hemlock and her staff.

Some demons aren't the sort you exorcise.

In any case, Raina has these intricate and detailed drawings of Hell and of me that she shouldn't be able to create. Supposedly, she claimed in an experimental therapy session earlier that she had been in Hell the entire time she was missing, and everyone took that to mean literally.

Is it wrong that I hope they're right? I know that means she's suffered—is suffering—but I can't help but feel excited and validated by her claim. I need to get her to say the same to me. I need to speak to the entity inside of her to discover the truth, which means delaying the exorcism until it's fully manifested.

I know you won't approve of what I'm doing, but I hope you'll forgive me. Everything I'm doing, I'm doing it for you. Maybe that makes me sick. Only a truly disturbed person would watch an innocent girl suffer to save a man everyone else believes is dead. But that just takes us back to the question I've been asking myself for a decade. Does a madman know how mad he is? If my mind was broken, would I even know? Everyone talks about the pain of a broken heart. Perhaps a broken mind is painless, or even euphoric. The insane always seem so happy. Sometimes, I wish I were one of them.

But I'm not. At least, not yet. For now, I'm just the same cold-hearted and selfish bastard I've been since you were taken. I've tried to tell Mrs. Hemlock the truth about what I mean to do, but she doesn't understand. They never do.

Perhaps I'll save the girl, and maybe she'll have the answers I want, but even if this all goes as planned, I have to wonder…will there be enough of me left to matter?

Love Always,

Felix

I closed the book. The pressure of an invisible hand rested on my back. I leaned into the arm that wasn't there and swore I could smell him burning next to me.

CHAPTER EIGHT

The staff brought everything I requested but left me to put it all on the bed. I guess my earlier spat with the housekeeper hadn't gone over too well. I left my gloves on and fought to get the mattress pad in place, and the pillow on the bed. They'd brought me one of those itchy blankets, but at least it was still in the bag, which meant it'd been handled minimally.

I'd say I didn't like being difficult, but that wasn't strictly true. I did, however, need to get a decent night's sleep if I was going to be useful to the Hemlocks, and that wouldn't happen if I was suffering through visions all night. As I finished fixing up the bed, I wondered if Raina had trouble sleeping too. I'd soon find out.

Once I'd finished, I left my room and went to find Raina. She was still in her studio, painting away furiously with her fingers. Occasionally, she'd lift her fingertips from the painting and push limp strands of hair away from her face, leaving a colorful streak behind.

I stood at her back, peering over her shoulder with

my arms crossed. I couldn't tell what she was painting, but whatever it was, it was very red. Honestly, I didn't care whatever image had enraptured Raina for the evening. We had work to do, and it began with getting her in a more tolerable state.

While she wasn't looking, I picked up the paint tubes one by one and tossed them into a plastic bag I'd brought with me. She didn't notice at first, just moving onto the next one instead. When there were no more tubes of red or orange paint, she pawed at the empty tray on the easel a moment before spinning around to glare at me.

"Looking for these?" I held up the baggie full of red paint.

"What do you want?"

"Your cooperation," I said. "I'm glad to see you can speak, or was that song and dance earlier for your mother's benefit?"

"You don't believe me?" Her fingers twitched as if they'd curl into fists, but stopped just short.

"I believe there is a God in Heaven and a Devil in Hell, and that most humans are so trivial, so unimportant that they aren't worth even the lowliest demon's time to possess." I tossed the bag aside. "What makes you so special, Raina Hemlock, that the Devil would want you? Even curiouser, why would he let you walk free?"

"I'm not free," she spat through clenched teeth. "I'm a prisoner in my own body. I can't eat. I can't sleep. The touch of soap burns my skin." Raina turned away and hugged herself, not caring that she was smearing bright red paint all over her dress and arms. "When they take me over, I have no control over what I say and do, but I'm awake. I can hear them and feel what they're doing to me. Do you know what that's like?"

"Yes," I answered.

Raina gave me another appraising look over her shoulder. "I don't know why they chose me, these voices in my head, and these things under my skin. I'm not special."

"You must be or they wouldn't want you." I eased onto an overturned box to sit. "If you believe the scripture, Heaven and Hell are at war. If you're possessed, then you were targeted for a reason. Some people get picked because they're stupid, messing with forces beyond their understanding."

"I don't have to listen to this." Raina stepped around her easel to open another box of paints, laying them out before her in a straight line.

"I was told you claimed to have been a captive in Hell, and that you said you escaped from there."

"People say all kinds of things when they're under hypnosis," she growled.

"So, you deny it?"

Raina opened a bottle of yellow paint and squeezed a drop onto her finger, smearing it over the canvas in a wide arc. "I don't know what I said. That time wasn't like the others. I wasn't awake inside."

Whoever had treated her would have recorded the session, or made notes. It wouldn't be easy to get those, not without a signed release from Laura, but convincing her to give me what I wanted wouldn't be too hard if I had results.

I drew my fingers over my chin. "Raina, answer me truthfully. Do you want this to stop?"

Her finger froze on the canvas a moment as she thought. "I want those fifteen years of my life back. I want the world to make sense again. I want to stop painting these damn pictures!" She pushed the canvas off the easel and melted into a hyperventilating pile of herself, gripping at her hair by the roots and tugging on it.

I stood and shrugged off my jacket so I wouldn't get paint on it. "I am addressing the entity inside Ms. Raina Hemlock. I command you to show yourself and manifest. Give me your name now, and we can do this the easy way."

"Please," Raina whispered. "Don't."

"Last chance," I said. "I'm going to count to three. One…"

"Please, please, please," Raina repeated and shook her head.

So, she could fight it. That was a good sign. How long she could repress the presence and under what circumstances, however, were what we'd discover together over the next day or so.

"Two."

Raina hugged herself and rocked back and forth, trembling.

On three, I marched over to wrap an arm around Raina's middle. She was thin enough that lifting her was like picking up a child. A very angry, long-limbed child that smelled like they'd rolled around in a sewer.

Raina shrieked as I grabbed her and hauled her toward the door, limbs flailing. "Stop! Put me down!"

"In due time." I wrestled her arms away from the door long enough to open it, but getting her through the doorway was another feat altogether. She was like a retriever I'd owned once, resisting going through the door by holding onto it with all her strength. I thought the demon would manifest itself there to keep me from removing her from the room, but I pried her weak limbs from the doorway without too much trouble.

Raina continued screaming bloody murder while I dragged her backward down the hall.

Laura stormed up the stairs. "What in God's name are you doing?"

"Step one of the process." I grunted and shifted my grip as Raina tried to throw herself to the floor. "We're going to get her cleaned up."

"But she screamed and nearly drowned herself the last time I sent her for a bath!" Laura stepped up onto the second floor, wringing her hands as she watched me struggle with her daughter.

I bumped into her. "Help me or get out of my way!"

Still apparently in shock, Laura stepped aside. I shifted my grip again and dragged Raina backward through the hallway to the bathroom.

In the Old Testament, Israelite priests were described as ritually washing themselves before entering the temple, which was a common practice in nearly every world religion. Long before we ever figured out the link between bathing and illness of the body, we understood there was a connection between cleanliness and illness of the soul. In Christianity, the same process manifested as baptism, and the little pools of holy water at the entrances to churches. Modern priests might claim dipping your fingers into the water and making the sign of the cross was simply meant as a reminder of faith, but once, that was the closest thing the faithful could get to a weekly shower. Not only did it do a little something to cut down the stink of peasants and pig farmers entering the Church, but it replicated a ritual passed down since the birth of human culture. Humans were expected to present themselves to their god in a clean state.

Traditional Catholic exorcism didn't require the demoniac (or victim, whichever term you prefer) to be clean. One of the hallmarks of possession was a refusal to maintain basic hygiene. But my goal wasn't to cast demons out of Raina quickly. For my purposes, it'd be better to irritate them a little first.

She clawed at my face.

I tossed her into the tub and quickly locked the door behind me. "You have two options, Raina: bathe or I bathe you."

"This is abuse!" she screamed at me. "You're a monster!"

I crossed my arms and put my back to the door. "Choose, Raina."

"I told you I can't! It won't let me! They won't let me!" She gestured widely.

"Who? What are their names, Raina?"

"I don't know!"

Laura was suddenly pounding on the bathroom door behind me. She must've found her spine. "You can't do this, Felix! Let her go!"

"I don't want to do this." My voice boomed through the tiny room, cutting through both Raina and Laura's protests. I nodded to Raina. "I want you to do it."

Her jaw trembled and she lowered her head, letting tears fall. "I can't."

I pushed away from the door and put my hand gently on her back. "I know it hurts. I know you don't want to, but our only goal here is to make your body uninhabitable for any forces that may be controlling you against your will. That means we have to do what it doesn't want you to do. You have to fight it with everything you have, in every way you can. That begins here. You're strong, Raina. I know you can do it, but if you doubt, my job is to help you. Do you understand?"

She nodded slowly.

"Will you do it, Raina?"

She lifted red, bloodshot eyes. "I want to try. It's just…" Her eyes flicked to the closed door.

"You're not comfortable with me in the room." I took my hand off her back and stepped away.

"No offense."

I was glad to hear it. A demon wouldn't care. I would have expected someone in the grip of possession to use the opportunity to seduce me. It wouldn't be the first time, and that was a trick they liked to play all the time.

"If I open the door and let your mother in here, would that be better?" I asked.

Raina considered it a long moment and nodded.

I carefully unlocked the door. "I'm still going to be in the doorway, Raina. Just in case."

The door swung open. Laura blocked most of the doorway with her body. She glared at me, then pushed past to go to her daughter.

I took up a sentry position in front of the door, blocking the exit with my arms crossed. "Get her cleaned up, Laura."

"But what if she—"

"Do it no matter how much it hurts her. Raina can take it." I glanced over my shoulder at them.

Laura stared at me for a long moment, a shocked and worried expression on her face. Then she turned to her daughter and helped her undress.

"You know," said Sean, suddenly beside me, mimicking my posture, "you catch more flies with honey than salt."

I lowered my chin to my chest. "What do you know? You're not even really there."

"Then why are you talking to me?"

I turned my head to look at him, but he faded to nothing, just dust dancing in the sunlight coming through the window across the hall.

Behind me, Laura ran the bathwater and helped Raina into it, despite Raina's tears. She sobbed at first, and Laura cooed at her daughter, gently trying to reassure her. Eventually, all Raina could do was breathe through the pain.

I stole a look behind me as Laura rose to collect a towel. Raina sat in the bath with her knees drawn, skinny arms wrapped tightly around them as she rocked back and forth. Her skin was bright red like she'd been in intense sun for hours and gotten a sunburn, though her chin trembled as if she were shivering. Her hair hung in damp, ropey strings, leaving her scalp exposed in some areas where she'd ripped out her hair.

There's a phenomenon in military psychology called the thousand-yard stare, that blank look soldiers get while disassociating during a flashback. Raina's face was fixed in one, staring at nothing straight ahead of her while her body went on.

She was suffering as I had suffered. Maybe more. I'd only been a prisoner in my own mind for a few days, and I'd certainly never been dragged to Hell, if that was what'd happened to her. Whatever she remembered of the fifteen years she was gone, it must not have been an easy time. Ten years out from my experience, I still couldn't sleep through the night without a light on. How long did it take to heal from something so horrific? Maybe never.

She tilted her head slightly to look at me. I turned around so all she would see is the back of my head. Her mother helped her out of the bath and dressed her in clean clothes. Raina stood and shivered, unable or unwilling to move her own body. It was hard to tell which.

Dressed in another white gown that hung off her body, Raina took her mother's hand and shuffled into the hallway, turning toward her room.

"What was the last thing you ate?" I asked Raina.

"She held down a protein shake two days ago," said Laura, patting Raina's back. "Just water since then."

"I asked Raina." I sped up so I could get to the studio door first and pulled it open for her. "Laura, have some dry toast brought up. Room temperature water and some plain broth as well."

"Oh, she won't eat that." Laura tried to smile pleasantly and shake her head.

"Bring it up," I repeated. "Otherwise, unless I call for you, I don't expect to be disturbed for the next two hours at least. Understand?"

A fire lit behind her eyes and Laura squared her jaw, but that pleasant smile never faded from her painted lips. "Of course."

I expected Raina to return to her easel, but she ignored it to sit on the edge of her bed. To keep her at ease, I left the door cracked open but stood in front of it so the message was clear. She couldn't leave unless I allowed it. If Raina wanted to go, I'd step aside and let her do as she wished, but not until I was certain it was what *she* wanted and not the entity trying to control her.

She stared up at me, distrust and anger in her dark

eyes. "What now?"

"Now, we talk." I crossed my arms and leaned against the wall, as far away from her as I could be and still be in the same room. "I explained to your mother how dangerous this is, but between us, I don't think she's that interested. Your mother's a bit simple. Likes her orderly world with easily explained events, I think."

She snorted and turned away. "She likes attention more than anything, but I'd bring her the wrong kind."

"Whose idea was the hypnotherapy?"

"My dad's. He's the only one who's really interested in where I've been or why I'm suddenly back." Raina wrinkled her nose and stood. "What's that smell?"

"If I had to wager, I'd say your bedsheets. Probably absorbed some of that awful sulfuric stink you've been emitting. Keep showering, two or three times a day. Perfume and scented lotions in between, if you'd like." I shrugged. "Doesn't matter. But the smell is a sensory thing. Demons like it, and it makes it damn near unbearable for your loved ones to be near you. Separating you from family and friends is a common tactic. Most people mistake the early withdrawal from friends for a symptom of depression."

Raina stood and stripped the sheets and blankets from her bed. "This isn't how I expected an exorcism to go."

"That's because I'm not an exorcist."

She paused while shaking one of her pillows out of a stained pillowcase to appraise me another time as if I'd suddenly changed with that announcement. "Then what are you?"

I shrugged and strode closer. "I've been called a demonologist, but I lack the certification from the Church to use that title professionally. They don't like my methods, and for good reason. While their exorcisms rely primarily on prayer to a single god, and their faith in His power to protect them, I know better. I know more about demons, Hell, and the Devil than the top three cardinals and the pope combined."

"That almost makes you seem overqualified." She wadded up the dirty linens and placed them in a ball by the door.

"I probably am too qualified to be called a demonologist. I've also been called a sensitive." Her posture straightened and her head jerked to the side toward me when I said the last line. "You've heard that term before?"

Raina nodded and gestured to the drawings all around her. "When I started doing this, the first person my father called was some psychic. Took me to her office where she held my hand, smiled a lot, and told me I was a gifted clairvoyant. She smelled like baby powder and cat piss."

I couldn't help but laugh at that. Wasn't that most self-proclaimed psychics though? Your average psychic was just really good at reading expressions and performing quick background checks once they had your credit card number.

"Before you were taken?" I pressed. "Did you have any premonitions before?"

She shook her head and sank onto the naked bed. "No. I was just a normal kid. I don't know what happened while I was gone, but when I came back, I was like this. The images I draw aren't places I've been or seen. Half the time, I don't even know what I'm drawing until it's drawn. I can't not draw them either. It's like…there's something inside my head, scratching at the inside of my skull, tapping, whispering in the dead of night to be let out. When I don't draw, I can't sleep. Can't eat. Can't breathe."

I spied a chair buried underneath a few empty canvases. After carefully removing the canvases, I dragged the chair to the center of the room and spun it around so I could sit and lean against the back. "Raina, I'm going to be honest with you. I think you can handle it, but it's probably not going to be easy to hear."

"I want to hear it." She nodded and mimicked one of her mother's poses, folding her hands neatly in front of her.

"I'm not sure if you're possessed by some demon. It's possible. You've met some of the criteria traditionally used to determine if someone is possessed or not."

Her eyebrows rose. "But?"

I sighed. "But not others. Your clairvoyance is troubling. Sometimes people with these sorts of abilities can act as beacons for spirits. It doesn't necessarily mean you're possessed. You could simply be channeling a ghost or spirit that's lingering around. In that case, there's little I can do to help."

"But you said you were a sensitive. If anyone can help me, it's you!"

"No, Raina. You'll have to help yourself. Whether we're dealing with a demonic presence or some malevolent spirit of another kind, only you can take the lead when it comes to expelling or embracing it." I folded my arms over the back of the chair. "I have no doubt that you're being tormented by something, and I aim to get to the bottom of it, but I also have a secondary interest in your case. A personal one."

She blinked twice. "What sort of interest?"

"I'd like to recreate the hypnotherapy session where you spoke about your trip to Hell."

"No," Raina said firmly, shooting to her feet. "Absolutely not."

"Why not?"

"Because I don't want to be out of control of my own body!" Her bony fingers twitched at her side.

"The answers to everything could be hidden in the memories you've lost. Where you got your abilities, why you, why did you return…we could answer all those questions with one afternoon session, Raina."

"I said no," she ground out through clenched teeth. Her eyes widened and a dark light flashed in her eyes. The shadows behind her grew deeper and twitched, splitting and growing into two separate and distinct shapes. They twitched and curled on their own like smoke for a moment before merging back together.

The door opened behind me and Laura backed through it with a tray of the food I'd requested. "Is everything all right in here?"

I flashed Laura a wide smile. "Perfect. Thank you." I stood, took the tray from Laura, and placed it on the chair I'd just been occupying, carefully turning the chair so the tray was facing Raina.

Laura stood behind me, wringing her hands. "Anything else?"

"No. I think that'll be all." I walked Laura to the door, and this time I shut it behind her. I turned back to Raina who was frowning at the tray of bland food I'd had brought up. "If you want to go back to your painting, I expect you to finish either the toast or the broth."

"I won't be able to keep it down," she protested. Nevertheless, she picked up the spoon and lifted some of the steaming soup to her lips.

CHAPTER NINE

Dinner did not go as planned. Raina got through only a few spoonfuls of soup before she vomited violently into the room's trash can. Considering her mother said she could only keep down water, she expelled a considerable amount of other substances, a whole rainbow of them.

After the first wave subsided, she sat in front of the can, sobbing and holding her stomach. I slid the tray aside and offered her the room temperature water. "Dry heaves hurt worse than actually throwing up. You're better off putting something in to come up."

Raina shoved the water away, gripped the sides of the trash can and heaved, though nothing came up. After a few tries, she made a choking sound.

I dropped to my knees beside her and pulled her still damp hair back from her face. "What is it, Raina?"

She continued to make gagging sounds until she reached into her mouth and slowly pulled out a matted thread of human hair. It would've been tempting to think Raina had only swallowed her own hair, except this hair was bright red. More disturbing, it was the same color as Sean's.

I let go of her hair and stumbled almost drunkenly away from her. It was impossible. Sean was gone, dragged to Hell long before I'd even met Raina, and there was no way she knew of him or his presence. *Plenty of people have red hair*, I told myself. *Maybe it's dyed. Maybe it belongs to someone else in the family I haven't met yet.* There were a thousand explanations for why Raina would vomit a wad of paprika-colored hair, and yet my mind had fixated on the one.

Raina pulled the hair from her throat, but that wasn't all. Shining in the center of the wadded nest of hair was a silver sewing needle. She stared at it wide-eyed and spat blood into the can. "What's happening to me?"

I finally came to my senses and swallowed the rush of fear that had bile surging into my throat. It'd been a long time since a scene had affected me like that. Was it because it'd reminded me of Sean, or because this was turning out to be anything but a typical possession?

"It's taunting me." I stepped away from the wall to grip Raina by the shoulders and turn her around. "I speak now to the entity inside of Raina Hemlock. Show yourself!" I shook her roughly. "Come on! Show yourself, you bastard!"

Across the room, the painted canvases began to rattle, tapping noisily against the walls and the floor.

"Let me go!" Raina shouted and tried to tear away.

I held her fast. "Answer me, demon, ghost, spirit…whatever you are, I command you to come forth!"

Several paintings fell over, slamming to the floor with a loud bang.

I placed my palm on her forehead, forcing her head back. "I know you're in there. Come forward!"

She stared at me with terrified eyes as her arms stiffened and pulled behind her as if someone held her with an invisible thread. Raina let out a single gasp before her eyes widened and her head snapped forward, pushing my hand away. A slow, sinister smile spread over her face while an inhuman snarl crawled from her mouth. "*Ne mandās me, peccātor.*"

"*Nōn territus sum per tuīs obscēnitātibus, daemon,*" I spat back. "You're going to have to do more than that if you want to scare me. Do something new."

"Scare you?" Raina's grin widened. "I don't give a shit about you. The bitch is mine, her and this whole fucking family!" Her arms sprang forward as if launched from a slingshot and struck my ribs.

I slid over the floor and crashed into another set of paintings that broke over my head. Horrible growls and snarls emanated from Raina while I fought to get free of the broken canvas, wincing every time I had to move my torso. When I freed myself, I found Raina standing on her tiptoes, arms and head hanging limply. It looked almost as if she were a corpse hanging from the rafters until her head snapped up.

She blinked and looked around the room as if she didn't know where she was. "Felix?"

My heart jumped into my throat. That voice…it was a dead ringer for Sean's.

"Felix, where am I?"

"You're not him." I pushed up from the floor, holding onto my injured side. "You don't even know him."

The thing inside Raina laughed in the wrong voice.

"Oh, but I do. We've gotten to know each other very well, Sean Yeats and I. He is ours, just like the girl!"

"You can't have her." I dragged myself the few steps across the room to take Raina by the sides of her face. "Fight it, Raina. You're stronger than this!"

Her whole body seized up as if someone had a rope around her neck, pulling her away from me. She gasped and flew out of my grasp to slam into the opposite wall. Boxes full of paint tumbled down over where she lay, still as death. I limped over to her side and shoved the boxes away to press two fingers to her neck. She had a pulse, but her lips held a pale bluish tinge.

"Raina!" I grunted as I dragged her away from the mess to lay her flat on the floor.

She didn't answer, not even as I slapped the side her face gently.

I pressed my ear to her chest. Despite the strong heartbeat, Raina's lungs were still.

"Christ," I muttered to myself and tilted her head back. "How the fuck do I always get into these messes?" I pinched Raina's nose closed and closed my mouth over hers to begin rescue breaths.

The second my skin touched hers, I tumbled into a vision.

I was no longer in Raina's room, or any room for that matter. Darkness pressed in from all sides except above where a blinding white light shone. I tried to move toward it, but my limbs were tied down. No, strapped down, and I was lying naked on an uncomfortably thin mattress. A familiar pressure closed around my bicep. A blood pressure cuff squeezing so hard it cut off circulation for a moment, leaving my arm in pins and needles.

Masked faces leaned over me, eyes shielded by thick

protective goggles. Latex gloves snapped into place and one of the strangers lifted a drill. Breath filtered through heavy ventilation in the protective suit as the drill-wielding stranger leaned in toward my face. "This will hurt."

I tried to scream as they drilled a hole in my skull between the eyes, but my jaw had been wired shut. Blood flowed from the fresh hole down into my eyes, stinging and blinding me. I thought I should pass out from the pain, or else the shock of losing so much blood, but somehow, I stayed awake, alert, and aware through the whole procedure. I felt the rush of air when they drilled through into my cranial cavity, the sting of what felt like antiseptic as they wiped away the blood from the hole with rough fingers.

I blinked and blood tears traced down my cheeks. "Why are you doing this to me?"

But the strangers in protective suits didn't answer, and once they'd drilled the first hole between my eyes, they placed the drill just below my right eye and repeated, "This will hurt."

I snapped out of the vision when Raina came around enough to push me away. She sat up, doubled over, coughing while I crawled into the corner away from her. Despite knowing I was back in my own body, back in reality, I could still feel the cold bite of the drill resting against my cheek. When I touched my cheek, my fingers came away speckled in scarlet.

What the fuck?

"Go," Raina whispered. Her arms trembled as she gripped a blanket to pull it down on top of her. "Please, just go."

In her state, she shouldn't have been left alone, but there was little I could do for her, especially as shaken as I was. I rose without a word and went out of the studio, having made virtually no progress.

***

I found my way to the back porch where I lit a cigarette and stared off into the forest beyond. The Hemlocks had decorated their back patio with white wicker chairs and a big stone fire pit that didn't look like it'd been used in ages. A big silver grill stood under an awning. I tried to imagine the senator and his wife out there hosting a barbeque and it didn't fit. He probably never manned the grill, and she probably didn't go around filling people's drinks. They had staff for that.

What would Raina's life have been like if she'd been allowed to grow up as a senator's kid and not in whatever hellscape she'd been in for the last fifteen years? And had she really been to Hell? It was the end of my first day with the family and I was still no closer to my answers than when I'd arrived. Tomorrow I'd have to make a harder push.

Raina had refused hypnosis though, and I didn't dare try it without her consent. Hypnosis was a funny beast. For it to work, the subject had to be open to it and believe it worked. Raina believed in hypnosis or the original hypnotist wouldn't have succeeded in the first place, and she wouldn't be so afraid of it now. I had to convince her to overcome that fear so I could find out where she'd really been.

There was no doubt in my mind, however, that I was dealing with a possession, and not just any possession. Raina was a clairvoyant, maybe even a medium. I still didn't know the extent of her abilities, and that was a problem. I was fighting my battle blind, which meant I needed someone else to be my eyes.

I crushed the cigarette on the smooth stone wall of the fire pit and sat down on top of the wall, frowning at my cell phone. While I knew who I needed to call, it was a call I wasn't looking forward to making. The last time I'd spoken to Jade, I'd promised myself it would be the last.

This is different, I told myself. It's business, and she owes me. Not that I could point that out, not to Jade. If I was being honest, I owed her a lot more than she'd ever owe me. After Sean, she'd given me purpose when no one else could. That didn't make the call any easier.

This is for Sean. I swallowed the dry nervousness in my throat and dialed.

The phone rang twice before a man on the other side picked up. "Mistress Jade's residence, Sloth speaking."

"Is the mistress available? This is Felix Cross."

"One minute." The phone creaked as he put it down.

A minute later it creaked again as someone else picked up. "Felix Cross," purred Jade on the other end, "I knew one day you'd come crawling back to me. How can I be of service?"

I tugged on the collar of my shirt. It was cold outside, but the air suddenly felt heavier at the sound of her voice. "This isn't a social call, Jade."

"*Onee-sama*," she corrected. "Come now, Puppy. I trained you better."

A lot of women in her profession liked to be called Mistress, or Madam, but not Jade. No, that was far too mundane for such a large and elegant personality. Even princess or queen wasn't big enough for her. She had to choose a Japanese honorific that not only elevated her to a position of awe, but reduced those who addressed her to being her bitch. Not wholly inappropriate, considering.

I sighed, lowered my head, and closed my eyes. "*Onee-sama*. I'm calling because I need your help on a case."

Jade hesitated long enough I wondered if she'd hung up. "What kind of help?"

I told Jade everything about Raina, the demon, the family. I told her more than I'd even written in my diary to Sean because I knew to hold back any information would make her unhappy. Old habits die hard.

When I was finished, she made a small sound somewhere between a grunt and a sigh. "And your empathy isn't working on her?"

"Not at all."

"You do realize what you're asking me to do?"

"Yes," I said. "Please, *Onee-Sama*. It could help me get Sean back."

"And what do I get out of it? I don't work for free, Puppy. Ass, grass, or cash. Nobody—not even you—gets to ride for free."

I shifted the phone. "Well, the Church is footing the bill for the case. I'm sure Bishop X will be ecstatic about writing a check to a dominatrix. Hell, you should come just to see his face when he has to pay you."

Jade laughed. "Oh, I do love a man of the cloth. They're good at groveling. Text me the address. I'll be there as soon as I can. And Puppy? Wear something black."

"Always." I hung up and sighed. It was cold enough outside that I could see my breath. I watched the cloud form and float away, wondering what Sean would think of me now.

CHAPTER TEN

THEN

I woke in darkness to find myself alone on the sofa. How long had Felix and I laid there? Long enough I'd missed all my classes. I sat up, rubbing my face, and picked up my cell. Three missed calls from Bishop X. Dammit all.

My thumb paused on the screen, just short of returning the bishop's call. Felix was retching in the bathroom. I eyed the bottle of vodka still sitting on the table. I'd had a little too much, but I wasn't drunk. Just on the edge of a decent buzz. Felix had drunk even less, so it couldn't be that, especially not after so long. Maybe he'd picked up a stomach bug, or eaten something that disagreed with him. He never was very particular about his food.

I cast the phone aside and walked through the darkened apartment to the bathroom door. A sliver of golden light told me the light was on. I rapped on the door three times. "Felix? You okay?"

The toilet flushed. Water splashed in the sink and

the door opened just wide enough that I could see his bloodshot eyes and pale sweaty face. "Probably best if you keep your distance, Sean. I'm not feeling so hot."

"What is it? Maybe I can help." I put my hand on the door and pushed it open. The whole room stank of sickness.

"The flu, I think." He drew an arm over his face. "Can't keep anything down. I'm sore head to toe too."

"Did you take your temperature?"

He shook his head.

I sighed and barged into the bathroom to open the medicine cabinet above the sink. "Of course you didn't. Typical Felix Cross."

"It's just the flu, Sean," he protested. "I need to sleep it off is all."

"I'll be the judge of that. Say ahh!" I popped the end of the thermometer under his tongue when he opened his mouth and waited by the door, arms crossed for it to beep. Even before the thermometer told me he was running a fever well over a hundred, I knew it. I could smell it on him. The stink of sickness and infection rolled off his body in waves, strong enough to make the eyes water. "A hundred and three? That's bad, Felix. Did you take anything for it?"

"Tried. Can't keep anything down long enough to digest." He glanced at the toilet, then closed the lid.

I ran the thermometer under the hot tap. "We should take you to the campus clinic, just in case."

"I'm fine," Felix insisted and pulled the door open the rest of the way. "I just need to rest." He staggered down the hall toward his room.

There was nothing left for me to do but follow him and make sure he got into bed. Felix's bedroom was the picture of order. Neither of us was a clean freak, but he was particular about how he kept his space. Books went on the bookshelf, the bed meticulously made, everything in its place. I was organized, but not like that. He had a whole system, but one that only seemed to make sense to him. For example, his books weren't arranged according to any system I understood, though he'd grumped at me once for putting one in wrong. Sometimes, I wondered if Felix just existed on a different wavelength than the rest of us.

He half-crawled, half-fell into bed, shoving the blanket down. "You shouldn't be here, Sean. Go help Bishop X."

"X can wait." I pulled the blanket up to his chest. "Someone needs to be here to look after you."

He shook his head and yanked the blanket up to his chin. "You'll just get sick too. Flu is contagious."

"I got my flu shot, dummy."

Felix grunted and turned over, curling into the fetal position. I sat on the edge of his bed until I was sure he was asleep, and then left the room.

For the next two days, I did hourly checks, putting my hand on his head to gauge his body temperature, waking him every once in a while to go to the bathroom and take some water. I even made him soup from scratch, but Felix couldn't keep anything down. Whenever he tried to eat or drink anything, he was in the bathroom within minutes, vomiting until nothing else would come up.

I knew we needed help when the muscle cramps and weakness became so bad, he couldn't get off the bathroom floor. The campus doctor wasn't willing to come to us, but I did convince one of my nursing friends, Damien, to have a look.

Damien came in his scrubs, donned his face mask and his latex gloves, and took Felix's vitals. He looked at Felix's eyes, his tongue, and did a quick swab of his throat before coming out to see me in the hallway.

"It looks like the flu," Damien said, pulling down his mask.

I nodded. "That's what he was saying."

"He's dehydrated, though. You should probably get him to the hospital for a liter of fluids, Sean. Dehydration is dangerous."

I frowned and rubbed the back of my head, glancing through the open door to where Felix lay in his bed. "Is he going to be okay?"

Damien shrugged and pulled off his gloves. "Felix is young and healthy without any serious underlying health problems. Chances that he'd die from influenza are pretty low. His lungs are clear, which is good. No pneumonia. Dehydration is the biggest danger to him now. You want my advice? Hospital. Now. Don't wait."

Damien and I loaded Felix into the back of Damien's little white coupe and drove him over to Mount Sinai Hospital, where we spent a miserable five hours in the waiting room before they called him back.

The nurse stopped me at triage. "I'm sorry. We only allow immediate family back with patients."

I leaned around her to watch as a nurse shuffled a weak and disoriented Felix further away from me. "I'm the closest thing to family he's got."

"Be that as it may, unless you're a blood relative, or a spouse, you're not allowed back." She closed in, putting a hand on my shoulder. The touch was gentle, but the message clear. If I pushed the issue, I'd have to deal with security.

I paced in the waiting area for another four hours, occasionally asking for updates they refused to give me. With each inquiry, I got more and more irritated. For all I knew, he was back there dying alone, though I hoped that wasn't the case. I tried not to dwell on it, alternating between pacing and praying, but it ate at me.

Outside, the weather shifted. Rain blew in sometime in the early morning, and by late morning, it'd shifted to thunderstorms. The worse the storm got, the more patients seemed to pour through the doors.

I bowed my head to pray as the clock ticked toward noon the next day and heard a strange beep. My cell was low on battery. Shit, the bishop! He'd think I'd given him the cold shoulder. I needed to call and explain things or else I'd have an awkward talk once this was all over. Not just that, but Felix's grade was on the line.

Since my cell didn't have enough battery to call out, I left the emergency department and found a payphone to call the bishop on. I expected to get voicemail since it was the middle of the day and he was probably in a meeting or teaching a class, but he picked up. "Bishop Xavier speaking."

"X, it's me. Sean Yeats."

He sucked in a deep breath, cleared his throat. "One moment." There was a muffled thump as he put the phone down for a moment only to return after another thud. Probably the door shutting. "I've been trying to reach you and Felix, Sean."

"I know. I'm sorry." I leaned into the payphone. "I saw you called, but something came up and I only just now had enough clarity to remember to call you back."

"I was calling about Marci's exorcism."

I sighed and rubbed my aching head. "I'm sorry we weren't able to continue assisting with Marci's exorcism. Don't take it out on Felix. I can explain."

"Marci Reed passed away, Sean."

A cold chill ran through me from head to toe. I shivered and swallowed, thinking I must have misheard. "What?"

"The girl is dead," X repeated.

I looked around the empty hallway, suddenly aware that I was alone. Then it hit me. This could all go wrong. Two untrained grad students, not even out of seminary, assisting on an exorcism without a doctor present...this was the sort of thing you went to prison for.

As soon as I thought it, guilt settled into the pit of my stomach like a coiled knot of vipers. A girl was dead, and here I was, worrying about my own skin. All our efforts that night in the Reed house had been for nothing. We'd lost. Whatever evil we'd been battling that night had won.

"Oh, no," I muttered into the phone. "No, no...how? When?"

"Shortly after we left the next morning," replied X. "Her mother found her. She was just gone."

"I told you she needed a hospital!" I shouldn't have shouted at the bishop, especially not while standing in a hospital hallway, but I couldn't help it. I'd warned him and he didn't listen and now a girl was dead. "Her blood is on your hands, X! If this falls back on us—"

"I will accept whatever blame there is for the situation." His tone was calm, measured. It was almost chilling to hear. "For now, the parents are grieving. The diocese and the school will assist however we can."

"I should hope so. You robbed them of a daughter,

X."

"Satan and his demons did that, Mr. Yeats."

I couldn't think of anything to say back, so I just stood there, numb and aching simultaneously.

"Sean?"

I shifted the phone against my ear. "Yes, I'm still here."

"Because of the nature of this, I must ask…what is it that came up and kept you from returning my calls?"

"Felix is sick," I said. "He came down with the flu. I'm at the hospital with him now. He's pretty bad off, X."

"I see." There was a long moment of hesitation before he asked, "Would you like me to come down there and pray with you?"

"I can pray just fine on my own," I said and hung up the phone.

A loud crack of thunder rattled the windows in their panes. Lightning flashed outside, distorting shadows and illuminating strange clouds. The lights in the hallway flickered and died for a moment. When they came back up, I turned away from the phone and gasped in a breath at the sight of Felix standing two feet from me. With his dehydration and illness, he looked like a shrunken, decaying version of himself.

"Felix!" I grabbed my chest. "You scared the snot out of me!"

He lowered his head and mumbled, "Sorry."

"Did they discharge you?"

Felix nodded slowly. "Nothing more they can do. Just fluids, rest, and Zofran." He waved a tiny slip of paper, a prescription, no doubt. Hopefully, it'd help with the nausea.

"Oh, good." I took the prescription from him and

we started down the hallway. "How'd you find me?"

Felix lifted and dropped one shoulder. "Just knew where you were. Lucky guess. Who was on the phone?"

"I was talking to X." I almost told him about Marci, but I didn't want him to worry. His only concern for the moment should be getting better. We could talk about Marci and the implications after he'd recovered. "Don't worry about him and Marci. I got it handled. Did they say it was flu?"

"Don't know what it is." He folded his arms and stifled a shiver after a particularly loud crash of thunder. "No elevated white blood cell count, which means no infection. No viruses. All the tests said I shouldn't be sick at all. They think it's some sort of food poisoning."

"You barely ate the day before though."

Felix just shrugged again.

I stepped in front of him and stopped his progress with a hand on his shoulder. "Are you sure you're okay, Felix? You know, sometimes they discharge people too soon. We could go back and ask for more tests."

"I'm fine," he insisted. "I just want to go home. Can we go home now, please?"

I sighed and nodded. I didn't have the heart to tell him otherwise. I could tell him about Marci and X after he was feeling better. Until then, it was my job to take care of him. Everything else could wait.

CHAPTER ELEVEN

NOW

I went back to my room, arranged the blankets, remembered I should check on Raina, and did so. Then I returned to my room and paced until it was time to check on her again. On both occasions, she was asleep when I cracked open the door. She'd wrapped a sheet around herself on the floor where she lay.

It wasn't until the third time that I worked up enough sense to enter the room and check that she was breathing. My experience earlier in the evening, coupled with an intense and unmet craving for another cigarette, and my empty stomach, left me scatterbrained and anxious. It took a while to shake all that off. I should've just propped open the window for a cigarette, but Laura didn't want me smoking in the house.

The floor creaked as I stepped into the room. Raina didn't wake. Not as I came closer, nor as I picked up some broken canvas and moved it aside, not as I stood over her body, twisted in the clean white sheets Willa had brought up. Her dark hair fell over her face in ropey threads, hiding all but her lips. The few loose and broken threads that lay over her mouth twitched in and out with steady breath.

I should've left her as she was. Instead, I decided I should pick her up and move her into bed. I knelt and slid my arms under her body. When I tried to stand with her in my arms, though, my back reminded me of the old injuries. It gave out with a strained pop and we fell together in a tumbled mess. Pain blinded me, drove me to double over at first, but the position was too painful. All I could do was lay flat against her, trying to remember how to breathe.

Raina never woke up. The earlier ordeal must've worn her out enough to put her in a deep sleep.

The pain faded to a dull throb instead of the sharp stab it'd been a moment earlier. I put a palm flat against the floor and pushed myself up, pausing at the sight of her. After her bath, her mother had dressed her in an unflattering white nightgown that buttoned down the middle. Either in my pained scuffle or while she was sleeping, half the buttons had come undone, leaving her pale breasts exposed.

I should have covered her up and walked away. That's what a good man would do, respect the poor suffering woman's decency. But then, I'd never been a particularly good person. Not since I lost Sean. I hovered over her, frozen, seized by a stupid fascination with two pale pink lumps of flesh the size of oranges. Part of my mind considered my stupidity, the consequences of getting caught in such a compromising position flashing through my mind. They'd toss me out on my ass, and be right for it, even though I wasn't doing anything but looking. I didn't

E.A. Copen

have permission to look. I knew she didn't want me to look because of our earlier discussion in the bathroom, and yet…here I was, gawking at her with her tits hanging out, letting my caveman brain indulge itself in a quick fantasy.

I wondered what it'd be like to fuck a possessed woman. It should have disgusted me, but then, everything else should have, too. The more taboo the subject, the more it'd always interested me. That was why I'd gotten into religion in the first place. So many things off limits. Once, I'd believed the tight restrictions would make me a better person. All my conversion did was give me new ways to sin.

A board creaked behind me. I had enough frame of mind left to turn my head. No one was there that I could see, but the hair on the back of my neck stood on end, aware of a presence I couldn't perceive with my eyes. Or maybe it was just guilt.

I swallowed the dry tension in my throat and adjusted Raina's sheet over her chest with trembling fingers. My back screamed at me as I forced my body to stand, but even the pain of the old injury wasn't enough to convince my caveman brain we had other priorities. I had to adjust myself just to walk out of the room. At least I didn't encounter anyone in the hallway.

Safe in my room, I locked the door behind me and leaned against it, letting the cool of the wood absorb through my clothes. Dammit, what the hell was wrong with me? What sort of monstrous person was I that I'd entertain such fantasies, even for a moment?

It's this place, I thought, touching my forehead. This case. Everything about it is wrong.

Despite Laura's wishes, I lit a cigarette and held it

pinched between two trembling fingers. I opened the window and sat next to it while I smoked. That'd have to be enough.

Demons attack whatever weakness they can find, I reasoned, staring out at the long shadows of naked willows and upright pointed hemlocks. Weakness of the flesh had always been one of mine. I'd never have made it as a priest. Even back then, I knew, but what else was I supposed to do? I'd been raised in the faith, my whole life shaped by my connection to the Church and the people in it. When I was lost, the Church had always seemed like it had the answers.

It was all a lie. There was no cure for the human condition. Our very nature was to sin, to seek out forbidden pleasures, and indulge. It wasn't the Devil that made us do it either. Mankind was born addicted to pleasure, and every time we indulged, that addiction got stronger. A life of chastity, poverty, and obedience to God was one long battle of denial, and I wasn't strong enough for it. Maybe I was a good enough con man to lie to my advisors, various bishops, priests, and even my parents, but even I wasn't egotistical enough that I believed I could fool the Devil. He knew my weaknesses and he'd exploit every last damn one of them to win.

I flicked glowing ashes onto the windowsill. "Joke's on you, pal. I don't feel the least bit guilty about getting turned on. It's called being human."

A light moved in the darkness outside, a little glowing yellow orb shifting through the long shadows of trees. If I squinted just right, I thought I could make out the silhouette of the housekeeper, Willa, walking into the forest behind the house. She paused at the tree line and turned, holding the old-fashioned lantern high as she looked behind her. The woman's eyes fell on me, dark and disapproving.

I smashed the cigarette against the windowsill before I shut the window and the curtains.

I turned out the light, fresh nicotine flowing through my veins, and climbed under the covers, but I couldn't sleep, not with the memory of Raina's body in my mind. What's a guy to do in that situation but scratch the itch? And why not? How many studies have been released over the years extolling masturbation as good for you? Good for your blood pressure, for your mental health, for your heart...it even supposedly reduced your risk for certain types of cancer. Jerking off's as natural as shitting, but nobody wants to admit that out loud.

The blankets next to me shifted, lifted, and the bed bounced as if someone were climbing into it with me. Sean's familiar musky scent filled the air around me. I didn't stop.

His breath tickled the side of my neck. "I saw you earlier, looking at her."

That was impossible. Wherever Sean was, I knew he wasn't in the house with me. He was never with me, even when I wanted him to be. Losing him had broken a piece of me, twisted my mind. His phantom was the result of that break, a coping mechanism I'd invented to survive a situation that might've destroyed a lesser man.

Foreign fingertips brushed against the line of hair in the center of my chest. "I used to wish you'd look at me like that. Used to wish we could be like this. Together. Except in my fantasy, you don't do this yourself." The familiar warm strength of Sean's hand closed over me.

I took my hand away, content to let a ghost who wasn't there finish all the hard work for me. It was a strange sensation, both knowing he wasn't there, but feeling him there in every way, hearing his steady breathing in my ear, smelling his breath. I turned my head and felt the touch of lips and tongue I knew couldn't be there, but they were as real to me as the bed and the house.

The bed moved. Sean's weight shifted, settling on top of me. How could that feel so real? Was I crazy? Maybe I'd fallen asleep in the middle of my own fantasy and this was just a wishful dream.

"I'm real," Sean promised. "As real as you want me to be."

The real Sean wouldn't say anything like that, but I was too lost in the moment, in what he was doing to me, to care that he wasn't real. Did it matter what was real and not? I was real, and what I wanted—needed—that was real, too, wasn't it?

"I can be her, too," he whispered.

The pressure on top of me shifted, lightening. Soft, feminine fingers wrapped around mine and took my hands to curved hips and firm breasts. Raina's voice gasped as I pinched and twisted skin between my fingers. Yet, I felt Sean with me too, his rougher hands on my chest and chin, touching, caressing, encouraging me to thrust faster, harder, make her scream louder. It all mixed, the hands, the voices, the touch, and the need, until I didn't know who I was fucking, or what. It didn't matter. Just that it was happening, and I couldn't stop, even if I wanted.

When other people describe climax, it's fireworks or an explosion of pleasure. That's bullshit. It's a profoundly lonely act, coming into nothing, alone in the dark, but more so when you have to invent ghosts and figments to do it with.

Still, this wasn't like the other times. It felt more real, more visceral, and the oxytocin high that came after was unusual, more like the real thing. Neither Sean nor Raina's bodies faded when I finished. They simply retreated into the dark, like a lover sneaking away to the bathroom.

I, however, remained frozen, unable to move. My hands pinned to my side as if someone were holding me. I tried to struggle, to turn my head, but it was no use. I was trapped, unable to do anything but breathe.

The bedroom door creaked open and a sliver of yellow light fell on me where I lay. My breathing quickened as I recognized the two silhouettes standing in the doorway. The first belonged to Laura Hemlock, the absolute last person I wanted to see at that moment. The second was another prowling mountain lion, this one larger, full grown. Both paced casually into the room to my bedside. Laura stood over me with a candle illuminating her perfect chin and the leopard print silk pajamas she wore. She held a small plastic vial in her other hand.

"Don't be embarrassed, Felix." My chest twitched as she ran her manicured nails over it. "Everybody does it from time to time. But not everybody's so damn useful. Just lie still and you'll forget all about this come morning."

I didn't have a choice. Whatever power held me wasn't one I could break free from.

Laura set aside the candle and slowly, delicately unscrewed the lid on her container. She scraped the opening over my stomach, over my sternum, collecting as much of the spilled seed as she could, shaking it down into the container. Her cat put its big paws up on the bed and purred at me, licking its big teeth.

"My, it's refreshing to have such a young and virile subject for once," she said. "There. That should be enough, although I do hate to waste the rest." Laura smiled the same debutante smile she'd offered when I first arrived. "Enjoy the rest of your evening, Felix. Come, kitty. We have what we need." Laura and her cat retreated to the doorway where Laura paused. "Sleep tight," she said and slammed the door shut.

CHAPTER TWELVE

I sat up in darkness, sweat racing down my back. The bedroom was empty, the door closed. Alone in the dark again. Had any of that happened? I put my head in my hands, trying to draw a line in my mind between reality and the dream. When had one ended and the other begun?

My head throbbed as I threw aside the thin, itchy blanket and put my bare feet on the floor. The night's chill spread up through my heels into my legs, a welcome break from the heat of the bed.

God, I needed another cigarette.

Before I lit up, though, I had to know. I pushed out of bed and paced across the floor to check the door. I'd locked it the night before, hadn't I? Maybe I hadn't. If I'd locked it, it was unlocked now. I let go of the doorknob and decided I must've forgotten to lock the door, a mistake I wouldn't make again.

I returned to the window and pushed aside the heavy drapes. The early hues of morning colored the sky in shadowy streaks of crimson, periwinkle, and gold. Roughly a hundred yards behind the house, the clearing died and the trees took over, crowding out all but the deepest shade. I watched the spot where I'd seen Willa earlier, or thought I had. It didn't look like there was any path leading into the woods. Going into them in the dark seemed like a stupid idea, an easy way to trip on something and break your neck. Then again, I hadn't grown up in rural Kentucky. I was a New York City boy, born and raised in Queens. Not many primordial forests in Queens.

After the cigarette, I grabbed fresh clothes from the bag X had packed for me—all black, of course—and went down the hall to shower. Of all the things I hated the most about staying with other people, the shower was the worst. There was something especially intimate about sharing a showering space with someone else, something that made it feel less clean, less private. Places like beds and bathtubs weren't supposed to house strangers, and yet here I was. I made sure the door was locked this time and hurried through cleaning up.

Willa was in my room when I returned, halfway through changing the sheets.

"Oh, you don't have to do that," I said, leaving the door open. I dropped my used clothes into a pile by the door. "Actually, I'd prefer it if you didn't. I can't share sheets and pillows with anyone else, so unless you've got an unused set—"

"It's my job to clean house." Willa yanked the last corner of the fitted sheet off without looking at me. "I've been doing it for decades, and I won't be told how to do it today." She wadded the sheets, blanket, and pillowcase into a ball and shoved them into a laundry basket she hefted up with a grunt. "I'll get these clean for you before tonight, sir. No need to worry about another set. The lady of the house shared your preferences with me."

I suddenly felt guilty for creating more work for the household. "Look, it's not a preference. I promise I'm not picky. It's just that I'm a sensitive. Makes it hard to share spaces with other people. When I touch certain objects, I have visions. I'd rather not have that when I'm trying to sleep is all. You understand."

"I do as I'm told." She paused by the door to collect the clothes I'd just dropped. "Mrs. Hemlock said to tell you breakfast would be served at seven. I suggest you hurry up if you want to make it." Willa backed through the open door and used her heel to pull it closed behind her.

I sighed. Better check on Raina first.

I paused outside her door on my way to the kitchen and knocked. "Raina, it's Felix."

She didn't answer, so I cracked open the door for a look. At some point in the night, she'd picked herself up and crawled into bed. She lay with her back to the door, curled into a tight ball. I could hear her snoring gently from the door, which was a good sign. She was breathing, at least. That was enough for me. I closed the door as quietly as I could and crept down the stairs.

I hadn't gotten a tour of the house the day before, so I didn't know precisely where the kitchen was, but I could follow the smell of bacon and eggs. I wandered down a long hallway lined with oil paintings. A small stand near the middle of the hall held a vase full of ferns. A photo of Laura posed behind her husband with her hand on his shoulder sat beside it. Both were dressed to kill in their matching blue blazers and wide, white smiles. An American flag hung in their backdrop.

They looked like the perfect senatorial couple. In a few years, the senator's face could be hanging on every post office wall in the nation over a plaque that read President of the United States of America.

Laura was in the dining room at the big table we'd sat at the night before to discuss my plans for Raina. She lowered the glass of orange juice she'd been sipping from and rose from her seat. "Felix! Glad to see you're up! Please, come. Sit."

I hesitated in the doorway, eying the two place settings. "What about Raina?"

She huffed out a breath. "You saw her last night. She wouldn't be able to keep any of this down. Besides, she needs her beauty sleep. You two have a big day today, don't you?"

"I suppose." The only other plate sat in front of the seat to Laura's right. I was uneasy sitting so close to her after the strange dream I'd had the night before, but my stomach won out. I shrugged off the unsettling feeling and sat next to her.

Laura smiled, pleased, and sank back into her chair. "Willa, darling, would you get Felix some coffee? How do you take your coffee?"

"Just black." I scooted my chair in while Willa poured dark coffee into a white mug. She'd gotten down there fast. "Are Willa and Jacob the only staff you have?"

"For now, yes." Laura nodded and leaned on her intertwined fingers. "With a house this size, though, I'd like to bring on a few more people, especially with John being away so much. It gets lonely in a big house like this, and I need help with Raina. Though Willa does a wonderful job." She beamed and put a hand on her maid's arm as she passed.

Willa placed the coffee pot back on the burner. The coffeemaker sat on a table in the corner along with several pitchers of juice. She returned to drop three strips of bacon on my plate along with an over-easy egg and two triangles of buttered toast. I could've served myself, but it seemed impolite to refuse, so I just sat there and let her do it, and thanked her when she was done.

She acknowledged my thanks with a slight bob of the head before shrinking back into the corner of the room to await further instructions.

"I was wondering when the senator would be back from Washington," I said.

She shrugged. "Who knows? Politics is boring but unpredictable. He comes and goes like a summer rainstorm, my John. The life of a public servant."

Laura sipped her juice while I pushed the egg around on my plate, thinking about the night before, and how disturbing that dream had been. It'd been a long time since I'd had a dream that odd, especially considering all the precautions I'd taken to prevent nightmares.

"Is something the matter?" Laura asked.

I lowered my fork. "You didn't happen to come into my room last night, did you?"

Her lips turned up in a tight smile. "Why on Earth would I do that?"

I shrugged and went back to pushing my eggs around. "It's nothing. Just a dream, I think."

She chuckled. "Well, I suppose I should be honored to be so in your thoughts that you'd dream about me."

My cheeks were suddenly burning. "It's not like that."

"Oh, sweetie, it's all right if it is." Laura's hand

closed on my thigh under the table.

My appetite suddenly vanished, and I had to suppress a shudder before I pulled my leg away. "As flattered as I am, I would never take advantage of your hospitality, especially not while your husband's away."

She rolled her eyes. "Oh, trust me when I say John's not a problem. The truth is, John and I have been in an open relationship for years. It doesn't work for everyone, but…well…once you've been married for so long, you have to do something to spice things up."

"I'm not interested, Laura."

Her smile faded. "I see. Then maybe my husband is more your type? Since you were asking about him."

I stood, pushing the chair out behind me. "Mrs. Hemlock, I'm here to help Raina."

"Ah, I see. My mistake." She cleared her throat. "My, now everything's going to be so awkward, isn't it? Can we just pretend this conversation never happened? I'd hate for you to feel unwelcome, Felix."

"Sure, whatever." I waved my hands and sat back down, just glad to get it behind me. At least now I could focus on what I'd come there to do, which was to deal with whatever was possessing Raina and get my answers.

"Well, if you'll excuse me, I do have some things I need to attend to." Laura stood and pushed in her chair. "It was lovely having breakfast with you, Felix. I'm afraid I'll be out of the house for most of the day today. I'm trusting you to care for Raina in my absence."

I nodded. "Of course."

Her smile widened. "Very good." Her heels clicked out of the room and down the hall.

I couldn't eat until she was gone. When I finished

my plate, Willa swooped in to take it from me. It was all I could do to grab a few extra triangles of buttered bread to take up to Raina. I wondered if they even tried to feed her before I arrived.

With the buttered bread in hand, I went upstairs to knock on Raina's door again. This time, she answered and invited me in. Raina was already at her easel, working on a new painting, more smears of black and gray with streaks of pink broken by bright red lines.

I took up a position behind her, studying the painting, trying to determine what she was working on, but the project was too early in to know. "What are you painting today, Raina?"

"I don't know." She shook her head. "Won't know until it's done."

"Can you put the brush down? I'd like you to try and eat again." I held out one of the toast triangles.

Raina's brush stilled, but only for a moment. "You know what happened last time."

"This won't be like last time. I've taken the time to bless the bread using an old ritual I know. You should be able to eat it." It was a lie, but I wasn't above a little fib if it helped her.

Like hypnosis, a lot of the power of exorcism came from the demoniac's belief that it worked. If Raina believed a prayer or a special ritual would give her the power to expel the demon, then she'd do it. My job was simply to facilitate that process. First, I had to get her to believe I had the power she believed she lacked. Then it would only be a matter of ritualistically transferring that power from myself to her. It was complicated psychology, or it was a lie. Maybe both. Did it really matter what it was if it worked?

Raina turned her head, eyed the toast with a frown,

and then scrutinized my face. "There's some sort of magical toast cleansing ritual? Really?"

"How do you think they make communion wafers?" I held it out to her more insistently. "Just try it."

Raina slowly put the paintbrush down and wiped her fingers over her white nightgown, leaving smears of charcoal black behind. She took the toast from my hand, sniffed it, and then took the smallest bite. While she kept it down for a moment, I wasn't ready to call it a victory until she got the whole half slice in her.

Raina's eyes widened and she stared at the toast as if it really were magic before taking a full bite.

I smiled. "How is it?"

"Good," said Raina with her mouth full of toast. She finished the first piece and snatched up the second, devouring it in a few bites.

I laughed. It's always good to see a plan work out. "Slow down. Let's make sure you can keep it down before we go hog wild, okay?"

She licked her fingers and nodded.

"Your mother's left the house for the day." I crossed my arms and sat down on the edge of her bed. "But we've got plenty of work to keep us busy. I've also got a friend coming to help us with the next stage."

"A friend?" Raina lowered her hand, suddenly on edge again.

I nodded. "Her name is Jade, and she's a medium, which means she's able to see and interact with spirits of all kinds."

"How will that help me?"

"Well, I've been able to confirm we're dealing with possession here, and I suspect there may be at least one entity, but I need to confirm that. There may be more.

Your case is exceptional for several reasons. Besides all that, I think another female presence would make you more comfortable, and Jade has some experience. She taught me a lot about power dynamics, self-control, self-respect…all things that will help. Would you be willing to talk with her when she gets here?"

Raina shrugged and went back to her painting. "Sure."

I sat on the bed and watched her paint for a little while, considering my next set of questions. There was still a lot I didn't know that I should have by then. I'd been so busy trying to deal with the basics, I hadn't done enough digging. "Raina, what do you remember about when you came back from wherever you were? Tell me how it happened."

She shrugged again. "I don't remember where I was or how I got here. Sometimes, things come in flashes or nightmares. Most of the time, it's just a void. I remember being eight, and even some of the day I was taken, but the rest is a blank space."

"Tell me what you remember on either side of that blank space, as much as you can. Even the slightest detail could help." I settled in, resting my hands on my knees and watching as she drew the brush carefully over the canvas in small, delicate strokes.

"I remember having dinner in the kitchen," Raina said. "I didn't like eating in the dining room, especially when Mom and Dad weren't home. They had somewhere to be. Somewhere important. They were always running off to do things like that. Sometimes, I wondered if they really wanted to be my parents because they spent so much time away from me. Anyway, Willa fixed me chocolate chip pancakes for dinner, and I ate them with blueberry syrup she made from scratch. I don't remember much after that, but I was very tired. And then…" Her brush froze. "Small, dark rooms. Cold, stony walls. So many needles piercing my flesh. Whispers, murmurs, screams…the sounds of hellish agony all around me. Pain…like holes in my head. They're putting holes in my head!" She screamed the last line. Her paintbrush clattered to the ground and she grabbed at her forehead, screaming and backing away from the canvas.

I leaped off the edge of the bed to catch her as she went down into a writhing, twitching fit of coughs and gasps. "Focus on my voice, Raina," I said, placing a gloved hand over her forehead. I didn't dare put my bare hand on her head after yesterday's vision. "Focus and fight. Keep control. Don't let it take you."

As she lay there, fighting, her body curling one way, and then the other, I closed my eyes and whispered a prayer. I wasn't big on praying anymore, especially after what happened ten years ago. Any god that would allow a good man like Sean to suffer wasn't one worth my worship, but I didn't know what else to do. Faith had been the cornerstone of my initial experience with the supernatural, so it was what came to mind first.

Eventually, Raina's body relaxed and she lay still, breathing hard. I thought maybe she'd fallen asleep until her eyes snapped open, eyeballs a pure white. "Felix?" The voice she spoke in didn't belong to her.

My fingers tightened around her shoulders and I paused my prayer, shocked at how well she'd mimicked his voice. "Sean?"

"Felix, where are you? It's so dark here." She reached for my face.

I dropped her to the floor and stood. "No," I said, backing away. "No, don't you dare pretend to be him..."

She sat up and stared at me with her white eyes. "What's wrong, Felix? It's me, Sean. Don't you recognize me?"

My back hit a wall and I shrank against it. I knew what I should be doing, how I should combat the thing inside of her that almost certainly wasn't Sean, but hearing his corrupted voice come out of her left me frozen.

Raina's head snapped to the side, away from me. "God, they're coming! You have to help me, Felix!" She looked back at me, arms outstretched. "Please! What are you waiting for, dammit? Take my hand and save me!"

Terror gripped my intestines and twisted them into a tight knot. What if it was Sean she was channeling? What if she could somehow communicate with him?

I launched myself away from the wall and gripped Raina tightly by the shoulders. "Where are you? Quickly, Sean! Tell me what you see!"

"Nothing! It's so dark here...dark and sweltering. I hear them coming! They're almost here! Please, you have to get me out before they—" She sucked in a sharp gasped and jerked her head backward, her arms going limp.

"Sean!" My fingers tightened around her shoulders. "Raina!"

Her lips turned up and she let out a hoarse laugh before lifting her head to smile at me. "They're not here right now. Please leave a message after the scream."

Raina shot out of my grip, flying toward the ceiling with a blood-chilling scream. Whatever force that held her slammed her face-first into the ceiling, pulled her away, and hit her again and again until her whole face was bloody. It let her go and I scrambled to throw my arms out to keep her from falling to the floor. Blood bubbled out of Raina's mouth. I turned her sideways so it'd spill onto the floor, but it wasn't just blood that came out of Raina. Small, round beads hung from her mouth. Raina made a choking sound and tugged on the beads with shaky hands. More blood came up, and with it, a familiar wooden cross.

A rosary, I realized, but it wasn't just any rosary. I picked up the blood- and mucus-covered thing, cleaning the cross off with a finger and turning it over. Somehow, the cross had been flipped upside down and reattached, but I recognized the rosary. It was identical to the one Sean had used to pray over me. *How?*

Raina doubled over, sobbing. "Make it stop. Oh, God, please make it stop. I can't do this!"

I closed a fist around the rosary and put my hand on her back. "Can you walk? We need to get you to the bathroom." I wasn't sure if her nose was broken, but it was bleeding. A lot.

She kept crying but nodded as I helped her up.

My primary concern had to be treating the damage to her body. I couldn't lose her, not before I figured out how to get to Sean. If this encounter had proven one thing, it was that Raina—or the demon inside of her, at least—knew something, and they'd been taunting me with that ever since I showed up.

My hand closed around hers as we hobbled slowly to the door. One way or another, Raina's possession would give me the answers I'd been searching for.

CHAPTER THIRTEEN

THEN

Felix didn't get better. He didn't get worse either, but he never made a full recovery. With midterms looming, I couldn't afford to stay with him all the time, but I spent all my free time making sure he ate enough to stay alive and changed his clothes at least once a day. The more time passed, the weaker he got.

He stopped going to class. I spent a week collecting his work for him and bringing it back to the apartment, but he couldn't get out of bed to work on it. After he missed all his midterms, his advisor stopped by and they discussed his options for graduating. Felix barely said two words to him.

As the bald priest advisor placed his hat on his head near the door, he shook his head and said, "He doesn't seem himself, does he?"

"He's been this way." I put my hand on the doorknob. "The hospital says he's not sick. I keep trying to convince him to go see one of the doctors on campus at the clinic, but he won't leave the apartment.

Not for anything. He just…sits there."

The priest cast a wary glance back at Felix's bedroom where the door stayed cracked open. "Not all illnesses are of the body, Sean. I think it's time to consider this may be a mental health problem."

"Felix isn't crazy."

"Now, I didn't say that." He adjusted his glasses and shrugged on his coat. "It's only natural to be facing some depression and anxiety with the end of his studies nearing. This is a difficult time for some students. Considering Felix's grades, and the difficult home life he's come from, I'm not surprised."

That difficult home life was the one thing we'd bonded over almost immediately, though Felix's experience differed from mine. My father was an overbearing and hateful man. Felix's parents loved him, but they'd separated. His father was sick, some autoimmune disorder, and his mom…well, she tried, but it was hard to be around when she had to work three part-time jobs. Felix had wanted so badly to escape the poverty he'd lived in, and becoming a priest was an opportunity to do that, and to minister to people who needed him. He'd been passionate about it once.

The priest pulled out a scrap of paper and a pen, scribbling down a set of numbers as he leaned against the wall. "This is the number of a friend of mine. She's a psychologist. Best one I know. Give her a call. Maybe Felix will find some comfort in talking with her." He held the paper out to me.

I took it and frowned at the name scribbled in messy handwriting. "Jade Haneda?"

"She can help." He nodded.

I pulled the door open for him and held it as he

exited. When he was gone, I considered the phone number he'd given me. Whatever was wrong with Felix, it didn't feel like depression, but I had to do something.

Most of his classes were willing to give him an incomplete for the semester since he'd missed so much, and let him make up for it during the winter break. We'd have to forgo our trip to Mexico, but we wouldn't be going if he was like this anyway. His education was more important than any trip. Neither would happen if Felix didn't get out of this funk he was in. Maybe this Jade girl could help him. I certainly couldn't.

I sighed and went back to knock on Felix's door. When he didn't answer, I pushed it open a little more and peeked into the dark room. "Felix?"

He sat in the same place he'd been for weeks, on his bed with the pillows piled up behind him. His laptop sat on his legs, playing another episode of some sitcom he was barely paying attention to. He'd let his beard grow in and badly needed a haircut. Felix's eyes slid lazily away from the screen to regard me. "What?"

"Can I get you anything?"

"No," he mumbled and went back to watching the screen.

I should've walked away and left him alone. I had a quiz to study for and several chapters on theology to read, but it all felt like it meant nothing in the wake of whatever he was grappling with. I stepped further into the room and flipped on the light.

Felix flinched and put his hands up. "Ugh, turn that off!"

I sighed and flipped the light back off. "I'm worried about you, Felix."

"You and everyone else." He plunged his hand into a box of cereal and shoved a whole handful into his mouth.

"Your advisor left the number for a counselor. I think maybe you ought to call her." I walked further into the room and held the paper out to him.

Felix stared at it. "I see. So just because I don't want to go to class anymore, I'm suddenly a basket case?" He moved the laptop to the side.

"That's not what I—"

Felix surged out of the bed, spilling cereal everywhere. "I'm not crazy, Sean! Maybe I don't want to be a priest anymore. Did you ever think of that? I mean, why the hell would I? After what we saw? What kind of god lets a child suffer like that?"

"It's God's will," I started. "We don't always understand it, Felix, but I'm sure there's a reason."

"So, God wanted Marci to die?"

My head snapped up. "How did you know about that?" I had made it a point not to tell him since he got back from the hospital. Bishop X had called several times to speak with Felix, but I hung up on him each time. Unless his advisor had told him, there was no way he could've known that.

"Answer the question," Felix demanded. "And while you're at it, let's talk about some other bullshit like your whole student career."

I blinked. "What?"

"You heard me." Felix took a step forward, got in my face. "Do you really want to be a priest, Sean, or are you just running away from admitting what you really are?"

"And what's that?" I knew what he meant, even before he said it. Of course I did. There were a lot of sins a priest might commit, but one stood above all the others, the one sin that couldn't even be talked about in seminary, let alone absolved.

"You're gay," Felix said finally.

It was almost a relief to hear someone else say it out loud, but the way he said it like a curse stung the same way the slurs in the schoolyard had. "That doesn't mean I can't be a priest."

"It does if I tell the bishop."

Cold sweat gathered on the back of my neck, but I kept my voice even. "So what? Half the men in seminary are gay, Felix. Probably a good third of all priests everywhere are, maybe as many as half. It doesn't mean anything. I can still keep up my vows. I can still serve."

"You don't want to take vows and wear a collar because you love God," Felix spat. "You want to hide behind that collar in a position of power. You'd be living a lie, Sean."

"That's not true!" I shook my head.

"It is!"

"It's not!" I shoved him and instantly regretted it. I just couldn't help myself. After all we'd been through, the laughs and fun we'd had, this was going to be the thing that destroyed our friendship? Once, I had thought...I didn't know what to think anymore. Everything I thought I knew about Felix was in question.

Felix stared at me, wide-eyed. "You're a liar!" he spat through gritted teeth and shoved me back.

Anger swelled in the pit of my stomach, adrenaline surging. All I could hear in my head was my dad screaming in my face to stop being a pussy; all I felt were his fists in my ribs, trying to toughen me up. All I needed was the snot beat out of me, some backbreaking work. Blood and sweat would make me a proper man, not more time on my knees.

I charged Felix, tackling him. He went down with his back to the bed. I drew a fist back to hit him but paused when I looked into his eyes. This wasn't my dad or some middle school bully. This was Felix. How the hell was I ever supposed to hurt him?

"Well?" he snarled. "What are you waiting for? Go on. Hit me!"

"No." I lowered my fist and let go of his shirt. "I won't do it." I started to stand.

Felix grabbed me by the shirt so I couldn't rise.

I struck out on instinct and slapped him as hard as I could. Maybe it would knock some sense into his thick skull. His head snapped to the side, but he didn't let go of the collar of my shirt. He blinked once, a stray tear falling from the corner of his eye.

Guilt tugged at my heart. "Oh, Felix. Shit, I'm sorry! I didn't mean—"

"Again," he said and turned his head a dark, hungry shadow in his eyes.

"What?"

Fingers tightened around my collar, yanking my face down to hover just inches from his. We were so close, I could smell the cereal on his breath and see the cinnamon-sugar dust on his cracked lips. When he spoke, his lips nearly brushed against mine. "You want to make me hard? You're going to have to hit me a second time, and put some effort into it."

I considered it. Maybe he wasn't so wrong about why I'd gone to seminary, and maybe he was there for the same reason. The world only felt right was when we were together.

The Church had warned us, though. Over and over, they drilled it into our head in class, in chapel, at every opportunity. "*Numquam duo, semper trēs.*" Never two, Always three, or so the saying went. We weren't supposed to be such good friends. Never alone. Always above reproach. We'd broken the rules, Felix and I, and when the bishop found out, there'd be worse laid at our feet than the crime of loving one another.

I wrenched free of Felix's grip and stumbled back several steps, shaking my head. "What the hell's wrong with you?"

He snorted. "So now you don't want to fuck me?"

"I want you to pull your head out of your ass and take your life back!" I gestured around the room. "This is insanity, Felix! This isn't you!"

"You don't know me." He stumbled to his feet like a drunk, brushed some cereal out of the bed and crawled right back into it.

"I know you're better than this."

He ignored me and turned back on the show he'd been watching before.

There's no point. I'm not going to get through to him. I left him alone in his room and slammed the door behind me. *Maybe it is depression*, I thought, putting on my coat, but even as I thought that, I knew it wasn't. There were more sicknesses than those of the body and mind. Something else was going on with Felix, and I had to rule out a spiritual problem.

As much as I hated Bishop X, he was the only one I could go to with this. After Felix's threat to push me out of the closet, though, it was a huge risk, bringing in the bishop. I could lose my seminary scholarship if we said or did the wrong thing. Yet if I did nothing, Felix could lose his life just as Marci had. I cared too much about Felix to let that happen to him, and whether he wanted to admit it or not, he did too.

CHAPTER FOURTEEN

NOW

I got Raina cleaned up as best I could and fed her a few over-the-counter painkillers before I walked her back to bed. It was the best I could do, considering. She needed to heal, and people did that best when asleep.

Alone in the big house with only my thoughts to keep me company, I decided it was time to explore while I waited for Jade to show up. Laura hadn't offered me a tour of the house, but I assumed I'd be fine to have a look around if I didn't open any locked doors. Even then, who would know if I opened a lock or two if I put everything back the way I found it?

The Hemlock house was a gigantic antebellum-style manor on forty acres just outside of Lexington; the place was so secluded, even the nearest neighbors were too far to reach on foot. With a house that size, I'd expect the Hemlock family to have a whole bunch of kids running around or a much larger staff. There should've been people everywhere. The house had enough room. Why have a big house like that if you didn't intend to fill it?

Although I had to say I was glad there weren't a bunch of kids to trip over. Kids and I had never gotten along too well, and Laura didn't strike me as the nurturing mother type. Still, I had to wonder. After Raina, why didn't they have more children? Maybe it was just too painful a topic. Marriages had broken up over losing a child, and yet, the Hemlocks stayed together, the very picture of happiness.

I was sure it was a scam. Relationships are rarely as perfect as they look from the outside.

All of this passed through my mind as I stood outside Mrs. Hemlock's bedroom, trying to break in. The lock disengaged with an audible click and I looked up and down the hall to make sure Willa wasn't around. I hadn't seen her since breakfast, but I was sure she was lurking somewhere. Wherever she was, it wasn't the upstairs hallway, so I pushed the door open, stepped in, and closed it behind me.

The room was a shocking mix of dandelion yellow and rose pink, the colors so prevalent throughout that it was like a slap, especially since the rest of the house was so dark. Yellow wallpaper colored the walls behind a pink canopied bed with a pink bedspread and pink curtains. A chandelier of flamingo-colored glass hung in the center of the room while mustard-yellow drapes hung heavy over the windows. A round mirror hanging above the fireplace duplicated the effect.

It was hard to imagine the senator sleeping there, but maybe she got her way because he was hardly ever home. Come to think of it, maybe the awful colors in the bedroom were why he didn't spend much time at the Hemlock house.

I went to the walk-in closet first. It was bigger than some New York apartments. Dresses from all colors of the rainbow lined the walls, and a three-tiered shoe rack stood in the middle with plenty of matching heels to choose from. There wasn't a single suit in the bunch. I didn't find any pants in male sizes tucked away in the dresser either.

That could mean nothing. He was on a trip, and he might have taken his entire wardrobe with him, though I couldn't see it. Even on an extended trip, a person has to leave something behind, some sign of their presence. Yet Senator Hemlock hadn't left so much as a sock in that bedroom, which could only mean one thing. Laura and the senator weren't sleeping in the same bedroom.

"Open marriage, my ass," I grumbled and left the bedroom behind.

I tried another door down the hall and found yet another bedroom, but this one was bare. A twin bed lay tucked in one corner with only a white sheet over it. Plain, white curtains hung limply over the windows. The lightbulb in the ceiling didn't even have a shade over it. It was just a lightbulb dangling from a socket on some exposed wiring. I almost left as soon as I saw what was inside, thinking I wouldn't find anything of interest. Curiosity, though, drove me to check the closed closet. Sure enough, three black suits hung on nails in the closet. A single pair of dust-covered leather shoes had been tucked into the opposite corner. How odd that she'd live in such grandeur and his room was a half-step up from a prison cell.

There wasn't anything else I could learn from the empty room, so I left and closed the door behind me, making sure I locked it as I went out.

The only other rooms upstairs I could get into were empty shells with no furniture. Some were filled with boxes of dishes or old clothes. Others were empty and waiting to be filled by something, anything. There was a lot of empty and unused space in that house, which was perhaps its most striking feature. More than enough space to have given Raina a studio separate from her bedroom.

The stairs creaked as I took them down, still searching for any sign of Willa. I hadn't seen her or heard her moving around. Maybe she'd gone with Mrs. Hemlock. I didn't know if I would trust a stranger like myself alone with my daughter if I were in Laura's position, but then everything about Laura was strange, slightly off in every way. She might have everyone else fooled but not me.

Downstairs, I walked through a den that lacked a television, and a study with an empty desk. Books sat in piles in front of empty bookshelves and Senator John Hemlock's golden nameplate had been tucked away in one of the drawers. It was out of sight, just like every other thing that could remind Laura he existed. If I didn't know better, I'd be tempted to think Senator Hemlock wasn't really in Washington, but rather buried in a shallow grave somewhere on the house's forty acres. But would Laura really hurt her husband? She was devious, conniving, selfish, and seductive, sure, but a murderess? That was a leap I wasn't sure I could make without any evidence. It was hard to believe a tiny woman like Laura Hemlock would be capable of hurting a full-grown man in good health.

In the hallway just off the kitchen, I found another locked door. Cool air emanated from a small crack at the bottom along with a slight musty smell. A basement maybe? What sorts of secrets would Laura have down there? The door had a simple key lock, which was easy enough to pick, especially when I had a whole kit to help me. After checking around to make sure Willa wasn't nearby, I broke out the kit and started fighting with the lock. It was stubborn and stiff, but the house was old. Maybe it was one of the original locks, which would explain why the mechanism was so stiff. A little oil would keep it from sticking like that.

"Just what do you think you're doing?" Willa's voice startled me so much I dropped my tools. They clanged to the floor. She eyed them with a disapproving frown.

"Just having a look around." I bent to pick up the tools and slid them into my pockets. "Laura didn't exactly give me the grand tour of the place."

"Locked doors generally mean an area is off limits." She turned her head to look at the door I'd been working on. "Especially this one."

"Why? What's back there?"

She grunted. "If Mrs. Hemlock wanted you to know, I'm sure she'd have taken you down there."

"You going to tell her I was snooping around?" I crossed my arms.

Willa looked me up and down, her upper lip twitching as if she wanted to smile but couldn't. "I believe in karma, sir. Whatever you do in this life comes back on you three-fold. I don't need to do anything for you to get what's coming." She folded her hands and turned her back to me.

"Karma's not exactly a Biblical concept, and neither is the three-fold rule," I pointed out. "And here I thought this was a Christian household."

Willa hesitated and gave me a lazy look over her shoulder. "I expect you to respect Mrs. Hemlock's privacy while you're on the grounds, Mr. Cross. If you don't, there will be consequences." She stopped in front of the kitchen window and moved aside the curtains, her permanent frown deepening as she peered out at the driveway. "Who on Earth has Jacob got in his car now?"

I came up behind her and looked over her shoulder. Jacob opened the back door of the Hemlock's limousine for Jade. She wore a long-sleeved black bodysuit with a high-waisted plaid skirt in green and black. The tops of her thigh-high knitted stockings showed as she climbed out of the car, taking Jacob's hand. Deep red lipstick, a tight French braid, and killer heels…it was a look only Jade could pull off naturally.

"That would be my assistant." It felt strange to call Jade an assistant, but I couldn't think of a better word to define her so Willa would understand her importance. "She's going to help me with the next phase of treatment for Raina."

"Well, she certainly doesn't *look* like the sort of person the Church would send to assist."

"That's because she isn't." I patted Willa on the back before rushing away from the window and racing through the house to the front door. She'd expect someone to open it for her and be waiting. I got there before she could even knock, and pulled the door open, breathless from my run.

Jade's mouth turned up into a smile that'd fit better on an excited kid's face than hers. "Puppy! Oh my! Have you always been this tall, dark, and handsome?"

"Time's been kind to the both of us, although I think you got the better deal." I started to step aside, but she pulled me into a long hug. Old feelings and memories forced their way to the surface, lesser now than they'd been all those years ago, but still there.

I hadn't loved Jade, not in any of the ways people were supposed to love one another. No, I'd loved her as people love the taste of ice cream after narrowly avoiding death. She taught me to appreciate life in the face of death and pain, and for a while, that had been enough of a reason to keep living. Like with everything and everyone else, though, even that wasn't enough forever. I'd needed *more*.

Jade kissed my cheek and pushed me back to stand at arm's length. "How long has it been?"

"Eight years," I answered.

"Eight too many. You should call more often. And this house…" She stepped past me without an invitation, looking up at the ceiling. "It is something else. Such a nice place. You know they say the country is good for the soul."

"It's not doing much good for Raina Hemlock's soul." I tucked my hands in my pockets and looked up the stairs to where Raina's room waited.

Jacob stopped at the front door and placed a large leather bag on the porch. "Anything else I can do for you, miss?"

"No, thank you." Jade flashed him a big smile and went to retrieve her bag. "I left most of my things at the hotel, but since you said this was a special case…" She opened the bag and drew out a length of bright red hemp rope, smiling at me.

"I hope we don't need that with her, but after this morning…" I shook my head. "Whatever's got a hold on her, it slammed her into the ceiling, Jade."

She was about to correct me again; I could see it in her face.

I cleared my throat to stop her. "Let's keep it

professional for now, please. This family's a bit…peculiar."

"Fine." She shoved the rope back into her bag, picked it up, and paced back through the front door.

I started to shut it behind her, but Jacob stopped me, putting a hand on the door.

"Sorry," he said, wringing his hands on the brim of the hat he'd removed. "I tried to tell you in the car. I wish I could've said more, but it's hard to put into words, isn't it?"

I nodded. "That's true."

Jacob glanced over his shoulder and around before continuing. "If you want to talk more about it, you're welcome to come to dinner. Me and my wife, we live in the guest cottage at the edge of the property. We'd love to have you while you're in town. Both of you." He didn't say it outright, but I suspected he had something he wanted to tell me, something he didn't dare say within earshot of Willa or Laura.

I nodded again. "I think I may take you up on that."

His smile widened and he replaced his hat. "Good. I'll tell Amanda to set an extra spot at the table for you."

I closed the door and turned around to find Jade standing in the center of the entry space, her arms out in front of her, palms turned up. "Anything?" I asked.

"Plenty." She closed her eyes and took a deep breath. "Don't you feel that? That infectious presence? Like a wound in the energy that's been allowed to fester and rot."

"I can't read a thing here. That's why I called you." I locked the front door and went to join her. "It's like I walked into a blind spot. I've never felt anything quite like it."

Jade dropped her arms loosely to her sides. "And there's the difference between an empath and a medium, Felix. I interact with spirits and energies on other planes, and you just get the vibes other humans give off."

"You make it sound so simple. You should try living with it." I took the stairs with her behind me. "There's a bit more to it than that. I'm not usually limited just to humans. I can sense other entities, or at least what they're doing to their hosts. It generally makes for easy exorcisms. Raina, however, is a complete mystery, though I believe I've confirmed the presence of a demonic entity."

"No name yet?"

I shook my head and paused at the top of the stairs. "Not yet, but it knows me. It's been using Sean to try to get under my skin. Just this morning, I heard her speak in his voice and then this." I produced the rosary from my pocket. I'd taken the time to clean it off in the bathroom, but it still held a strange sulfuric stink that made her nose wrinkle.

Jade wrapped her fingers around the beads and promptly withdrew her hand with a hiss. When she showed me her fingers, they were red as if the rosary had burned her. "Where did that come from?"

"Inside Raina." I wrapped the beads around my hand and put them back in my pocket. "I've seen a lot of demons do a lot of things, Jade, but this…this shouldn't happen at this stage. Raina is still aware, still fighting it. It's as if the thing already has her and everything I'm doing is pointless. All I can do is watch and react."

She put a sympathetic hand on my arm. "You haven't lost this battle, Felix. We'll get to the bottom of this."

"Tell me, Jade. Is there a chance she could be channeling him from...wherever he is?" I almost didn't want to ask, but I had to know.

"Anything is possible," she said with a shrug. "When dealing with the demonic, impossible is just another word for unlikely." She put her hand on the doorknob.

I stopped her with a hand on her shoulder, prompting her to look at me with her dark, brown eyes. "I need the girl to agree to a session of regression therapy."

Jade's perfect eyebrows shot up her forehead. "Hypnosis? On a demoniac? Do you realize how risky that is for you and her?"

"During the last session, she claims to have been in Hell and returned. Now she's potentially channeling Sean. Their cases are similar, Jade. Both gone for ten plus years, both taken by demons, only Raina's been returned. Why? How? I have to know. If there's even a chance I can get him back—"

"You're willing to risk the girl's soul for your answers?" Jade tore her shoulder away from my grip. "You haven't changed a bit, have you? You're still a monster."

"Open that door and see what a real monster looks like, Jade. If something is taking people, don't you want to stop it?"

"You're one man, Felix!" Jade exclaimed. "You can't take on all of Hell by yourself!"

"I can and I will. I might not win, but I'll be damned if I'm going to stand here and do nothing while a good man suffers. That should be me!" I pointed to my chest emphatically. "Whatever Sean's going through should be happening to me, not him. Don't you get it, Jade? I'm responsible. I can't just leave him there. Not if it's within my power to save him."

"Even at the cost of one innocent girl's soul?" Jade asked.

I looked at the closed door separating us from Raina. "Without pain, there can be no growth. You taught me that. I don't want to sacrifice Raina for Sean, and I wouldn't take the risk if I didn't think she was strong enough to withstand it. The girl's been to Hell and back literally. That's not something the weak survive. But let's hope it doesn't come to that."

I pushed open the door for Jade and held it.

Raina was awake and painting again. She stepped back from her easel when we entered. "Just in time. I think it's done. Now I just need to figure out who it is." She picked up the canvas and turned it around so we could see.

The painting was of a pale man wearing a dirty blindfold. He hung upside down in a dark room, arms stretched out and nailed to a beam with rusty nails. Blood poured from the gag in his mouth, trailing in detailed lines up his face and underneath the blindfold. Grotesque black sores covered his chest and arms. Even with all the horrific details and much of his face obscured, I recognized him. Raina had painted Sean.

CHAPTER FIFTEEN

THEN

"He hasn't been himself since the day after we assisted on the exorcism." I considered the pool of brown, steaming liquid in my cup. To call it coffee would be an insult to coffee beans everywhere. It'd come from the tiny, lime-encrusted coffeemaker sitting in the faculty break room of Aquinas Hall. It tasted like water that might've been in the same room as a coffee bean once rather than actual coffee.

Bishop Xavier, who sat across from me at the chipboard table, leaned into his hand and rubbed his chin. "Is he showing any signs?"

"Of possession?" I shook my head. "Maybe. It's hard to tell. But is that even possible? I mean, Felix is a lot of things, but one thing we both know he's not is without faith."

X was the last person I wanted to talk to after what happened with Marci. I was still furious with him for letting the girl die. If we'd taken her to a hospital, she might still be alive. Of course, that was all conjecture.

Some part of me knew his argument might be just as true, that Marci would've died either way. I just couldn't bring myself to believe that nothing could be done to help her. Good won and evil lost. That was the way it was supposed to go. We must have done something wrong for it to turn out the way it had.

"It's a myth that demons can't inhabit the faithful." He picked up his paper cup, sipped some coffee, and cringed at the taste. "One doesn't have to be engaged with the forces of evil to be taken, Mr. Yeats. Do you think Marci was dabbling in the occult? A child?"

I spun the cup in my hands. At least I could enjoy the warmth if not the taste. "How should I know how demons choose their victims?"

"No one knows the how or why. Not even me. All I know is that cases have been steadily on the rise, especially among children of a certain age. Felix wouldn't fit that profile, but Marci certainly did."

I finally looked up from the cup. "Are you saying it could've left Marci and gone into Felix? Is that possible?"

The bishop sighed. "For someone of faith, you believe surprisingly little is possible. God may be omnipotent, Mr. Yeats, but the other side is powerful too. It wouldn't be much of a war otherwise, would it? Anything is possible when dealing with demons, angels, and the faith of man."

"Yes, but how?" I leaned into the table, eager to hear his explanation.

It must've crossed my mind a dozen times on the walk across campus. Felix wasn't showing all the signs of a possession such as superhuman strength or knowledge of the unknown, but his sudden change in personality was troubling. Felix's advisor had suggested subtly that his problems were mental, but I'd never seen a depression come on like that. Not in anyone. Least of all with Felix. His normal coping mechanism for dealing with stress was to laugh it off. He wasn't the type to crawl into his shell and hide in the dark.

But when and how could it have happened? Unless…

"Oh, no." I cradled my head in my hands.

"What? What is it?" X pressed.

"It's my fault." I wiped my hands down my face and let them rest flat on the table. "We left him alone in there, X. I pulled you into the hallway, remember? He was alone against that thing. Who knows what could've happened in those few minutes? It got to him, X. I know it did."

"Calm down, Mr. Yeats." X raised his hands in a gesture that was meant to calm, but it just made me more anxious. "We don't know anything for certain, but just in case, I'll come by and talk to him. I'm supposed to hold office hours shortly, but I'll put a sign up instead."

I nodded and stood. "Thank you, Your Excellency."

"Of course." He dumped what was left of his coffee into the trash along with the cup. "I should also mention something that came up during my last meeting with some of the other professors. They've noted the two of you have been spending a considerable amount of time together. I assured them it was because of Felix's illness. There were mumblings that it's gone on far longer than the last few weeks."

I hesitated at the door and met the bishop's eyes. He knew. I could tell from the way he was looking at me, the way he phrased it. "Nothing is going on between me and Felix."

Bishop X crossed the room and put a hand on my back, guiding me through the door. "Quite frankly, I don't care. Between you and me, no one cares what you do with your time so long as it stays behind closed doors, Mr. Yeats. These days, the Church is concerned about its image. Too many scandals in the news. Christ may not judge, but the American public certainly does. Just be careful, is all I'm saying."

I nodded and we said no more on it. There was nothing else to say because it was an unwritten rule in Catholicism. If you didn't talk about it, it wasn't real.

The bishop printed out a sign with a generic apology and his cell number if any students had an emergency, taping it to the door of his locked office. Rather than walk back to the apartment, we took his car. I'd been away from Felix for several hours already, and I was nervous about the state I'd find him in when we returned. He hadn't progressed past just lying around and eating junk food in the dark, but that could change at any moment.

My anxiety spiked higher with every passing minute. It was all I could do to focus on the parked cars we passed, counting the blocks, the house numbers, the seconds ticking away. I had this awful sinking feeling in my gut that something was terribly wrong, though I didn't know what. It'd only been a few hours. How bad could things get in a few hours?

The weather outside had gone from gloomy to dark and foreboding. The wind picked up, pushing dead leaves along the sidewalks. Charcoal colored clouds hung low, rolling and crashing against each other. A plastic grocery bag flew by and got caught briefly on the side mirror before the wind jerked it away and it went sailing down the street. It was only four o'clock in the afternoon, but it was already dark enough that the streetlights had come on.

Bishop X parked his car on the street in front of our apartment. No lights were on inside. He frowned and turned off the car. "How was he when you left him?"

"Lying in bed, watching some show, and eating cereal, just like I told you." I unbuckled my seatbelt. "Why?"

"Just a feeling. After a few hundred exorcisms, you learn to trust those." He got out of the car and adjusted his collar, straightening it, before opening the trunk and retrieving a briefcase. "Just in case," he said, patting the briefcase.

The feeling that something was wrong intensified as I slid the key into the lock. "Felix?" I called after pushing open the door.

No answer.

I stepped inside. The smell hit me a moment later. Not the sulfuric, rotten egg stink I'd smelled in Marci's house either, but the sweet decay of rotting meat. I gagged and covered my mouth. Bishop X put a hand over his nose.

"It wasn't like this when I left," I said.

"You said you confronted him before you left?"

I nodded. "We argued."

Bishop X dropped to his knees and opened his briefcase right there to shrug on his purple stole. "Demons may like to hide, but when confronted, they tend to lash back. It may view you as a threat to its continued existence and therefore has accelerated the situation. We must proceed, quickly and carefully." He stood and made the sign of the cross over me, speaking the words of absolution before handing me a small leather-bound book of prayers.

"Bishop, I'm not sure I should assist. Not after what happened last time."

"The demon is in a weakened state." He shoved the book into my hands. "We've driven it from its original host and into a servant of God. It's been forced to the surface, not because of anything you've done wrong, but out of a sense of self-preservation. At this stage, it's desperate and will do anything. If you wish to save Felix's soul, we must do this now. We cannot afford to wait the weeks or perhaps months it will take for the Vatican to approve an exorcism, Sean."

It was the first time he'd called me by my first name, a testament to how serious he believed the situation to be.

"You do want to save Felix's soul, do you not?"

I swallowed, nodded, and closed my fingers tightly around the prayer book.

X patted my arm. "Good lad. Now, as before, you must not listen to whatever it says. Remember that the being we go to confront is not Felix, but that Felix is still in there. We must help him fight."

I nodded again and showed Bishop X to Felix's room. "Felix?" I knocked and pressed my ear to the door. Something rustled around on the other side, but Felix didn't answer.

I braced myself for the worst and turned the doorknob. Nothing could have prepared me for what I found on the other side.

Flies buzzed everywhere. More flies than could have gotten into the room by normal means, especially in the limited time I'd been gone. Felix had stripped himself naked and sat on a bare mattress with the contents of our fridge spilling out onto the bed in front of him. Every container had been opened and emptied onto the bed. Strawberry jelly, mayonnaise, mustard, raw hamburger, tomato sauce…he'd mixed it all into one filthy heap for the flies to breed in.

With shaky hands, I fought to flick on the small flashlight on my keychain. The dim light moved over the rotten pile of food where little white specks like rice writhed, two for every speck of other foodstuffs. Maggots. Everything was infested with them.

Felix's thin fingers sank into the disgusting pile and he took up a handful, maggots and all. His head snapped toward me and an animalistic snarl escaped his bloodstained lips as I moved the flashlight to his face.

"God on high," I whispered and crossed myself. I had to turn away as he shoved the whole handful of it into his mouth.

"Your God has no power here," Felix ground out. "He is mine!" Felix leaped from the bed for the window.

I don't know how I got there before him, but I did, and I was in his way, blocking his attempt to jump out it. Felix snarled at me and clawed at my face, ripping three burning lines across my chin.

"Help me restrain him!" X shouted and grabbed Felix from behind.

Felix fought and twisted in X's grip, but between the two of us, we managed to get him to the floor. He spat a mouthful of mucus and blood in my face, tipped his head back, and laughed like a madman. "How'd you like to fuck me now? Come on, pretty boy! Put your pretty little cock right in my ass!"

X pinned his legs while I held his arms, but Felix was strong, too strong for the two of us to hold him.

"Do something!" I screamed.

X shifted himself so his legs held Felix down. He kissed his fingers and placed them on Felix's forehead. "*Pater noster, quī es in caelīs...*"

Felix snarled and snapped at both of us while X began a Latin rendition of the Lord's prayer, but X held fast. I had to do the same.

"*Adveniat rēgnum tuum. Fīat voluntās tua, sīcut in caelō et in terra...*" Even with both of our voices joined together, we barely drowned out the awful, inhuman sounds coming out of Felix's throat.

We made it through the prayer and the beginning of another that I didn't know quite as well before Felix's limbs finally relaxed and he quit fighting. He made a gagging sound and his body surged up. I had no choice but to let him go so he could turn his head and vomit maggot-infested filth onto the floor.

I'll never forget the raw, agonizing scream that came after. No demon could make that sound. Only a man whose soul was being tormented by creatures not of this Earth.

Felix rocked back into my lap, all the energy suddenly gone out of him. "What's happening to me?" he sobbed. "Oh, God, it burns!" He clawed at his chest.

I watched in horror as three deep gashes slashed across his chest and stomach, appearing out of nowhere. Blood welled to the surface. Felix's head snapped to the side as if he'd been slapped.

"Make it stop! Please! Please, stop!"

I had never heard a more desperate plea. I looked to X who had paused his prayer to stare, aghast at Felix. He faltered, hands shaking as he retrieved his book and flipped through several pages. "We must not stop,

Sean. No matter how he begs, no matter what happens, we must see this to the end, or else his soul is forfeit."

I nodded and ran my sleeve over Felix's chin, wiping away vomit, snot, and tears. "We're going to help you, Felix. I promise."

CHAPTER SIXTEEN

NOW

I took the painted image of Sean from Raina and held it in front of me at arm's length. Though I knew it was just the demon taking another dig at me—albeit a creative one—I couldn't help but feel at unease. Such detail…she'd gotten every shadow, every curve, every slight blemish just right. Even if I had wanted to deny that it was him, I couldn't. A photograph couldn't have been more accurate.

I dropped the painting and gripped Raina by the collar of her nightgown. "I am addressing the entity inside of Raina Hemlock!"

"What are you doing?" Jade put a hand on my shoulder and tried to pull me away.

I pushed her back and tightened my grip on Raina. "In the name of God the Father, I command you to show yourself to me! Manifest, you son of a bitch!"

Raina let out a cry and desperately tried to pull away. "Stop it! Let me go!"

"I demand a response!" I moved one hand to grip

her by the head so she couldn't pull further away. "Why this girl? She's nothing special. Unexceptional."

"Felix!" Jade again pulled on me but I didn't let go of Raina. I almost had it! I could feel it!

"If you wanted an artist, you could've had any of your choosing. Why this pathetic nobody's child in this backwater state? What do you gain by using her to taunt me?"

The lights flickered and the foundations of the house trembled. Jade let me go and took a step back, giving the ceiling a worried look. "Felix, stop! You'll bring the whole house down before you conjure that thing!"

"Let the house crumble then," I said, squeezing Raina's shoulders tight. "It's only a house, and Raina is only one girl. Look at you, demon, trying to prove how powerful you are! But you've done nothing I haven't seen before. You demons, all the same."

A power exploded out of Raina, throwing me back and knocking over several canvas paintings. The terrible, choking power flew through the room, rattling everything that wasn't nailed down. Raina lifted onto her tiptoes and then an inch off the floor. "*Non sumus īdem*," the demon within spat. *We are not the same.*

I lowered my arm from my face. "There you are. Name yourself, demon. Who are you, then?"

Raina's mouth smirked, but it wasn't her smiling at us. "Sean wanted me to say hello. It's too bad you slipped away from us. You two could be in cells next to each other. You could listen to him curse your name as we rip the flesh from his body and feast upon it!"

Jade was suddenly beside me, gripping my arm hard enough to leave bruises. "The girl," she whispered, staring at Raina. "The poor child!"

Raina's head tipped back. The wind ceased and she fell into a heap on the floor. Jade pushed away from where I sat, frozen, and ran to the girl's side. "She's breathing. I think she's okay."

"Do you still have that rope?" I stood and dusted myself off. "I think it's time we put it to use. That's the second time I've seen her levitate. If we let it have her a third time, there won't be a fourth."

Jade laid Raina's head down gently and stormed across the room. "You shouldn't have conjured it. You, of all people, know the danger of bringing a demon to the surface like that!"

"I need answers!" I leaned in, my face hovering inches from hers.

"She needs help! If you're not going to help her, then get the hell out until you can get your head on straight, Felix!" She pointed emphatically to the door.

"And leave you alone with that thing? Not a chance." I tried to push past her.

Jade held me back with her palm flat on my chest. "I can handle Raina. I handled you at your worst, Felix. Do I have to remind you how to obey?"

I looked past her to where Raina lay. If anyone besides me could handle a demon, I had no doubts it would be Jade. In some ways, she was probably more qualified than me to do the job. At least she was even-tempered.

"Fine, but make sure you tie her up tight. I don't want to come back and find her floating on the ceiling." I adjusted my collar and sleeves, straightening my clothes before I went out the door.

Outside, the air held that sweet earth scent native only to spring. Humidity hung in the air, making it seem warmer than it was. When the wind blew, it was still cold enough I was glad I'd stopped to grab my jacket. That's where my lighter was anyway. I lit a cigarette and instantly relaxed at the first pull of nicotine into my lungs.

"You really should consider quitting," Sean said, suddenly beside me.

I didn't look at him. Every time I did, he'd disappear, so I remained content in catching the occasional glance in my peripheral vision. "Never should have started." I considered the cigarette pinched between my two fingers. "But it was either this or the bottle. The last shrink I saw told me I had an addictive personality, and he didn't mean it as a compliment. I suppose that's where everything went wrong to begin with, isn't it? All the singing, the praying at church, it ticks those boxes. The brain thinks it's getting meaningful positive interaction. You can be addicted to religion. How do you think cults happen?"

"And people," he added.

I nodded. "And people. All my life, I've been trading one addiction for another. That's what this quest is really about. Deep down in my psyche, I know it is. I need that thing, that spark, to keep me going, Sean. Without it, I don't even know who I am."

"I never would've thought you were an adrenaline junkie."

I laughed and tucked the cigarette into the corner of my mouth. "Have to be for a job like this. There's a certain excitement to the danger. What's the fucking point of living if you don't flirt a little with death?"

He shrugged. "Maybe that's how you think of it, but not everybody does. Raina doesn't want to suffer anymore, Felix. She doesn't need to."

"Don't you think I know that, Sean?" I had to stop

myself from facing him while I shouted at him. "Regression therapy will get my answers. I just need one session. One goddamn session, but she won't agree to it."

"Because she doesn't trust you. You need to make her trust you."

"Fine job I'm doing of that." I sighed and stood in the cold, smoking with Sean's ghost for a long moment. "Raina's never going to trust me. Considering the progression of this possession, I don't think I have the time it would require to build that kind of rapport with her either."

"You're hoping Jade does your work for you. That's sly, Felix."

I raised my eyes to the second-story window above my head where Jade and Raina were alone together. It would all be easier if I had that damn white collar. There was a lot of talk at seminary about what the collar meant, what it symbolized. That was all bullshit, just like everything else. The collar was power. Putting it on gave you authority over every other believer. It elevated its wearer one step closer to Christ in the eyes of the masses. In times past, the collar demanded blind obedience, as if priests, cardinals, and popes were the hand of God Himself. Walk into any home in America with a collar and you're instantly entitled to respect. Didn't matter what you did behind closed doors, as long as it didn't leak into the public eye.

But I didn't have a collar. I had taken no vows. Even if I had wanted to, that door closed to me because I had done as I was asked and stayed behind to pray. It was prideful, but difficult not to compare my suffering and Christ's as he prayed alone in Gethsemane.

"There you go again, Felix," Sean said, tucking his

hands into his pockets. "Feeling sorry for yourself. No one could've predicted what would happen to you that night. No one knew what we were really dealing with. We all thought it was just some demon. Even X."

I shook my head. "This isn't him. Whatever's inside Raina is far lower on the food chain, but that doesn't mean I don't fear it. It knows about you. It's using you to taunt me. The hair, the needle, the vision, the picture…All this time, I've done everything I could to keep myself from imagining what sort of torture you might be suffering through, and now it's all there in black and white. I can't ignore it."

"You're here to help Raina though, Felix. Not yourself."

"Regression therapy might help her too. You never know." Raina herself didn't seem to know what'd happened to her in the fifteen years she'd been absent. When this was all over, she'd want answers. It had to be difficult, living with a fifteen-year hole in your memory. Once we understood her past, both Raina and I could move forward.

"This isn't a normal exorcism," said Sean. "You know that. Something else is going on here. The mother is involved."

I had that feeling, but I wasn't sure how yet. "Then the regression therapy might tell me plenty of useful information." I flicked the finished cigarette down onto the pavement and ground it in with my shoe.

"It will help, but it's not going to tell you everything. You need to dig deeper, Felix."

"What's that supposed to…" I trailed off as I realized I'd mistakenly turned to address a man who'd never been there in the first place. *Dammit all.* I rubbed my forehead. *I really do need to get my head on straight.*

Jade had Raina restrained in her bed by the time I returned. To levitate, she'd have to move the whole bed. If I'd had my way, we'd have nailed the bed to the floor too, just in case. For Raina's safety, and ours, Jade helped me stack all the paintings in the hallway and empty the room of everything but the essentials. We got Willa to bring us extra sheets and blankets, which we tied around the bed frame to keep Raina from hurting herself should the entity show itself again.

Raina lay awake during all of it. Jade did her best to explain everything we were doing as we did it, but it wasn't Raina who was at the surface. I had called forth the demon inside, and it remained in control. That would make any attempt at hypnosis difficult, but both Jade and I agreed it had to be done.

"Go on, make 'em nice and tight," the demon spat at Jade as she tugged on one of the ropes.

"Why?" I asked. "Are you planning on getting free? Have another little performance for us, do you?"

Cracked lips grinned, pulling so wide that her lips split and bled. "Perhaps, but you'll have to let me loose to see it."

"I'd be more than happy to loosen the straps for Raina." I placed my briefcase full of equipment on the end of the bed and undid the snaps. "Why don't you let me talk to her?"

"First you want me. Then you want her. Make up your mind, you cum-swilling cuck." It spat a mouthful of yellow phlegm at me, but missed; it hit the wall instead.

I pretended not to notice. "We've been through this, demon. There's nothing you can say or do that will shock me."

The demon strained Raina's body against the restraints, pulling her upper half away from the mattress as far as the ropes would allow. "Oh, is this the part where you say your little prayers? Because that worked so well before. What was the girl's name? Marci? So delicious. She was a virgin, you know. A pretty little virgin and now her soul's being fucked in Hell. Your prayers are worthless. You're no priest."

I pulled out a small, round bottle and held it so the demon could see.

Its eyes widened. "What's that?"

"Give me your name, demon, and you won't have to find out."

"*Legiōnem autem multī sumus!*" The demon fell back against the bed, cackling.

"Jade, how many spirits are there inside of Raina Hemlock?" I pulled the stopper out of the bottle.

"That's a more complicated answer than I think you were expecting." Jade folded her hands. "There is one other, a dark and foreboding presence. Certainly demonic. But I sense another. One that isn't whole."

"So two at best. Doesn't sound like much of a legion to me." I splashed the holy water on the demon in the sign of a cross.

It screamed and recoiled, twisting and pulling against the ropes.

"As I see it," I continued, "you've got two options. Either you give me Raina back to speak to right now, or I force you out. I need Raina. I don't give a fuck about you."

"*Puella mea est!* I will have what was promised!" The demon tugged one arm hard. The rope twisted and seemed to fray a little, but it would hold. Jade's ties always held, no matter how much you struggled.

"Who promised you the girl? When did you first make contact with her? What do you want with Raina?"

The demon laughed at my questions and shook Raina's head back and forth, flicking her tongue out and making grotesque sounds in the back of her throat.

"You want to do it the hard way? That's just fine with me." I took out my book of prayers and flipped to the page I wanted and began the Lord's prayer, exactly as it had been uttered over me ten years ago.

CHAPTER SEVENTEEN

THEN

Felix fought us as we carried him from his bedroom to mine. His was too destroyed to be of use, and neither Bishop X nor I could stand the smell. I had to hold him down by throwing my entire body across his waist while the bishop tied up his kicking legs, and then his flailing arms. It took all of our combined strength just to move and hold him.

For his part, Felix thought our exhaustion was hilarious. When he wasn't screaming outright, he was laughing as if someone had just delivered the punchline of the funniest joke he'd ever heard.

I turned away. "Now what?"

X drew his sleeve over his forehead, wiping sweat from his brow. "Now we begin in earnest." He crossed himself and began again with the Lord's prayer. "Our Father, who art in Heaven—"

"Faggot!" Felix screamed. "Cocksucker!"

No, not Felix. The demon. Felix wouldn't ever be so cold and unkind.

X ignored him. "Thy kingdom come—"

Felix lifted his upper body from the bed and spat blood at the bishop's face, then leaned back, cackling louder.

I fumbled to find something he could clean his face with and placed it in the bishop's hand. To his credit, the bishop never faltered through the prayer, not even as I helped him wipe his face clean.

My voice joined the bishop's as the prayer came to a close. "And lead us not into temptation, but deliver us from evil."

X got out the holy water and splashed it over Felix again.

The demon forced Felix's body to recoil, but he didn't scream this time. The growl that had formed deep in his throat earlier grew to a crescendo and his body bucked against the restraints. I watched as Felix's body contorted in impossible ways, joints stretching and pushing to their limits. The pain he must have been in...

"Sean!" X snapped.

I lowered my head from watching Felix and found him thrusting the prayer book at me.

"Read," he commanded. "Follow." Then without waiting for me, he launched into the next prayer. "Saint Michael the archangel, defend us in battle! Be our protection against the traps and snares of the Devil."

Felix suddenly stopped laughing. I quit thumbing through pages of the text in search of Saint Michael's prayer and looked up again, a feeling of horrible dread settling in the pit of my stomach. He lay in the bed, panting, his head turned toward us. His eyes rolled back in their sockets, exposing bloodshot sclera. The sound of death itself bubbled and croaked out of

Felix's throat. For a moment, I thought I felt the temperature in the room drop, but that wasn't possible. All the windows and doors were closed, and the thermostat set to kick on at sixty-eight.

I turned back to the prayer book and found Saint Michael's prayer just in time to speak my lines. It felt like a theater performance. None of it was real. This couldn't be happening, not to Felix. Not to me. Not to any of us.

"…and all the evil spirits who prowl the world seeking the ruin of souls," X finished. "Amen."

"Amen," I repeated, half-stupefied.

X turned to the next page, prompting me to do the same. "Lord, have mercy. Christ, have mercy. Lord, have mercy on us."

I repeated each line, mimicking X's words, even if I could not match his confident tone. I was certain now that the temperature had dropped in the room, falling far below what was naturally possible. Felix's panting breaths came with clouds, as did my own. The chill in the air left me trembling severely enough I nearly dropped the prayer book. My fingers tightened around the pages until my nails left little indentations and I was afraid I would tear it.

"Holy Mary, pray for us," X continued.

"Pray for us," I echoed.

"Holy Mother of God—"

"Pray for us."

"Holy Virgin of Virgins—"

"Pray for us."

"Saint Michael…"

"Pray for us." And so on and on it went in a cycle with X invoking the name of every saint imaginable and imploring they utter a prayer for the three of us locked in that tiny room.

How many times had I mindlessly parroted the same Litany of the Saints and thought nothing of it? In seminary, we were taught that prayer was a deep and meaningful conversation with God, and yet the prayer seemed to leave no space for Him to answer. We filled the room with requests, begging every saint in creation to pray for us, and yet I had never felt so utterly alone in my prayer. Not even as I lay bruised and weeping beside my bed the last time I let my father lay hands on me.

No. I swallowed and repeated my next line, "We beg you to hear us." I must not think of that now. That time is over. I don't have to go back. This will work. I must have faith.

And so I tried. I believed with everything I had in the power of the words that came out of my mouth, be they practiced and worn or not. Every prayer in the book of exorcism rituals held more power because I lent my voice to it and because I believed. It had to be so. I had not come through all those years at seminary, all the suffering of my past, all the pain and misery of life for nothing. If this was my purpose, then so be it.

We reached the end of the book, but X did not pause in his prayers. "Lord Almighty, Father most high, You who cast Lucifer into the fiery pit…" He opened a small vial of holy oil and dabbed some of it on his finger, using it to draw three crosses on Felix's forehead. "We humbly ask now that You extend your grace to this son of God, Felix Mason Cross."

Felix rocked back as he drew, writhing and shaking his head back and forth to keep X from completing the crosses.

X was unshaken and completed his drawing while

speaking his own prayer for Felix. "Give unto your servants courage abundant that we may stand firm in the presence of evil." He moved his hand to Felix's bloodied chest.

Felix began to shake violently and spit up blood and chunks of rotten food laced with dead maggots. A few that had survived their bath in stomach acid wiggled and writhed against Felix's broken skin.

"Drive out this unclean spirit!" X's voice worked into a crescendo as he turned his face Heavenward. "In the name of God, I cast you out, demon!"

Felix's mouth grinned, showing bloody teeth. "Go on. Do it again! That tickles."

The live maggots wriggled and squirmed, forcing their way under X's palm.

"You have no power here, demon!" X shouted, unmoved. "Felix is under the dominion of Heaven, and so with God's aid, I command you to flee him, body, soul, and mind. Christ himself commands you to be gone, deceiver! Liar! Vile snake!"

"Come on!" Felix spat in a voice that was not his. "Is that the best you can come up with? Insult me, bitch! Whore! Cunt slurping fuckface!"

"Tempter of man! Father of lies! Prince of murderers and accuser of God's people!"

"Oh, those are creative, but I still think I can win. How about assface lobotomite slutfucker?" The demon laughed manically and traded more insults with the bishop.

Neither seemed to make any headway, though the demon continued to be amused as the bishop reached further and further. He even dipped into some Latinized descriptors for Satan himself, but not one of them made the demon inside Felix flinch.

The demon rolled Felix's head toward me. "This is boring. Suck my cock."

"Begone from this man!" X shouted. "Return to your palace of darkness, to your pit of snakes, and your lake of fire, demon! You will not have this servant of God!"

The demon snapped Felix's head toward Bishop X. "But I've already got him. Nothing you say or do will force me out. He is mine and I'll do with his body as I please." The bed rattled back and forth on the floor. Wood creaked and groaned as it flexed in the demon's grip. The wooden legs clattered against the wall, against the floor, like the feet of clog dancers, rattling so loud I couldn't think.

"He is not yours," I shouted firmly. "You will not have him!"

"Oh no?" The rattling stopped. The demon's white eyes widened. "You don't think so?"

"Do not speak to it directly," X urged.

I ignored him and snapped closed the useless book of prayers, tossing it aside. Nothing X was doing worked, so why not try a different approach? If exorcism really was all about imploring the demoniac to expel the demon themselves as he taught, then we were wasting our time.

I moved forward to grip the sides of Felix's face and kneel beside the bed, close enough that it took a will of iron to suffer the revolting stench of vomit on his breath. "Felix, I know you're still in there. I'm here. I accept you, and forgive you all your wrongdoings. Do you hear me?"

His head tilted back and the white eyes rolled away, revealing Felix's familiar brown irises. For a long moment, I thought I had finally gotten through to him, though the chill in the air didn't fade. "That's a touching speech, pretty boy." The headboard snapped and Felix yanked one arm free from where it'd been tied. He put his hand on the back of my head and shoved it downward.

I fought away from his strange new strength and threw myself to the floor and the window shattered. Gale-force winds tore through the room like a hurricane, smashing the lightbulb and spreading papers throughout the room. Wood splintered as Felix pulled his other three limbs free.

Felix rose out of the bed, his back stiff and limbs stretched out in all four directions as if he were being drawn and quartered. He rose two inches from the bed. Six. Two feet! Felix screamed and turned his head, watching as an invisible force pulled his right arm out of the socket. It flopped down limply and a moment later the left arm did the same.

X lowered his prayer book and backed away.

"Do something!" I shouted.

Felix's ankles twisted and popped while he levitated and sobbed, begging for our help.

With shaky hands, Bishop X removed the crucifix hanging around his neck and brought it to his lips for a kiss. Cautiously, he extended it out in front of him like a shield against the storm. "Let Christ's precious blood cleanse this man!"

He might as well have been whimpering in the corner for all the good it did. The demon dislocated Felix's right kneecap before spinning him in a full circle. His head and legs sagged, back curving and stretching to its limit.

"Help me!" Felix pleaded.

I left the safety of the doorway and climbed up onto

the desk beside my bed, hoping to push him back down, but the same invisible force that held him slapped me back. My head hit the opposite wall and bounced off.

Felix broke with the same snap as a celery stalk, folded in half the wrong way so that the back of his head touched his lower back. Satisfied with the destruction, the demonic force dropped him back to the bed. The wind stilled and silence followed.

"Felix!" I pushed myself to my feet and stumbled dizzily to Felix's side.

"Sean? I can't…" He let out a muffled sob. "I can't feel my legs. Help me!"

I turned around to glare at the bishop.

His pale face blanched further. "I-I…it should have worked. I don't know why…"

"Shut up and call an ambulance before this thing kills him!"

X rushed from the bedroom.

I closed my fingers around Felix's. "You're going to make it. I'm here, Felix. Try not to move, okay?"

His fingers twitched weakly wrapping around mine. Scabbed over, dry lips parted. "It's still in there. I can feel him. Like…worms in my blood. He's infecting me."

"You can fight him. You're strong."

His throat swelled as he swallowed. "I'm not. I'm weak. So damn weak. And the things I've done…shit, I can't die like this."

"You're not going to die." I shook my head, but even as I did, I didn't believe it. I could feel him slipping away from me, inch by inch. The demon was draining the life out of him before my eyes, just as it had done to Marci.

"Last rites?" his voice was a whisper, but his grip tightened into an iron vice. "Can I still…?"

"No." I shook my head. "I can't. I won't!"

Felix's eyes rolled back into his head, turning snow white again. His mouth split open into the demon's smile. "Told you he was mine!"

"You!" Rage bubbled to the surface. I let go of Felix's hand to grab him by the shoulders, but instead of shaking him like I meant to, a thought occurred to me. There was still a way to save Felix. One way left. "You want a body?" I spat through clenched teeth. "Take mine, asshole. You leave him and come into me, dammit!"

A blinding pressure erupted behind my eyes, building to a blinding crescendo. I let go of Felix and stumbled back several steps as the pressure increased, weighing my whole body down. Voices laughed and cackled all around me. Claws raked at my back, at my sides. I spun, trying to fight them off, but there were too many. A dark presence stepped out of the shadows of the room and pushed me to my knees. It forced my jaw open with a vice-like grip and slithered into my mouth.

I looked down and a fiery chasm opened beneath my feet. Talons gripped my ankles and pulled me into it so fast, I didn't even have time to scream.

CHAPTER EIGHTEEN

NOW

The demon flinched as I spread holy water over Raina's body, making the sign of the cross. Her body strained against the ties holding her to the bed, and against Jade's strength as she held her stomach flat. I knew firsthand what could happen if the demon were allowed to flex the demoniac's body beyond its normal limits. A solid restraint across the middle would solve the problem, but I didn't have anything on hand that would do the trick. Jade's weight was the best solution at the moment.

"What is your name, demon?" I commanded with as much authority as I could muster. "Give me your name, and we can end this."

"End it?" Raina's demon snarled through clenched teeth. "Why would I want to end this girl's sweet suffering?"

I gripped Raina's forehead, pressing in with a thumb and forcing her head back so she had no choice but to look me in the eyes. "I'm getting tired of playing games, demon. You and I both know I can expel you at any time."

"Yes, why don't you then?" The grin widened and her tongue flicked out between her teeth like a snake tasting the air. "Ah, because you want something. Information, is it? Tell you what. Give us the girl, and we'll tell you exactly where your loverboy is."

"He's in Hell, and your kind took him there."

Raina's bloodshot eyes widened and the demon pursed her lips. "Oh, is he now? So certain…"

Of course he was in Hell. Where else would he be? Bishop X had been outside the apartment when it happened, standing right in front of the door, according to him, calling an ambulance for me. He would've seen it if Sean left out the front. I'd reviewed the security footage from the parking lot out back a thousand times too. He hadn't left that way. There was nowhere for Sean to go, and yet he had disappeared. All that'd been left of him were deep scorch marks on the carpet.

My memory from that time was hazy though. I remembered waking in the ambulance, in more pain than I'd ever been in. My shoulders hurt so bad I wanted to throw up, but everything from the mid-back down felt like it was gone. When the doctors had told me I'd broken my back, they told me I also might never walk again. Their mistake was underestimating how stubborn I was.

All the therapy and rehabilitation that followed left the next year a blur, but I knew that much was true. Jade had walked me through my own regression therapy, and together, we discovered I remembered a lot more than I thought. I remembered the smells of the possession, the sickly-sweet rot my body gave off.

At the end, there was a moment where the familiar foul stink of rotten eggs cut through everything. Sean screamed, and then he was just gone.

I had never actually seen him vanish though.

What if he'd found a way to sneak out? To run? In the ten years I'd been seeking Sean, I'd never once considered that he'd left me by choice.

"Felix?" Jade frowned and shifted her weight across Raina's middle. "Remember why we're here."

"I know why I'm here," I snapped at her. I'm here to get answers. I'm here to find out how to get Sean back. This demon is offering it to me. What do I care about some dumb girl's soul? If I exorcise it, the demon will just be back in someone else. It was a losing war, a tireless, thankless job. Surely over the last few years, I'd cast enough demons out of people that I deserved to get something besides a few bucks. I deserved to get what I wanted just as much as Raina, didn't I?

Jade turned her head away, focusing again on Raina. "Liar. Be silent, demon!"

"I can't tell you my name if I'm silent, so which is it you want?" The demon cackled. "Seems like you two need to get on the same page if you want to continue."

Jade let out an exasperated grunt and stood.

"What are you doing?" I gestured to Raina. "You have to hold her, Jade!"

She grabbed me by the elbow and dragged me toward the door. "We need to talk. Now."

"Don't worry," the demon said. "I'll wait." Then it threw its head back and howled with laughter.

I pulled my arm away once we were in the hallway. "What the hell, Jade?"

"What the hell yourself?" She pushed my shoulder.

Hard. "Tell me you didn't just seriously consider that thing's offer? Demons are liars, Felix. You of all people should know that!"

"What are the chances that we'll be able to pull this off, huh?" I crossed my arms. "An exorcism is one thing, but we have to toe the line. We can't pull that thing out of her, Jade. Not yet. Not until I have my answers."

"Raina has the answers you need, Felix, not some demon!"

"You don't know that! Nobody knows it! We could be about to throw away the best lead I've had in a decade, and for what? Some poor little rich girl? Tell me why I should feel one ounce of sympathy for her? So what? She had a shit life. Well, guess what. Some of us have had shit lives without having senator fathers and mansions to hide in!" I paused to catch my breath, intending to continue my rant, but the shocked expression on Jade's face gave me pause.

"This jealousy is beneath you, Felix Cross." She gripped my arm. "What happened to you, the life you've led, and the troubles you've had, they aren't her fault. Think hard. Would Sean want you to trade Raina's life for his? Even if he is suffering in Hell?"

I turned my head away, staring at the floor. The earlier rush of anger had left me, transforming into the weight of guilt. Jade was right. Raina didn't deserve what was happening to her any more than Sean deserved what was happening to him. No one deserved the pain and anguish a possession brought with it.

Jade's fingers squeezed hard on my shoulder joint. "The regression will work, Felix. Even if you've lost your faith in God, believe in me. Have I ever let you down?" She crooked a finger under my chin and made me raise my head.

I swallowed. "No. Never."

"Then trust in me. I can do it. I can help her remember for you, for her. For Sean. But first, you have to do what you do and send that demon straight back to Hell."

I nodded, took in a deep breath, and turned toward the door. "You know what? You're right." I tugged off the leather gloves that kept my abilities safely tucked away and stormed back into the room.

It hadn't worked the last time I'd laid hands on Raina, but the last time I hadn't wanted to feel, hadn't wanted to see. The demon had made the mistake of pissing me off, and now I was going to enjoy watching it squirm.

The demon strained against the restraints. "Come back for your answers?"

I ignored the demon, folded my gloves together, and tossed them aside before rolling up my sleeves. "I'll need an anchor."

Jade nodded and went to her bag. She came back with a small foam ball.

Intense empathic visions overwhelmed my psyche rather easily. I'd had more than one seizure in the past, and at least one good fall where I knocked myself out. There was no easy way to come down from it, but I'd learned through experimentation that I could use certain objects and textures to remain grounded in reality. The lightweight foam ball was flexible enough, I could clench my hand around it without it hurting. If the vision intensified, all I had to do was drop the ball and Jade would know to help me. It wasn't the most eloquent communication method, but it was one we'd used in the past.

The demon's amused smirk faded. "What are you doing?"

I handed Jade the vial of holy water, just in case. "Ready?"

She nodded.

I crossed myself—an old habit—and pressed the flat of my palm against Raina's forehead. At first, nothing happened, just as before, but I felt the wall wearing away, eroding under my grip. The demon rocked Raina's head back and forth with a scream. I held fast and concentrated on the touch. Only the touch mattered. Not the screaming, the sweat, the vomit, the trembling, clammy skin beneath my fingers. Only the transfer of invisible energy from me to her.

The resistance cracked like a crumbling dam and I rushed through.

It was dark in Raina's mind, and not the sort of darkness one would associate with nighttime. No, this was a pervasive, living, insidious thing with weight and gravity. Every time it drew a breath, the darkness flexed, pressing in.

"Raina!" I cupped my hands to my mouth and screamed her name again. Despite the crushing feeling of the darkness, my voice echoed freely. My legs were leaden with every step forward. "Raina, where are you?"

A rumble of thunder shook the darkness. I had the distinct feeling of being watched, though I couldn't see anyone in there with me.

I turned a half-circle. "Raina, it's me. You can come out."

"No!" Her scream was distant and everywhere. An echo from the other side of a canyon. "It'll hurt me."

"Then call to me, Raina. Help me find you." I put

my hands out in front of me, feeling the pull of too strong gravity try to push them down.

"What do I say?"

"Anything!" I shouted back and turned toward where I thought I'd heard her voice the loudest.

There was a slight pause before Raina's voice echoed through the space, singing: "Jesus loves me, this I know for the Bible tells me so. Little ones—" She cut off with an abrupt scream as the thunder clanged even louder.

I zeroed in on a direction. "Keep singing, Raina!" I stopped. "Raina?"

A breath. Two. What if something had happened to her?

And then a small, shaky voice rose out of the darkness. "Little ones to him belong. They are weak, but He is strong."

"Yes, that's good. Keep singing. Louder, Raina!"

A howling wind pushed through the space while invisible fingers clawed at my body, pulling me back, trying to keep me from reaching her. I shed them all and pressed forward.

"Do you think you can free her, sinner?" whispered a voice in my ear.

I turned my head but whatever had been there was gone, just a wisp of smoke in the dark.

"She was promised to *me*," whispered the demon on the other side of me. "But we can share her. I don't need the body. Much." The thunder became laughter, rolling through the heavy darkness.

Sean's voice cut through the darkness, louder than Raina's song. "Felix? Felix, don't leave me!"

It's not him. I closed my eyes and forged ahead, following Raina's voice.

Something bit into the back of my left leg. I stumbled and fell with a shout. My knees struck what felt like hard cement with a loud crack. I rolled onto my back, hugging my knees to my chest and blinking tears from my eyes.

The demon laughed. "I thought a Church bitch would be more comfortable kneeling, but you're not even that, are you? You didn't abandon your God. He abandoned you. He left you for us in a Hell of your own making. That's how much your Jesus loves you."

Raina's singing stopped.

"Keep singing, Raina!" I threw my hand out, gripped the darkness in front of me, pulled myself forward inch by inch. "Sing it louder!"

"Jesus loves me this I know as he loved so long ago…"

Yes, that's it, I thought, pulling myself along. As long as she kept singing, I could find her. But her voice broke as she reached the refrain, and she started crying. At least that was loud enough I could keep following the sound. "Just keep making noise, Raina. I'm coming for you."

"Run, Raina," whispered the demon on the wind. "He'll kill you if he catches you, just like he killed Sean. Everywhere Felix goes, death follows with him."

"I don't believe you!" Raina shouted back. "Go away!"

I tried to pull myself along another inch, but the darkness had grown thicker. It was like trying to move through fast-drying cement. My body felt as if it weighed three tons. I knew I didn't have the strength to go on, but I couldn't quit. Not now. She was so close. *I* was so close. She sounded like she was only a few feet away, and yet there might as well have been a continent between us.

I stretched my hand out as far as I could. "Raina! Take my hand!"

"No, I can't!"

"You must!"

The wind and thunder were deafening, and new sounds had joined the mix. The gelatinous splatter of fresh, wet meat against something solid. The buzzing of flies. The moans of the dead and dying. The awful chorus rose around us, choking out every other sound, and still, I called for Raina to take my hand.

Fearful fingers crawled through the dark and brushed against mine, then darted away. I grabbed for them, closing my entire fist around a single clammy, cold finger.

It was enough.

Light erupted from our combined grips like an atom bomb exploding. The weight of the darkness lifted and the sounds rose along with the black maelstrom, spinning above our heads in a storm of light and darkness.

Raina lifted her head, her hair whipping against her face. "What is that?"

"It's you, Raina. You're doing that." I pushed myself forward and squeezed her hand tighter. "You're in control. You can make it leave anytime you want. You can have your life back."

She stared up at the maelstrom. "How?"

"Stand up and order it to go," I replied.

Raina looked back at me, waiting for me to give her an encouraging nod before she slowly pushed herself to her feet. She swayed, and I thought maybe the ordeal had been too much for her, but she held on. Her fingers curled into little, white fists at her side. Raina's head snapped up. "Get out! I command you to leave!"

"But child—" The storm flashed with every syllable. "—you were promised to us. Payment for services rendered."

"You can shove whatever services were bought. Get the *hell* out of my body, demon!"

The demon in the maelstrom screeched in a hundred dark voices, spinning wildly as the light burned away the dark.

I released the foam ball and fell back into my body, staggered by the sudden change. My hips, shoulders, and back ached as if a bad storm were coming. Battle scars. Reminders that the battle may have been won, but the war was far from over.

Raina choked out a sob, turned her head and tugged at the restraints. "Mother? Mother!"

Jade steadied me.

"Go." I nodded to the girl.

Jade left me to undo the restraints keeping Raina tied to the bed. Though Jade wasn't her mother, Raina was so desperate for comfort, she threw her arms around Jade and wept into her.

"Is it over?" Jade asked, patting the girl's head.

I put a hand on the wall and slid to sit on the floor. "For now."

The demon had claimed Raina was payment for services rendered, but what services? And who had traded her life to the legions of Hell? There were still too many unanswered questions.

"How long until we can take the next step?" I asked.

Jade squeezed Raina protectively. "I think she's been through enough today. Don't you? Let her rest, Felix."

I didn't want to. I wanted my answers, and to move on. I certainly didn't want to spend another night in that house with Laura around. Something about her was off. Maybe I could bum space in Jade's hotel room.

No. I shook my head. Bad idea. I don't want to go back there. I said this was business, so let's keep it businesslike. Besides, I needed to stay close to Raina in case something else happened.

"No," said Raina, pushing away from Jade. She drew a hand under her bruised eyes, wiping away tears. "I can do it now."

Jade combed her fingers through Raina's hair. "Honey, you don't have to."

"I want to help." There was more resolution in Raina's voice than I'd heard since we'd met.

"Are you sure?" Jade asked.

Raina nodded.

I sighed and looked at the mess around me. "Let's get this room—and you—cleaned up first."

CHAPTER NINETEEN

Jade helped Raina through a shower and a sandwich while I cleaned up the mess in the room. There wasn't much to be done for most of the paintings. The canvases were cracked, broken, or the paint smeared. I stacked what I thought could be saved—if Raina even wanted to keep them after what'd happened—and put the rest into big black contractor bags.

Once the trash had all been picked up, I went looking for new linens to put on the bed, but I couldn't find where they were stored. Couldn't find the maid to ask her either, despite knowing she was around somewhere. At least, she had been earlier. The best I could do was pull the blanket from my bed and use it to cover the stained mattress in Raina's room.

I had just finished sweeping the floor when Jade brought Raina back. Raina's pallid complexion had brightened a little. In her jeans and t-shirt, with her hair pulled back, she almost looked like a different person. A happy person. Someone with their whole life left to live.

Guilt stabbed at my heart. I'd almost destroyed her to get what I wanted. What kind of monster had I let myself become that I would put my own needs before that of an innocent girl? Jade was right. I had gone too far. Sean wouldn't care for the person I had become.

Raina's eyes widened as she scanned the room. "Wow, it looks nice in here. A lot less crowded."

"I didn't know what you wanted to do with those." I gestured to the paintings I'd stacked in one corner.

Raina's face darkened. "Burn them," she said simply. "I just want to forget all of this happened."

"Unfortunately, what I'm about to ask of you will be just as difficult." I smoothed my hands over the blanket and got out of the way so Jade could help her into bed.

"Let's get you comfortable." Jade fussed with the blanket and the bare pillows behind Raina for a moment while I pulled the chair close to the bed for her to sit in.

As much as I wanted the answers, it would be better if Jade did the actual hypnosis. She was clinically trained as a psychologist, after all, and had done it a thousand times. I'd tried hypnosis a few times with mixed results. Raina would also likely be more comfortable with Jade. Nothing was more important in a hypnosis session than Raina's comfort. At least we knew she was a good candidate for hypnosis since she'd already been through it once with a different therapist.

"There, Raina. Are you comfortable?" She placed a hand on Raina's knee.

Raina nodded. "I suppose so."

I crossed my arms and moved behind Jade, keeping as far back as I could stand. Though Jade would be directing the session, I would have to help her with the line of questioning.

"Did Felix explain to you what was going to happen?" Jade asked, and then launched into an explanation when Raina shook her head. "I'm going to hypnotize you and guide your subconscious through several exercises. It'll be a little like falling asleep, but not quite. You'll still be aware and completely in control at all times. Just to put you at ease, I am a licensed counselor in the state of New York. When I had my own practice, I used hypnotherapy several times a week to help lots of people deal with past traumas."

Raina took a deep breath and frowned. "Have you ever used it on someone who's been possessed?"

"Yes," said Jade, glancing at me. "It's not going to fix all your problems, Raina, but it might help explain what happened to you, where you went fifteen years ago. It might help us find whoever took you so they can be punished."

"Mother says that doesn't matter. That I shouldn't think about it." She played with a loose strand of hair.

Listening to her speak, watching her movements, it was difficult to believe she was a twenty-three-year-old woman. She reminded me more of a ten or eleven-year-old child. Maybe that's as old as her psyche was. After all, trauma had strange effects on people. It wouldn't be unheard of for her to have a delayed mental age after all that'd happened to her.

"Well, what do you want, Raina?" Jade put a hand on Raina's back, waiting.

Raina turned her head away, staring at nothing on the wall. "Nobody's asked me that before. I don't know if I want to remember everything that happened to me. I have this awful feeling in my stomach when I try, like I know it was something bad. It was a bad place with bad people. I have nightmares sometimes, but I never remember them either." She turned her head back to meet Jade's eyes. "But I also believe that bad people should be punished for being bad. If I was hurt, I want whoever hurt me to suffer. Does that make me a bad person?"

"No, sweetheart," said Jade, rubbing Raina's back. "It makes you human to want justice. Maybe we can find the answers that will lead to justice together."

Raina nodded.

Jade sat back in her seat. "Okay then. Let's get started. Raina, I'm going to ask you a series of questions. Some of them might seem silly, but answering each of them honestly is very important. Do you understand?"

"Yes," answered Raina.

"Raina, do you wish to be hypnotized today?"

Raina nodded.

Jade frowned. "I need a verbal response."

"Yes," Raina repeated.

"And do you wish to be hypnotized by me?"

"Yes."

"Okay, very good. Now, during this session, I may touch the top of your head, your hand, your arm, or your knee. This is only to gauge your responsiveness to the therapy being performed. Is that okay, Raina?"

"Yes, that's okay," Raina said.

Jade pressed her lips together a moment and repositioned, crossing one leg over the other and resting her hands in her lap. "I want you to put your hands on your legs like so. Yes, very good. Now, please close your eyes and focus on the sound of my voice as

I guide you. There is nothing but my voice, and yours. Everything else is just going to fade away. But before I do that, I want to give you a special tool that will help us both."

Jade opened the bag on the floor next to her and brought out a remote control, sliding it into Raina's hand. "Just hold onto that for right now and focus on the sound of my voice."

She guided Raina first through a series of relaxation techniques, designed to put Raina at ease. She had Raina do everything from relaxing her muscles with verbal prompting, to breathing and counting backward from one hundred. It took a long time, longer than I remembered it taking.

Occasionally, Jade would pick up Raina's arm and let it drop to test how relaxed she was. Then, they would start a new exercise. It went on and on until Raina's shoulders drooped, her arms hung limp, and her eyelids were so relaxed, I would have thought she'd fallen asleep if she wasn't still responding to Jade's prompts.

When she was satisfied with how relaxed Raina was, Jade removed her hands from Raina's body. "Now I want you to picture the day you came back. The very first memory of when you returned. Build it up in your mind brick by brick, detail by detail, and when you have that moment firmly in your mind's eye, I want you to raise your finger, Raina, just like we practiced."

Raina's fingers twitched. I wouldn't have called that a finger raise, but I wasn't the expert in the room.

"Wonderful. Now, describe it to me."

"It's dark." Raina's voice was groggy, as if she were about to fall asleep. "The air is humid like it might rain. I can smell it in the air. Crickets are chirping in the grass. Tall grass. It's making my shins itch." A small smile sprouted. "There are lightning bugs in the grass."

"What else?" Jade pressed.

Raina's smile faded. "My feet hurt, and so do the backs of my legs. I think I've been walking for a long time but I can't remember why or when. I'm in the woods now. My woods. I know this place. I can see a little cabin at the back of the property. The lights are on. I'm scared because no one used to live there. It's confusing me, but I know I need help. I can smell something else. Garlic. Tomatoes. Herbs. I smell spaghetti. My stomach growls and I'm so hungry. I just need to eat something, anything. I knock on the door."

"Who answers?"

"A man," Raina continued. "Someone I don't know."

"Jacob," I said. "The Hemlock's driver. He lives in that cabin, but he's only worked for the family a few years. There's no way Raina would've known who he was until after."

Jade just nodded. "Okay, I want you to pause that memory like you'd pause a movie."

Raina pressed a random button on the remote.

"Now rewind it. Let's go back to the beginning and further back. Further. Even further, Raina. Now, press play."

Raina's finger pressed a button and her breathing changed, speeding up. Her eyes twitched as if she were flinching.

"Raina," Jade said, leaning forward, "what do you see?"

"They're hurting me!" Raina cried out.

Jade placed a hand gently over Raina's. "No one's hurting you, Raina, remember? We're just on the outside looking in."

"Who?" I uncrossed my arms and gripped the back of Jade's chair. "Find out who it is."

Raina's breathing became even quicker, heavier, more panicked. She rolled her head from side to side. "No, they're putting sticky pads on my face. It's so cold! A blanket, please!"

"Raina, come back to my voice!" Jade squeezed Raina's hand. "Be calm."

Raina's breathing slowed slightly as Jade guided her through a few more breathing exercises.

"There you go." Jade nodded though Raina couldn't see her with her eyes closed. "Okay. Now, tell me what's happening to your past body."

Raina swallowed. "I'm lying naked on a table. I can't move. I think they must've drugged me, but I'm completely awake. They keep telling me I have to be. That it's important."

The chair groaned as I leaned in harder. "Who is they?"

Jade waved me off. "Can you see the people doing this to you? What do they look like?"

"Men," Raina whispered, "in black suits and white coats."

Men in black suits and white coats? That didn't sound like demons to me.

"They're putting the sensors all over me. The table is hovering over a tank. Oh no! They're putting me into the icy cold water! It's so cold, it hurts! It's burning my skin. Oh, God! I can't breathe. I can't move! I'm going to die in there!" She thrashed her head back and forth a moment before going still.

"Raina?" Jade carefully touched the girl's arm. "Raina, what do you see?"

"Hell." She was whispering again. "I have to be quiet in my cell or the monster will come for me. If I'm quiet, if I'm good, and if I do whatever they say, they won't hurt me and it won't come out and make me do those awful things."

Jade looked at me. I shook my head. I had no idea what she was talking about either.

"What do you see, Raina? What does it look like where you are?"

Raina's fist closed around the remote. "It's a small space. The size of a prison cell. All I can hear is screaming. They're torturing people, just like they'll do to me. Every day, all day, that's what they do. They hurt me to try and make *him* come out."

"Who? What's his name?" Jade leaned in, listening as if her very life depended on the answer Raina would give.

Raina's lips moved but no sound came out for a long moment until she spoke in a croaking voice: "Belial."

Belial, one of the primary demons mentioned by name in nearly every demonology text ever written, going as far back as the Gospels themselves. Belial, the first demon made by Lucifer himself, a Lord in Hell with eighty legions under his command, and fifty more legions of vengeful spirits to do his bidding. Named in Milton's *Paradise Lost*, in the Dead Sea Scrolls, in every list of the most vile, evil entities ever to taint creation with his existence, and here they had put him inside a *little girl!*

To what end? And who? Raina's testimony created more questions than it answered, but one thing was for certain. If it was indeed Belial who we were dealing with, we were all still very much in danger.

I stepped back. "End the session, Jade. Now!"

She twisted in the chair to look at me, frowning. "Don't you want to ask about Sean?"

"I do, but the longer you have her under, the more danger we're in. Belial is not some small soldier demon, Jade. He is Lucifer's second in command. In his time, he has claimed more human lives and cause more suffering than any of us will ever know. And he absolutely will not stop coming for her until he claims his prize."

She gripped the back of the chair, fingers closing until her knuckles were white. "I thought you said the exorcism was a success?"

"It was," I agreed, nodding. "For now. But her soul was promised to a high demon with legions to command. He won't give up easily."

"Then we'd better hurry." Jade's chair creaked as she turned back around. "Raina, I want you to hit the rewind button on your remote. Take us back to the first day after you were taken, when you were first brought to this...torture facility."

"To Hell," Raina corrected, but pressed the buttons on her remote.

I stomped forward to stand in the narrow space between Jade's chair and Raina's bed. "What are you doing, Jade? We need to end this. Something more is at work here. I was right when I said I suspected this wasn't a normal possession."

She looked at me, her expression hard, the no-nonsense gaze that demanded I back off. "We won't get another chance to hypnotize her, Felix, and I didn't come all this way just for you to chicken out at the last second. One more scene. Just let me try one more."

I took a deep breath in and glanced over my

shoulder to where Raina lay, her fingers pressed on the power button of the remote. We'd promised her answers too, answers we still didn't have. I wasn't sure what one more scene would tell us that we didn't already know, but it was worth a shot.

I stepped aside. "Okay, but if she shows any signs, I'll terminate the session myself."

Jade nodded, folded her hands, and leaned forward again with her elbows resting on her knees. "Okay, Raina. Press play. Now, what do you see?"

"Nothing." Raina shook her head, and then squinted, eyes closed. "No, wait. There was something on my head. A bag or a blindfold maybe? But they've removed it. I'm inside a building. It smells awful. Like rotten eggs." She wrinkled her nose. "There's a tiny waiting room with those plastic chairs they have at airports, all sitting together on this long beam. There's a lady at the receptionist's window. She's on the phone. We don't stop to talk to her. She presses a button and there's a loud buzzing sound that makes me flinch. It echoes really loudly through the whole building! A metal door slides aside and we enter a long hallway. There are no doors. I'm scared. I don't want to go."

"This is pointless!" I threw my hands up. "That could be anywhere."

Jade pressed a finger to her lips. "Let's go back, Raina. Back to the waiting area. Are there any windows you can see through? Anything at all?"

Raina turned her head to the right and then the left as if she were searching for something. "Yes. They're really high up, though, so I can't see through them very well. Nothing but the tippy-tops of trees."

That might be useful. I uncrossed my arms, suddenly alert. "Ask her what kinds of trees."

"Raina, what do the trees look like?"

"Like Christmas trees," Raina answered. "Except without the Christmas lights."

Pine trees grew all over North America. That didn't rule out many places, and it still didn't tell me if Sean was there, or somewhere else. How in the world would he be there anyway? It was all a pointless gesture. This girl's case had nothing to do with Sean's disappearance. We were wasting our time.

A sudden pounding downstairs made me uncross my arms and frown at the door. Footsteps crossed the floor below and the front door opened. I forgot all about the hypnotism and went out into the hall to see what was happening.

The maid had finally showed back up. Of course she would now that I didn't need her. She stood at the door, holding it open, her other hand perched on her hip. She didn't look happy to see whoever it was.

"I apologize to come unannounced," said a distinctly male voice with a southern drawl. "I only came by to check on Senator Hemlock since he's been out ill."

Ill? Laura said John was in Washington, not sick. Something didn't add up there.

"I'm sorry, but Senator Hemlock isn't taking any visitors at the moment," replied Willa. "He's resting, but I'll be sure to tell him you stopped by."

"I see. And do give him my wishes for a speedy recovery. Oh, and if he's well enough, let him know I sent some documents for him to look at."

"I will." Willa swung the door closed.

I ducked back into Raina's bedroom before she could turn around and see me eavesdropping.

CHAPTER TWENTY

I shut the door behind me and locked it. "I think it would be best if you ended the session and got out of here, Jade."

"Why?" she asked. "What's happening?"

The pieces of this puzzle had begun to come together, but I still didn't have them all. I didn't know where the senator really was, for example, or precisely what Laura was up to. What I did know was that Laura Hemlock was bad news. The longer we stayed in the house, the more danger all of us were in. I needed to find a way to get Raina out of there, and I had the perfect excuse.

"We need to go. All of us. The sooner, the better." I folded my arms.

She hesitated, balking at being told what to do at first. I'd tried to put enough urgency in my voice that she'd see I wasn't trying to order her around. I only had her safety in mind. After waiting a moment to make sure I understood she was still in charge, she turned back to Raina and began talking her up out of her unconscious state.

"Raina?" Jade touched Raina's shoulder gently. "In a moment, I'm going to count to five. Not yet, but when I do, you're going to emerge from this state and return to your normal level of consciousness full of joy and happiness. One…"

When Jade reached five, Raina opened her eyes, blinked twice, and smiled wide.

I took a step away from the door. "Raina, I hate to ruin the mood, but I need to ask you something. Has your mother been acting strangely since you returned?"

Her smile faded. She let go of the remote and it dropped to the mattress with a dull thud. "Strange how?"

I shrugged. "Anything out of the ordinary."

Raina raised her eyebrows and tilted her head to the side. "I'm not sure I know what ordinary is."

"Fair point. How about your father? When was the last time you saw him?"

"About five days ago, I think," she said, putting a finger to her bottom lip in thought. "Before he went to Washington."

"Felix, what did you find out?" Jade stood and rubbed her palms on her stomach as if she were smoothing out the fabric, but it didn't have any wrinkles.

I debated not telling them. After all, if something sinister was going on, they might be safer not knowing. In the end, however, I figured my next moves would be easier if everyone was on the same page. "I just heard the maid tell a visitor Senator Hemlock was sick."

"Maybe he's sick in Washington," Jade suggested with a shrug.

I shook my head. "No, the guy thought he'd come for a house call. I think he was someone else who worked in Washington. He was talking about some papers he sent for the senator to look over."

Raina sat up, away from the pile of pillows at her back. "What are you saying?"

"I'm saying I don't think your father is in Washington, Raina. I don't think he's sick either. I don't know where he is really, or what reasons your mother might have to lie, but I'm concerned. The things you said while you were under hypnosis, combined with the missing senator, Laura's strange behavior…I don't think any of us is safe in this house."

"But she's my mother. She wouldn't hurt me." Raina swung her feet over the side of the bed. "She's been taking care of me all this time."

"You couldn't eat any of the food she brought you, Raina," I pointed out. "Yet you ate just fine when I brought you food. Food neither she nor the maid wanted me to bring up, I'll add. It's also not the most disturbing thing I've experienced in this house since my arrival. Something here isn't quite right and I think it would be best if you got away, Raina. Is there anywhere else you can go? Any other family?"

She shook her head.

I muttered a curse under my breath. Of course it wouldn't be that easy. Removing her from Laura's care would be difficult, especially since Raina didn't seem to know how to care for herself. She might've been in an adult body, but she was still very much a child. Set loose in the world, someone would take advantage of her.

Maybe I couldn't get her off the property, but I had an excuse to get her out of the house. Jacob had invited

Jade and me to dinner. I was sure he wouldn't object to us bringing Raina along. He'd seemed like he wanted to tell me something. It could be he was just as wary of Laura Hemlock as I was.

"Right, so here's the plan." I clapped my hands together. "Jacob extended an invitation to me earlier today. I felt like he had something he wanted to get off his chest. Something he was too afraid to say here, where prying eyes and ears might catch on. We're going to take him up on that offer. Raina, you're going to come with us."

"Hold on." Jade raised a hand. "I didn't say I was going."

"Well, what else have you got to do tonight?"

Jade raised an eyebrow. "Sleep? I've got a flight back to JFK at four tomorrow morning."

My heart sank into my stomach. I swallowed to get it to bounce back up. "I thought you'd stay and help me see this through."

"Oh, Felix." Her heels clicked as she crossed the room to pinch my cheek and smile. "You don't need me. You're an expert demonologist, remember? I'm sure whatever else needs to be done to wrap this up, you can do it without me getting in your way."

"I'm not sure I want to go either." Raina folded her hands in her lap and stared down at her intertwined fingers. "I don't know Jacob very well and…well, I don't know. Maybe this is all just a big misunderstanding. Maybe you misheard what Willa said, or maybe she was just saying that to make the man go away. It seems like such a big reaction to a small bit of information."

I left Jade and went to kneel in front of Raina. "It might seem that way, but I would rather err on the side of caution, Raina. If Jacob doesn't have anything to add, I'll bring you right back home, okay? I promise."

She frowned. "Pinky swear?"

"Pinky swear." I offered her my pinky finger.

She hooked hers around it and we shook on it.

Satisfied, I stood and nodded. "Now get your coat. It's cold outside."

While Raina dug her coat out of the closet, I walked Jade to the front door. "Are you sure you don't want to catch a later flight?"

She smiled as I held the door open for her. "You just can't let me go, can you? It's true, I am a catch. But our time is over, Puppy. You long ago learned everything I had to teach. There's nothing left between us but fond memories of a different time. Besides, we both know Sean Yeats is your true love." She hopped up on her tiptoes to plant a kiss on my cheek. "I hope you find him, Puppy. I really do."

I sighed, letting all the air out through my nose. "I just wish this case had gotten me a little closer. Bishop X seemed so sure Raina's kidnapping was connected to Sean's disappearance, but Raina's never been to Hell."

"Sounds to me like she's certainly been through a version of Hell." Jade buttoned her coat and tugged on a bright red hat. The temperature outside had dropped since her arrival.

"Not literally though," I pointed out. "Which means I learned nothing that will help me find a way to save him, Jade."

"You know, they say Heaven is a place on Earth. Maybe Hell is too."

"That's just a song," I said as Raina started down the stairs behind me. She'd found a faded blue coat that seemed several sizes too large for her skinny body.

Jade smiled and was about to say something smart back, but paused when we heard car tires on gravel. I thought it might be Jacob, coming to pick up Jade and take her back to the airport. I'd planned to slip into the back of the car with her and then just go straight to Jacob's place. We could call Laura later from the house to let her know Raina was okay and where she was.

But when the Hemlock limousine pulled to a stop, the back door opened, and Laura climbed out with a cell phone glued to her ear. "I don't care, Tom. Run the numbers again. There's no way he could be polling that low, not after yesterday's numbers." She paused right in front of us. "Just fucking do it or I'll fire you and hire an intern who'll do it for free." Laura hung up the phone, removed her sunglasses, and flashed the three of us a plastic smile. "Oh, hello! Who's this…woman? And Raina! What are you doing up?"

I gestured to Jade. "This is Jade. She was assisting me with the exorcism today, and I'm pleased to report it went extremely well."

Laura's smile faltered for just a moment. "It's done?"

I nodded. "It's done. The demon's been exorcised."

"Momma?" Raina pushed past me and embraced her mother.

Laura patted Raina on the back and rested her cheek on the top of her daughter's head. "It's good to have you back, sweetie. But what are you doing up? And out here in the cold no less! You should be inside, recovering! What an ordeal you've been through."

"Jacob invited us to dinner," Raina said.

Laura's grip on her daughter loosened. She stood up straighter and cast a questioning glance back at her driver, who'd gotten out of the car to carry Laura's shopping bags to the porch.

Jacob hesitated, put down the bags, and removed his hat, putting it to his chest. "That was before, child. When you were still…not yourself. I mean no offense, but I only meant to be polite to Mr. Cross. Extend him some hospitality."

"I should hope so. Raina's in no condition to be going anywhere." Laura put her arm around her daughter and led her back toward the front door.

"But Momma, I feel fine."

"Hush, child. Mother knows best."

I didn't miss the way Laura's fingers tightened protectively around Raina's shoulders as she led her back into the house. I also didn't miss the apologetic glance Raina gave me.

Laura paused inside. "What about you, Felix? You are, of course, still free to join Jacob and his family if you choose. You're also welcome to dine with us."

I knew I should stay with Raina. Alarm bells were going off in my head, especially with the way Laura was behaving now that she was back. Raina was in danger and there was no doubt in my mind that she should not be left alone with Laura.

But I also knew if I stayed, I wouldn't get any more of the story. If Laura was going to make a move, she'd wait until after I packed my bags and left in the morning. There was nothing I could do to stop her from hurting Raina if she chose to do so, not without some irrefutable proof. I hoped I was right about Jacob's intentions.

I gave Laura my best innocent smile. "No, thanks, Mrs. Hemlock. Jacob did invite me first. I'm going to see Jade back to her hotel safely anyway."

Laura's smile shrank slightly. "Okay. Be safe."

"We will." I nodded and opened the car door for Jade.

Laura left Raina inside and stepped back out, closing the front door behind her. She gestured for Jacob to come over. The two shared a quick and whispered conversation before Jacob begrudgingly nodded and hurried back to the car. "Might not have been wise to refuse the lady's invitation," he said when we were on the winding road.

"I know Laura's not who she's pretending to be." I leaned forward. The leather seat creaked under my shifting weight. "I know she's up to something, Jacob. That's what you wanted to tell me before but couldn't, isn't it?"

His head jerked to the side. "Not here," he said through clenched teeth. "There are ears here."

There are ears here. I glanced around the car, searching for any listening devices, though I knew they'd be far too small or well-hidden for me to spot. Someone like Laura would've made sure of that.

Jade put a hand on my leg. "I can reschedule my flight if you need me."

I considered it. Something was coming. This whole thing—whatever it was—was about to unravel in front of me. I could feel it in my bones. When that happened, I didn't want to face whatever was coming alone. Yet I also didn't want Jade caught in the crossfire. She was a damn good psychic, and a good person. One of the few I'd come across in my journey to educate myself. For all that, she wasn't a fighter. While Jade didn't scare easily, I didn't know how she would handle true horror once it was staring her in the face.

I picked up her hand and kissed her knuckles before letting go. "No. Other people need you more than me.

There's nothing more for you to do here. I've got this handled, Jade. Let's just get you settled back at your hotel and you can forget this whole thing ever happened."

She chuckled. "Typical Felix."

We dropped her off at a Holiday Inn. She gave me her new cell number, just in case. I tucked it into my back pocket and trudged wearily back to the limousine.

"She your girlfriend?" Jacob eyed me in the rearview mirror.

I stared out the window at the small-town setting, wishing I had an excuse to stay with her. "Jade and I have been a lot of things, but a couple's never been one of them. It's not really who we are."

He nodded as if he understood, but I was sure he didn't. I didn't blame him. It was a difficult concept to explain to an outsider, to have needed someone like I had once needed her.

"Amanda and me have been married for eight years," he said. "Two kids. Thought they'd each be the death of us. Kids are hard. You ever have any?"

I shook my head.

"Kids'll change you," Jacob continued. "People say they make you grow closer together, make you stronger. But that's because having kids is like getting a scar. Hurts at first. All the arguing. The exhaustion. The figuring out who you are outside of changing diapers and warming up bottles. When they get older though, and when they're quiet, there's this moment. You look at your kids and you think, 'wow. I helped make that.' Having kids is like getting a second chance at life."

I turned away from the window. "Is that how Laura thinks of it too?"

Jacob's fingers flexed around the steering wheel as he considered his answer carefully.

I moved to the closer seat and leaned forward to speak to him. "I don't care about ears anymore. I need answers, Jacob. Something isn't right about that woman, about this family, and you're the only one who's been straight with me. Tell me the truth. Where is Senator Hemlock?"

"I can't tell you that, Mr. Cross."

"Can't or won't?"

He sighed. "Not yet. Let's get back to the cottage first and have some dinner. I think what Amanda has to say about it will be good for you to hear."

I pressed my back to the seat and crossed my arms letting out a small frustrated growl.

"Look," said the driver, "I know you want your answers, but trust me. If you want to make it through the night alive, you'll wait until we're back at the cottage."

If you want to make it through the night alive? I was suddenly surer than ever that I'd done the right thing by sending Jade on her way.

Just what the hell was going on in the Hemlock household?

CHAPTER TWENTY-ONE

Jacob turned the limo off the highway and onto the state route that would take us out to the Hemlock property. "So, Miss Raina's better? You finished the exorcism?"

"Yeah. Earlier today." I got out my crumpled pack of cigarettes, knowing I couldn't light up in the car. Once we stopped, however, I planned on smoking two before moving on. It'd been a hell of a day.

"Then no offense, but why not just leave?" He lifted his eyes to the rearview mirror. "Your job's done. I wouldn't be offended if you skipped out on dinner and just had me take you right to the airport. I'm sure Mrs. Hemlock wouldn't mind either."

I paused midway through tucking a cigarette behind my ear. Jacob was right. I'd technically done everything I'd set out to do. I'd saved the girl from her demon, determined that her case had nothing to do with Sean's disappearance. All I had to do was call the bishop and collect my payment. We could part ways and everything could go back to the way it was before.

Except I didn't want that. When Bishop X had found me, I was at my lowest point, ready to just lay down and die. This job had reminded me I could do more with my knowledge, even if it hadn't done anything to help me find Sean.

"I can't walk away," I said. "Not when I know Raina's in danger. She's not safe in that house, Jacob. I know Laura is up to something. I just don't know what."

Jacob nodded. "I can respect that."

Rather than turn into the Hemlock driveway, we went a little further down the curvy road and turned onto an unmarked gravel driveway. Hemlock and ash trees lined either side of the road, which felt like it stretched on for miles. When Jacob told me he lived in the guest cottage at the edge of the property, I expected to be able to see the Hemlock house from his place. I must've underestimated the size of forty acres. The only thing I could see in every direction was more trees. More leaves. Underbrush and forest.

I tried to imagine Raina coming this way two years ago when she first returned. It would've been so easy to get lost in those primordial woods. How had she even found the place?

I stuffed my empty cigarette package back into my pocket and dug out the lighter. "So why do you live in the Hemlock's guest cottage, Jacob?"

He shrugged. "Easier to do the job, I guess. The Hemlocks need driving at all hours of the day and night sometimes, and I needed a place to stay. Can't complain too much about them taking the rent out of my paychecks since I don't have much of a commute. Overall, the Hemlocks have been good to me and mine. As long as I keep doing right by them, it'll probably keep going that way. But I've seen what happens to the people who cross Laura. It's not pretty."

"And yet you're willing to help me? Why?"

He shook his head. "The truth will come out either way. Sometimes, you just do what you've got to to survive. That's all I'm doing, Mr. Cross. Whatever I have to do to keep me and my family safe."

It was an odd way to answer the question, but I shrugged it off. Jacob had always acted a little weird. Maybe he was just nervous about whoever might be listening in on our conversation.

The guest house appeared at the end of the gravel road, a small, blue cottage with white trim. It didn't look big enough to house four people, but looks could be deceiving. It had a good-sized deck that wrapped around one side, dropping off into a balcony that overlooked a wooded hillside. An American flag hung out front, shifting lazily in the slight breeze.

As we parked, the front door opened and two children—a boy and a girl about seven or eight—scrambled down the steps to throw their arms around Jacob, screaming, "Daddy!"

He greeted them with a big smile and kisses and lifted the smallest of the two—the boy—up onto his shoulders. "Felix, I'd like you to meet my kids. This is Trevor and that one's Emily. Kids, this is Felix Cross."

The little girl's eyes must've doubled in size. She shrank behind her father. "The exorcist?"

"Sure, kid." I lifted the cigarette from behind my ear and waggled it in my fingers. "Mind if I have a few of these before we head inside?" I'd need more than one if I was going to be dealing with kids. They were noisy, messy, and nosy. Even the best-behaved ones were a pain in the ass.

Jacob nodded. "Just be sure to pick up the butts. Amanda will flip her lid if she finds them. I'll be inside. Feel free to come on in when you're done."

The boy slid down from his father's shoulders and tugged on Jacob's jacket. "Daddy, can I stay outside with Felix?"

"Do you mind?" Jacob asked me.

Yes, I mind. But I didn't say that. That'd be rude, and I wanted to stay on Jacob's good side so I could get information out of him later. "Sure. Whatever floats his boat, right?"

Jacob hesitated a moment but went inside with his daughter.

I turned my back to the kid and lit my cigarette, wishing it was a little colder outside. Then the kid would've run inside with his father instead of standing next to me, staring at me like I was a museum exhibit. I moved away from him. He scooted closer, still just staring up at me with those big, brown eyes.

Eventually, I had enough and plucked the cigarette from between my teeth. "What is it, kid?"

"Smoking is bad for your health."

"Yeah? Well, so is being a smartass." I put the cigarette back and puffed at twice the speed.

The boy stuck his tongue out at me and pulled down one eyelid. "I know you are, but what am I?" he chanted before running off, giggling.

And that was why I considered all kids to be miniature assholes.

As I finished my cigarette and started another, I tried to put together what I knew. Raina had been possessed by a demon that claimed she'd been promised to him. While demons were liars by their very nature, that might have been true. She'd also described a place, a facility with many cells where she was tortured in hopes of bringing him out. The demon claimed to be Belial, who was no small entity. He was a prince in Hell and Lucifer's second in command according to some texts. In others, Belial is called the Angel of Darkness. The *War Scroll*—one of the *Dead Sea Scrolls*—specifically states that Belial is accursed by God and his people, perhaps even more so than even Lucifer himself. The *Damascus Document* called him the patron demon of necromancers and wizards.

He was a demon invoked by those brave or foolish enough to seek wealth and power, but an invocation of Belial was particularly dangerous. To keep the demon placated, he required frequent sacrifices of human blood. Few would attempt to summon him, and Laura certainly couldn't do it by herself. It would take a whole coven of witches just to attempt it. Besides, what would she get out of it? She'd gotten all her wealth and power from marrying the senator. Without John, she was no one but an ambitious socialite.

Speaking of John, what did this have to do with him? If Laura was somehow behind Belial's possession of Raina, had she been stupid enough to offer John as a sacrifice? No, Laura was too smart for that. Someone would miss John. She wouldn't be able to keep that charade up long. Besides, she had much more attractive offerings all around her. A smart woman like Laura would go after her staff before she turned to the source of her lavish lifestyle. Where, then, was Senator John Hemlock?

What fate awaited Raina once I was out of the way? Laura had certainly seemed less than thrilled with my successful exorcism. It almost seemed as if she was hoping I would fail like all of Raina's other treatments.

I didn't know if Jacob had all the answers, but if he was willing to fill in just one of the holes, it might be enough to make this dinner worth my time.

I dropped the cigarette butt to the ground and stomped it out before I picked it up and deposited it into one of the garbage cans at the side of the house.

Inside, it smelled like roast chicken and fresh herbs. The scent was good enough to make my mouth water. I couldn't remember the last time I ate a decent meal, a fact my stomach reminded me of with a loud grumble. No one heard it though since the kids were running in circles around the table, giggling and playing a game of keep-away with a hacky sack.

"All right now, you two," said a middle-aged woman I took to be Jacob's wife, Amanda. She was a lean woman with streaks of silver in her shoulder-length dark hair. "Go on and wash up."

The kids ran from the kitchen like two stampeding elephants.

"Sorry about them." Amanda smiled and stepped away from the stove, wiping her hands clean on the front of her pink apron. She offered me a handshake. "I'm Amanda. You must be Felix."

"That's me." I took her hand and squeezed.

Her smile faded and she looked down at my gloved hand. "Is it too cold in the house for you?"

"Oh, no. I always wear these." I retracted my hand and made sure the gloves were on tightly. "I'm something of a sensitive. It keeps me from having sensory overload when I come into contact with people or items that may have strong emotional connections associated with them."

"Oh," she said simply.

She didn't understand. Almost no one did. It was a difficult curse to explain that simple human touch was often painful for me. Since most of my interactions were brief—like this one—I'd never bothered to come up with a more succinct explanation for it. I wore gloves when I could, but more often than not they'd been a luxury I didn't bother with in recent years. Maybe this gig with Bishop X would help me change that.

"Well, I'd best get this chicken cut up." Amanda nodded and went back to her work, carving up the chicken she'd baked and plating vegetables.

Dinner was pleasant. The children were too busy stuffing their faces to do much talking, and when they did, they kept their table manners decent. Their parents had done a good job of teaching them not to speak with their mouths full, and not to eat too fast. Either that, or it was a nice performance put on for their guest.

The food was simple but delicious. Amanda's chicken was the best I'd tasted in a long time. She paired it with some red potatoes, carrots, and squash, all quartered and roasted together in a big pan. Her handmade yeast rolls were the star of the show, though. I unashamedly ate three without any butter. If she'd offered to bag me some to take with me, I probably would have. Unfortunately, they were popular with everyone so there weren't any left.

As dinner wound to a close, Amanda sent the kids to go play. I pushed my plate full of chicken bones to the middle of the table. Amanda stood and leaned over to collect it.

"I can help," I said as she went to scrape the plate into the trash.

"Hush, now! I won't have it. You're a guest here,

Mr. Cross. In my kitchen, guests don't work." She scraped the plate and piled it with the rest before turning on the faucet. "I was waiting for the kids to go, but I've got to ask you. How do you like Laura?"

"Amanda," Jacob ground out in a warning.

"What? It's only a harmless little question." She used a fork to scrape untouched carrots into the garbage. "I'm not going to lie, though. It's no secret I don't care for her. I think she's a little crazy."

"Crazy's not the word I would use." I picked up my water glass and frowned when I found it empty. "She's smart. Probably dangerous."

"What makes you say that?" Amanda lowered the plate into the sink.

I folded my hands on the table. "I know Senator Hemlock isn't in Washington. I know he's not sick. Laura's telling two different stories about where he is, and I want to know why. I also think she might've been involved somehow in Raina's disappearance. Now, if I'm right, that connects her to two disappearances in her immediate family. That woman's up to something. I'd bet on it." I leaned back in my seat. "But you two would know her better than me. What do you think?"

Jacob exchanged a glance with his wife.

Amanda nodded slightly and smiled. "How would you like some hot tea, Felix? Bad news is always easier to swallow with a little tea, I find."

"I'd love some."

"Perfect." She got right to work on making it from scratch, pulling ingredients from the cupboard and the fridge to throw together in a pan.

"She's a witch, you know," Jacob said, his voice hovering barely above a whisper.

"Who? Laura?"

He nodded. "There used to be rumors around town that was how she got with the senator. You know before she was the Laura you met, she was just a waitress. Poor as dirt. John was out of her league and engaged to marry someone else. People say she put a love potion in his drink and that was that. She had him all to herself."

I smiled and stifled a laugh. "Well, people say a lot of things."

"They sure do," he agreed, nodding. "Still, can't help but wonder if there's some truth in that fiction. As for if she was involved in Raina's disappearance, I couldn't say. I wasn't with the family back then. I can tell you, however, that I never drove Mr. Hemlock to the airport. Not to the bus station, or anywhere else."

Finally, we were getting somewhere. "When was the last time you saw him?"

"Two weeks ago, it must be." He leaned back as Amanda placed a steaming mug in front of him. "He and Laura were in the back of the limo, having it out over some bill he was sponsoring. I don't know the details. All I know is that Laura didn't like him being all wishy-washy when it came to his political platform. She was mad that he was trying to lean more moderate and wanted to push him to lean further right with the rest of his party. Said if he didn't, the party could turn their backs on them. Like I said, I don't know the details. But they shouted all the way back from the airport until I dropped them off at the house. Next day, he wasn't around."

So, the driver takes him home with his wife, and he disappears inside the house? It was starting to sound more and more like Laura was involved in some foul play. "What about Raina?" I pressed as Amanda put my cup of tea in front of me.

Jacob gripped his mug with both hands. "Can't say much about that, like I said. At least not about when she went missing. But I can tell you about the day she came back."

CHAPTER TWENTY-TWO

THEN

The air smelled of garlic, tomatoes, and herbs because that's all we'd been eating. It was three days before a payday when Raina Hemlock knocked on my door, which meant money was scarce. Back then, the Hemlocks paid me weekly instead of monthly, and I didn't make quite as much. We were always just scraping by.

I was in the living room, in my favorite armchair, flipping through the funnies when the knock came. Trevor and Emily were watching cartoons on the ratty old couch we'd brought with us on our move from Henderson. It'd been second-hand when we got it, maybe even third-hand.

The knock was faint at first, like whoever was on the other side didn't want to be heard. I lowered the paper with fear clawing its way up my back. Mrs. Hemlock wouldn't come all the way out there on foot. She'd have called if she needed me. Who else would be knocking on my front door? Maybe I hadn't heard anything at all.

I glanced over at the kids. Neither of them had moved from their spots, their eyes wide and focused completely on the animated characters dancing on the screen. Amanda hadn't stopped cooking and humming in the kitchen. Maybe there hadn't been a knock.

But then it came again, more solid and demanding. Loud enough Trevor blinked and looked at the door.

With a sigh, I set aside the newspaper and stood, straightening my shirt. *I should get my jacket and put it on if it's Mrs. Hemlock*, I thought. Then I remembered I'd put my jacket in the laundry when I'd come through the door. If she wanted me to drive her somewhere this late, she'd have to accept I didn't have a jacket.

Before I opened the door, I pushed aside the thin drapes next to it and peered out onto the porch. "What in the world…?" The words fell out of my mouth and I found myself reaching for the doorknob to open it.

Outside on my porch stood a waif of a young woman, thin as a scarecrow and wearing nothing but one of those ugly, polka-dotted hospital gowns and a pair of ankle-high socks. She had to be freezing in that weather, as it was just barely above forty degrees out there. Leaves and sticks decorated her matted hair.

My first thought was that maybe she was an escaped mental patient, but I didn't think there were any asylums around for her to have escaped from. The nearest hospital was a good forty miles from there. No one could've made it that far on foot. Not without getting picked up.

She looked up at me with those big, brown eyes, her skinny arms crossed tight across her chest.

I've seen those eyes before, I thought, though I

couldn't place them.

"P-p-please," she stammered out. "Please help me."

My gut said I should take the girl in, dress her in warm clothes, feed her whatever we had handy, and fix her some nice, hot tea to warm those cold bones, but I was too confused to react. I leaned forward, looking first one way and then the other to see if maybe there was some car that'd dropped her off. "What are you doing here, miss? Who are you?"

"My name is Raina Hemlock, and I'm very hungry," said the waif.

Raina Hemlock? The missing girl! The one whose picture and story had been all over the news? I'd heard the senator talk about her on occasion. It was a painful subject though, and not one he brought up often. The paparazzi had been hounding the family ever since she'd gone missing.

But if this was her…after all this time? Could it be? It'd be a miracle if it were true.

"Jacob?" Amanda's voice came from the doorway between the living room and the kitchen. "Who is it?"

I stepped aside so she could see.

Amanda's eyes widened. "Oh my! Well, don't just stand there! She must be freezing. Get her in here!"

The girl practically barged past me to grab the nearest blanket from the back of the sofa and wrap it around herself. The whole bundle, blanket, girl, and all trembled. "Have you got anything to eat?"

"Sure," I said. "You stay right there." I grabbed my wife by the shoulder and led her into the kitchen. "She says she's Raina Hemlock. *Raina Hemlock*, Amanda!"

"That poor thing?" Amanda pressed her lips into a straight line and shook her head. "Do you know how unlikely that is? Raina's probably dead, Jacob."

"I know that. But what if it is her?"

Amanda leaned back to watch the girl shiver in the living room for a moment. "Even if she isn't who she says she is, who would know? That girl's worth a fortune."

The thought hadn't crossed my mind, but now that Amanda had brought it up, it was all I could think about. The interviews, the movie deals, the fame and publicity…whether she was the real Raina Hemlock or not wouldn't matter. Once the press got wind of her, they'd want the full story, and that story might just be enough to change our lives for the better.

"What about the senator and his wife?" I whispered. "They'll want to know. We can't just call the papers without talking to them first."

"Oh, what have those people ever done for us?" Amanda snapped. "The minute you bring them in on this, we lose our chance. If you go to the papers first, they'll remember you and talk to you. They'll buy the story, Jacob, and we can get out of here for good. You can call the Hemlocks right after, so long as you're the first contact. That's all that matters, Jacob. We've got to look out for ourselves."

"What if it was Emily?" I pushed. "Or Trevor? What if it was your kid, gone for all those years and then suddenly someone was back saying they were them? Wouldn't you want to know right away?"

"Of course I would!" Amanda went to the pot of spaghetti sauce on the stove and stirred it furiously. "But we're not talking about our kids. We're talking about theirs."

I frowned. "Senator Hemlock's been good to me."

And he had. He was nice enough, always saying please and thank you. He had good manners and a pleasant demeanor. They'd given us the cottage to live in when we lost our last apartment. The rent came out of my checks, but we got by. That was more than I could say for a lot of families in the area.

Amanda, though, didn't see it that way. She hated Laura Hemlock, hated the Hemlocks' big house, their fancy car, their designer clothes. Being poor had made her bitter, and part of me wondered if she didn't like that bitterness just a little. It gave her purpose.

I went to the phone hanging on the wall and picked it up. "I'm calling them."

"You're making a mistake," Amanda said, shaking her head, but she made no move to stop me.

Laura picked up the phone on the third ring, her pleasant, high-pitched voice ringing out in a, "Hello?"

My throat constricted. How do you tell someone news like that over the phone? I had to. She certainly wasn't going to come all the way out to the cottage for any other reason. Laura Hemlock didn't trouble herself with the problems of others.

She sighed. "Jacob, I know it's you. What is it?"

"I'm sorry to disturb you, Mrs. Hemlock, especially at this hour. It's just that…well, something's happened."

"What's wrong?" Her voice was suddenly tense. "The toilet's not leaking again, is it? Because I told you if it happened again, you'd be responsible for the repairs."

"No, no. It's not that at all." I shifted my grip on the phone, my palms suddenly damp with sweat. "It's about Raina. She's here."

Silence on the other end. Had she hung up on me?

"I'm sorry," she said at length. "What did you say?"

And so, I explained to her what had just happened,

how the girl had showed up at my door, how she didn't seem to know where she was, or even that so much time had passed. I thought about sharing my conjecture with Laura that the girl sitting in my living room was likely a fake, but that wasn't my place.

Laura cut in before I was even finished. "That's impossible. Raina's been gone for years. Thirteen years, Jacob. She'd be an adult!"

"Yes, ma'am. I know that. I don't pretend to understand. I'm just telling you what happened."

"This obviously won't do. We can't have impostors going around, using her name. What does she want? Did she ask for anything?"

I shook my head before I remembered I was on the phone and Laura couldn't see me. "No, ma'am. Just a blanket and some food. I think you ought to come down here and meet her, though."

The phone creaked as if Laura were changing positions. "Well, I can't very well get out there, can I? It's dark and John's already gone to bed. I'm not going to walk through the woods in the dark by myself, Jacob. If you think there's some credence to this, put the girl in the car and drive her up here. Otherwise, don't waste my time." The phone clicked and a dial tone followed.

"Well?" Amanda crossed her arms. "How'd it go?"

"She hung up on me."

"She doesn't believe it's her any more than we do, does she?"

I shook my head. "She wants me to drive the girl up to the house so she can have a look at her."

"At this hour? Dammit, Jacob. You're not at their beck and call!" Amanda sighed. "I guess we can feed her and clean her up first. Make her presentable."

The girl—who I had to call Raina, despite not believing it was her—smelled awful, but didn't seem to understand how to work the shower. I had Emily show her twice before Emily finally lost all patience and just ran the bath for her. She also helped Raina scrub the mud and leaves out of her hair.

Raina was tall, but very thin, so finding clothes that would fit her was a challenge. Amanda was too curvy for her wardrobe to be a good fit, and Emily too short. Eventually, after much searching, we found one of Amanda's older shirts would work alongside a pair of Trevor's sweats. They were short enough to show off her shins, but that was the best I could do.

When we sat down at the table, she didn't wait for us to say grace. Didn't pick up a fork either. Just started scooping spaghetti into her mouth with her fingers.

"That's not how you do it!" Emily exclaimed and shoved a fork into Raina's fist. "Use a fork. Like this!" She demonstrated for Raina how to twirl up the noodles.

Raina struggled to imitate her and eventually wound up just scooping noodles with her fork, shoveling them into her mouth.

I cleared my throat and forced myself not to watch. "So, Raina. I hate to ask, but where have you been all this time?"

Her answer came out muffled through chewing a mouthful of food.

"Sorry, I didn't quite get that."

She swallowed and licked her lips clean. "I don't know. I don't remember. I was just here suddenly and your food smelled so good. Tastes good too."

Amanda didn't answer until I elbowed her. "Oh, thank you, dear."

Trevor frowned. "Why's she like that?"

"Trevor!" Amanda snapped. "Manners."

Raina shrank back from the table and immediately grabbed her napkin, cleaning herself up. "Sorry. It just feels like it's been so long since I ate real food."

After dinner, Amanda got her cleaned up again. I loaded Raina into the limo and slowly drove down the darkened lane, glancing at her in the back seat. She seemed so lost in thought, staring out the window at the darkness.

What if she *was* Raina Hemlock? Everything would change. Maybe John and Laura would finally stop fighting and get along. The family could heal. I couldn't imagine what it must've been like, losing a child, especially not one as young as Raina had been. And then to have the media storm on top of it all? It seemed like the Hemlocks were always popping up in the news, more often because of their missing daughter than anything John did in the Senate.

I watched her reaction as we pulled up to the house. She didn't seem surprised or overwhelmed by its size and grandeur, but overjoyed. I couldn't stop the car fast enough to keep her from leaping out of it and rushing up the stairs. The front door opened just before Raina made it and Laura appeared.

Raina hesitated just a moment before she threw her arms around her mother. "Momma!"

Laura did not hug her back. At least, not at first. When she did, it was a stiff imitation of the real thing. Not at all the sort of reaction a mother should've had to being reunited with her missing daughter.

"Momma, I missed you so much!" Raina squeezed tighter.

Laura wriggled free and pushed Raina back, forcing

a smile. "It's so good to see you! Your father will be so pleased!"

"Can I go inside?" Raina beamed.

"Yes, of course you can." Laura let go of Raina as the girl raced through the front door as if she were still a child and not the full-grown adult that had returned.

I thought Laura would close the door, and my small part in the story would be over, but the woman hovered at the top of the stairs, frowning at the girl running through her home. She gestured for me to come closer.

I removed my hat and complied. "Yes, ma'am?"

"Who else knows she's here?" Laura demanded.

"My family. I don't know if anyone else saw her. I didn't see any cars drop her off or anything. She just sort of appeared in front of my door. Odd, isn't it? Do you think it's really her?" I leaned to the side to catch another glimpse of Raina.

"How should I know?" Laura's cold demeanor seemed excessive, even for her. She was watching Raina run up the stairs. "This will ruin everything," she muttered.

"What? Shouldn't you be happy?"

Laura turned her icy glare on me. All I wanted to do was slink away. "Once the reporters hear about this— and they will—they'll be all over the front lawn. We'll be hounded to no end. She would've been happier if she stayed wherever she was. Now, she'll never know peace."

"But you got your daughter back." I lifted my hat to my chin as if I could hide behind it.

"Yes." She frowned. "But at what cost?" Laura sighed and crossed her arms. "I suppose you'll want something for your assistance?"

"Oh, that's not—"

Laura closed the distance between us with a single step. She was a petite woman, but strong. In a fight, she'd be no match for me, but I wasn't the sort of man who'd ever lay hands on a woman. "Let me be perfectly clear, Jacob. If you tell anyone else—any reporters, news outlets…anyone—that Raina is here, I will cast a curse on you and your family, one so cruel that you will cry out against the day you opened your door to her. Do you understand?"

I swallowed. There was no doubt in my mind that Laura Hemlock would do as she promised. "Yes, ma'am."

She grunted and stepped back. "Good. Now go home."

Every time I dropped the Hemlocks off at the end of the day, I thought I raced back to my family. Never before had I sped down the rocky road as fast as I did that night. I knew my Amanda, knew her intention. I could only pray I got back fast enough. Dust flew around the wheels of the limo like a black cloud. It drifted ahead of me as I slammed on the brakes in the driveway to the cottage. I didn't even pause to turn off the engine or close the door before I sped up the walk. The front door slammed open.

"Amanda!" I shouted. "Amanda, come here!"

"What is it?" She appeared in the doorway, her hand on the phone's speaker.

My heart sank into my knees. I'd come too late.

CHAPTER TWENTY-THREE

NOW

Jacob finished his story and I lifted my cup of tea only to find I'd already emptied it. Strange, considering my mouth still felt dry. An odd feeling of weightless anxiety had also settled in the bottom of my chest.

"I don't understand," I said, frowning into my empty cup. "Who was on the phone?"

Amanda and Jacob exchanged a look before Amanda turned away. "I called the local news station. You have to understand we were in dire straits at the time. Poor as dirt. I've got two kids' futures to think about."

"What about the curse?" I licked my lips. During dinner, I'd drank two glasses of water, and I'd just finished a cup of tea. Why, then, did it feel as if I had had nothing to drink for days? "Why are you telling me all this? Especially right after telling me how good the Hemlock family had been to yours? Doesn't seem to add up."

"More tea?" Amanda lifted the steaming kettle.

"Yes, please. A bit dry in here." I offered her my mug and she refilled it.

Jacob folded his arms on the tabletop and leaned forward. "I'm telling you all this, Felix, so you'll understand what comes next. I'm not a bad man. We're good people. We made one mistake—just one—and we've been paying for it for years. I've got my family to think about. It's nothing personal."

"Nothing personal," Amanda repeated as she handed my steaming mug back.

I looked down into it. The light brown water spun counterclockwise and then rose out of the cup like raindrops in reverse. Droplets of tea floated in fat globules before my eyes. I tried to reach for one, but a familiar heaviness had settled into my limbs. As my body slouched lazily in the seat, my brain sent out one last alarming word: paralyzed.

I had been paralyzed before, when the demon took my body from me. It left me awake and aware, unable to move. You'd think having your back broken would leave you in agony, but the body is an amazing machine. Adrenaline kicks in and shock blocks out most of it.

This paralysis, however, was different. Nothing in me was broken, and yet I had been robbed of my ability to move or respond. Still awake, still completely aware. I could feel the pressure of the chair digging into my lower back from the slouched posture, the slight discomfort of a full stomach, and the ever-present ache in my shoulders and hip from the old injury. Words still flew through my mind, but they had no escape. I was a sentient doll, malleable to the will of my new captors. The only things I could move were my eyes, and even that felt sluggish.

Jacob sighed, pushed his chair out, and stood. "Sorry, Felix. I did try to tell you that you should get out while you still could. I gave you every chance to walk away. It isn't like I want to do this. I got no choice. I have to save my kids, and Laura said this was the only way. I have to break the curse she put on them, don't you see? You'd understand if you had kids of your own."

I watched, helpless, as Amanda opened one of the kitchen drawers and retrieved a small glass vial, handing it to Jacob. It was a replica of the vial Laura had used during that strange dream I'd had my first night in the Hemlock house. At least, I'd thought it was a dream. Now that I was completely awake and seeing another vial, I'd begun to doubt that.

Jacob removed the cork top of the small vial and leaned over me. Powerful fingers pressed in on either side of my jaw, forcing it open. He left my mouth hanging open like that. Whatever they'd given me had the wonderful side effect of increased salivation. In short, they left me paralyzed and literally drooling on myself. After waiting a few moments for the effect to kick in, Jacob scooped up some of my saliva in the small vial, capped it, and handed it back to Amanda.

"Call Laura. Tell her we got what she wanted." He moved around behind me, strong arms hooking under my armpits and lifting me from the chair with a grunt. "Sorry, man. I really am. But it was you or my kids. I didn't have a choice."

He dragged me away from the kitchen table, through the living room, and down a hallway. Doors opened on either side of the hallway and the kids peeked their little heads out, watching their dad take me away. Jacob shouted for them to get back in their rooms and doors slammed shortly after, but I wasn't there to see it. He'd already dragged me into his bedroom. With another grunt, he hauled me onto the bed.

Jacob shifted my hands so they were crossed on my chest, then leaned over me. "Comfortable? I don't want to be cutting off any circulation or anything."

I glared at him, unable to answer.

"Blink twice for yes," he said. When I didn't respond, he sighed heavily. "Look, this is going to go easier for all of us if you just cooperate. Laura won't like it if you fight. People are going to get hurt if you fight. If you just go along with it, do whatever she says, we can all just go home. Things can go back to the way they're supposed to be. The way they were before Raina came back."

I refused to blink. Whatever he and Laura had in store for me, I'd rather go down defiantly than willingly.

"Suit yourself," said Jacob, but he still adjusted the pillows behind my head before leaving and closing the door behind him.

I didn't have much time before Laura came. Amanda was probably calling her right then, and Jacob was likely putting on his coat. He'd drive the short distance from the cottage to the house, pick her up, and bring her back. I didn't know what she wanted from me, but it couldn't be anything good.

Now that I knew Laura was a witch, everything started to make sense. When Jacob said she was a witch, he hadn't meant it in the modern-day sense, talking about followers of Wicca or the hippies that collect crystals and talk to houseplants. He meant she was a true witch, a medieval woman of power who had drafted and signed a contract with a demon for the power she and her coven held. She had magic, but her power didn't come without a cost. Spells needed ingredients, ingredients she'd slowly been collecting from me.

Belial was probably the demon she had a contract with, which made sense now that I had the time to think clearly. I recalled reading an obscure text that stated he was the demon to invoke for political success. The price of Belial's binding to a witch's will, however, was among the highest one could pay. He demanded the sacrifice of a blood virgin, a pre-pubescent and virginal girl related to any who dared conjure him.

Laura had traded Raina to Belial to win John's Senate seat, and in doing so, launching her ambitions forward as a socialite. Raina's disappearance brought her fame, fortune, and a position of power as the sympathetic wife of a Kentucky senator, and all she had to do was sell her daughter's soul to a demon.

The one thing I couldn't fit into the story yet was where Raina had gone once the demon took control of her body. Someone had taken her. Maybe Laura knew all along where Raina was, knew that she was being tortured. Yet she did nothing to stop it.

What kind of sick person did you have to be to sell your child like that? It spoke volumes about how far Laura would go to get what she wanted. Whatever she wanted next involved me, which meant I needed to figure out how to get the hell out of there before she showed up.

The paralyzing agent Amanda had slipped into my tea wasn't a strong one since it left me conscious. It must've been something hallucinogenic though because as I lay in the bed, the ceiling began to melt.

White textured paint dripped like a leaky faucet, splashing paint onto my still body. The stitching in the quilt beneath me came alive, transforming into thousands of tiny ants crawling over my skin.

It's not real. I squeezed my eyes shut, but it didn't help. I could still feel them there, their little legs marching over my arms and legs, clawing their way into my gloves.

I opened my eyes and the world was an oil painting in an oven, colors dripping one into the next. The window drooped and the closet door sagged open. Voices echoed as if I were in an empty factory and not in the back bedroom of a tiny cottage, each of them distinct but distant. Though I strained, I couldn't make out what was being said.

Not until Sean's voice rang out startlingly close to my ear. "Felix, wake up!"

I turned my head. Or, I thought I turned my head. My vision changed but my body didn't move. It was as if there was another version of me inside myself, and this version was able to move and interact while my body stayed numb and distant. "Sean?"

He squatted next to the bed, the only thing made of color that wouldn't bleed. "Come on. We have to go. Now." He cupped his hand under the flowing colors of the window and parted the flow, creating a small opening.

I sat up out of my body. "Where are we going?"

"As far away from here as we can," he answered and dipped through the window.

"Wait! Don't go!" I pushed off the bed, but my legs wouldn't work right and I stumbled into the window. Glass crashed all around me. Shards dug into my arms, legs, and face. They sliced open my skin, leaving heavy drops of crimson to join the dance of melting color. But it didn't hurt. I still felt nothing.

"Come on!" Sean called and disappeared behind a tree.

"Wait for me!" I pushed up and staggered through the brush to lean on the tree I'd just seen him walk behind. There was nothing there but moss and stone. The laughter of children echoed behind me. I turned, wobbly on my legs, and saw one of the children slide behind another tree.

"Hurry!" Sean called. "This way!" His voice sounded like it was coming from somewhere further away and off to my right.

I turned to limp after it.

A thick fog settled on the forest floor. The moon and stars spun on a low ceiling above, closer than they should've been, and moving too fast to be natural. The Earth was spinning at light speed. No wonder I couldn't keep upright. Moonlight reflected off the fog, casting strange shadows between the trees. Shadows that seemed to come alive only to dive and melt back into each other. The laughter of children rolled through the uneven landscape, bounced off the bark of ash trees, and encircled me.

My knee hit a thorn bush and buckled. The rest of me fell into it, the bush's teeth digging deep into my flesh. Whatever had left me numb to pain was still in effect, so I wrapped my palm around the thorny arms and yanked them out of my skin. Crimson welled to the surface of my clothes in curved lines, one after another, but I crawled out of the bush and into a small clearing. Trees towered above, leaning in, whispering to each other.

I rose to my knees and put my hands to my mouth,

calling, "Where are you, Sean?"

The scream of a mountain lion answered. Glowing yellow eyes appeared in the bushes all around me, and a moment later, two of the cats crept through the bushes, shoulders hunched.

The children, I thought, staring into the glowing cat eyes. *Laura's mountain lions. She's transformed them all.* The horror of what she'd done to Jacob's family struck me along with the last thing Amanda had said to me. "It's nothing personal."

I could die there. Let them take me, end the curse. Jacob's family would live if Laura kept her word. Yet sacrificing myself so that Jacob's family could return to normal would mean letting Belial take Raina again. It would mean letting Laura and her coven win. Was it fair to trade Raina's life for the lives of Jacob's children? Mine for theirs?

In the moment, fairness didn't matter. Fear reigned supreme and my desire to live forced me to my feet.

I limped back the way I had come as fast as I could. At least, I meant to. I'd gotten turned around somehow and couldn't be sure. Everything in the forest looked the same. Had I passed the tree with the roots like an old man's knuckles before? Maybe two trees looked like that.

Bushes rustled and one of the cats leaped out onto the path, this one smaller. Practically a cub. Another joined it, this one and adult. "It's nothing personal." Jacob's voice bounced off the trees all around me.

I turned around to face them but kept backing away. "Stop this, Jacob! You don't have to do this. I can help you."

The big cat crept closer, panting.

I didn't know if I could undo the curse Laura had

laid upon him and his family, but I would try as hard as I could if only he'd give me the chance. "Please!"

Another mountain lion jumped out from behind a tree at my back.

I turned, shifting directions and still backing away. Even in prime condition, I was no match for one mountain lion, let alone four, even if two of them were cubs. They'd rip me apart. At least it'd be faster than whatever Laura wanted to do to me.

My heel caught on a protruding root and I fell backward, sliding down a steep embankment. Vines, branches, and thorn bushes all whipped at my face and body as I tumbled. I tried to grab onto them, but they slipped through my palms, leaving them raw and bloody. At the bottom, my back slammed into a fallen tree.

I lay there for who knows how long, just blinking and trying to remember how to breathe again. There was no pain, but even in my drugged state, I knew it'd feel like hell once the drugs wore off. Fog floated above me, a silky sea of smokey white. I stared into it. Maybe if I just laid there, completely still, they wouldn't find me. I could stay hidden in the fog, in the foliage of the woods.

And then what? Where would I go? I didn't know my way around these woods. Even if I did find a road, what would I do? Who would I tell? What would I say? I couldn't tell the first motorist that stopped I was an exorcist being hunted by a witch and her mountain lions. Even I wouldn't have believed that before coming to this godforsaken hollow.

The fog shifted above me, forming into Sean's familiar face. "You have to get up, Felix. Right now. Run!"

I swallowed. "I don't think I can."

"You must," he responded. "Go. Hurry! They're coming!"

But even as I tried to will my body to rise, it wouldn't respond. My limbs flopped uselessly back to the ground, lying in wet, rotten leaves. A stream of icy water flowed beside my spine. No, not water. My legs were warm. I must've pissed myself. Great.

"There you are." Long, feminine fingers reached through the fog. Both Willa and Amanda hauled me to my feet and held me in front of Laura.

Laura had put on a brown coat, knee-high boots, and a hat. She held in her hands a .22-gauge shotgun and wore a crooked smile. One of her lions rubbed up against her side. She petted it affectionately. "You're lucky they found you before I did."

The mountain lion moved away from Laura and knelt on the ground. Bones cracked. Skin split. Bloody fur melted into a crimson puddle on the mossy forest floor. Human shoulders emerged where leonine ones had once been. The snout shrank, bones cracking, popping, reforming into Amanda's pained human face.

It took only moments for the lion to fall away and the woman to return, but it left the air stinking of blood and sulfuric power long after. Amanda stood and shook blood from her naked body.

I tried to stand but my legs weren't working right. The world was still spinning too fast. My heart hammered away in my chest as if I'd just finished running a marathon. "Are you going to kill me?"

"Eventually, yes. We can't have you running off and telling everybody the truth, now can we?" She pinched my fingers with gloved hands. Thank God for small miracles. "But not yet. I have further uses for you." She took a step back and aimed both barrels at my head. "Now, strip."

I stared at her, dumbfounded. "What?"

"For the hunt," she said as if I should have already known. "Animals don't get to wear clothes."

I shook my head. Even if I'd wanted to comply, I was too drugged to be coordinated.

"Poor thing." Willa ran her knuckles across the side of my face. "I think he had too much of your special tea."

Laura sighed and lowered the shotgun. "Well, I'm not going to wait for him to fully recover. We have to complete this part of the ritual before dawn. Help him."

They grabbed at the collar of my shirt and the waistband of my pants. I pushed Willa away, but the momentum sent me stumbling backward.

Amanda hesitated. A look crossed her face, one that told me she knew this had gone too far. She wanted it to stop as much as me.

All I could do was appeal to that side of her. "Please," I said, backing away. "Please, don't."

"Do it," Laura demanded and shifted her grip on the shotgun. "Think of the children."

Amanda lowered her eyes to the ground. She didn't look at me as she pulled off my shoes and socks, moving as slowly as possible.

Willa, on the other hand, giggled the whole time, clawing and ripping clothes from my body as if she were opening a birthday present.

Laura's smirk reappeared. "Don't be too unkind, Willa, dear. It *is* cold out tonight."

Stripped naked and shivering, they pulled me to my feet.

"What do you want from me?" I asked, teeth chattering.

Laura lifted the shotgun and pointed it at me again. "I want you to run."

CHAPTER TWENTY-FOUR

My back, legs, and feet were already sore from running through the underbrush earlier, and I'd been still long enough for the adrenaline to wear off. Jumping through the glass earlier in my drugged state had left me with gashes all over my right arm, which I must've put out in front of me. None of the bleeding was bad enough that I would die. Not unless the cuts got infected, which was a real possibility the way I'd been rolling around on the dirty forest floor.

None of that would matter if the lions caught me, or if Laura landed a shot.

Thunder boomed through the woods, the crack of her shotgun nipping at the mud just behind me. I stumbled and covered my head, stunned by the noise.

"Run!" she shouted with hideous glee. Her voice echoed through the foggy forest from nowhere and everywhere all at once. "Run faster, Felix! You'll never get away like that!" Her shotgun boomed again and the shells took a bite out of the tree bark to my right.

Panting, I pushed myself to my feet and took off

again, limping through the trees. Panic pounded away in my chest, my heart a jackhammer and my lungs twin flames. Bile crept up the back of my throat. Did it even matter that I was running? Laura wanted me to run, which meant this chase was fun for her. She knew she could catch me at any moment, that I wasn't getting free. Why, then, was I bothering to exhaust myself?

Because I can't just lay down and die, I thought. I have to survive. I have to try.

I missed a step and slid down a shallow embankment where a wide patch of thorn bushes waited to break my fall. I tried to direct myself to fall into a thin section, and only hit the edge. Still, the thorny branches bit into the side of my head and clung to my hair. The only way to get free was to grab the branch and twist it, which opened the healing wounds on my palms. I dropped the thorned branch to the ground as another gunshot rang out, this time more distant. Maybe I was losing her. I had to hurry.

Hurry to where though? I didn't know the geography of the area well enough to decide which direction to go. Even if I did, my sense of direction was a mess without street signs or GPS to lead me. In the woods, I was hopeless.

Maybe I could double back to Jacob's house. The limo was parked there. If I was lucky, he'd left the keys behind and I'd be able to find them, but where? I probably wouldn't have time to search the house. Still, it was my best option. No one would be home, and the limo was my only possible escape from whatever gruesome fate awaited me at Laura's hands.

What about Raina? I'd be leaving her behind to fall victim to Laura's plans. The worst part was, I didn't have a choice. My only chance of saving her relied on my escape. I could drive into the nearest town and find the police. They'd take one look at me and...well, probably call me a madman. I was, after all, about to tell the cops a senator's wife had fed me drugs, stripped me naked, and chased me through the woods with a shotgun, and that was only half the crazy truth.

So, I ran. I weaved around trees that trembled in the foggy dark, through shadows so cold the air itself should have frozen. Branches reached like fingers to scrape against my skin and voices called my name from every direction. Human-like shapes darted behind thick tree trunks along with the giggling of children.

In reality, only occasional gunfire or the screaming of mountain lions broke the sound of my labored breathing. I was alone in those woods against Laura and her people. No shadows, no demons, no angels would be coming to help me. Whatever I was seeing, I knew it to be a hallucination thanks to whatever drugs Amanda had fed me, and yet I couldn't stop reacting to what I saw.

A shadow stepped out from behind a mossy pine tree. I turned and limped to the right to avoid it. Thick, feminine laughter snaked through the trees, curling around my neck like a noose. I shook it away and tucked my head under a hanging vine.

Two glowing green eyes appeared just ahead and the head of a mountain lion lowered, sticking out of the bushes with shoulders hunched. I couldn't outrun a mountain lion, but maybe it hadn't noticed me yet. I turned again, this time weaving left. Branches rustled and paws padded against the underbrush as the big cat leaped on something behind me. I didn't dare look back to see how close it'd come.

Something in my side pulled and I went down to

the ground, rolling into another small divot in the land. Fog flowed over the little impression of earth, moving overhead like the surface of water. Pale moonlight struck the fog and bounced back, leaving me in darkness but for the slight light of my breath in the cold. I wrapped my arms tightly around myself and scooted back, huddling in the curved roots of a tree. The small divot was so narrow, I'd have missed it in the daylight. Maybe they'd wander right by too and I could hide there until morning. That was, if I didn't die of cold. The blood loss probably wasn't helping that fact either.

My hand went down on something squishy with hard bits. I gagged and held back vomit as I realized I'd put my hand in the rotting corpse of a dead animal, an opossum, maybe. Most of it was already gone. Only a few bits of liquified guts remained inside the fragile bones. Scraps of grayish fur clung to the skull. Empty eye sockets stared at me.

I wiped my hand over the bed of damp leaves and scooted as far from the corpse as I could. It wasn't far, considering the space was maybe four feet wide and three feet high.

I stayed curled up in the roots of that tree for what felt like years, my arms wrapped around my knees. Maybe it was only minutes. My perception of time was still off thanks to the tea. I kept my teeth from chattering by forcing my chin against my knees as hard as I could. The run had left me sweating, despite the cold, but that was working against me now. Sweat and blood clung to my bare skin, leaving me feeling like I'd just climbed out of freezing water. Could you get hypothermia from your own bodily fluids? I didn't know, but I was certain I would die in those woods, one way or another. Either Laura and her people would catch me and kill me, or I would die from exposure.

As I sat there, huddled in a fetal position, trying to keep my breath calm and silent, an odd euphoria settled into my bones. I had to bite my arm to keep from erupting in laughter. It was ironic, though, wasn't it? That I would spend ten years wishing I had died, and then—after finding the one thing that made me want to live again—I was facing death. Now that it was before me, I didn't want it. Why didn't I want to live until I knew death was coming for me?

It was the great irony of the universe, probably one that had played out time and time again. The young and healthy didn't appreciate life, did they? It's only when they face losing what they have that they even realize they had it in the first place. Life feels like a choice until that choice is taken away.

The very thought made me giddy.

I bit down harder.

All the amusement drained out of me when I heard a scraping sound next to me. I turned my head and stared at my double. He looked like me in every way, except for the flies. They swarmed around his head like a dark halo. He was also armed with a knife. A knife he was using to carefully strip the last of the flesh from the dead opossum's bones.

"When you die today," said the other me, "do you think you'll go to Heaven or Hell?"

I squeezed my eyes closed and whispered. "You're not real."

"Yeah, I wouldn't want to think about it either." My double drew his blade over the opossum's ribcage, slicing through the last bits of stubborn sinew. "On the one hand, you were raised a good Catholic boy. You've been baptized. Even tried to be a priest. But that was before. You've got a whole new batch of sins to confess and atone for."

"N-no one's here to take a confession," I whispered.

My double nodded. He lifted the knife, pointing the blade at me. "And even if there were, you wouldn't give it, would you? After all that's happened, the way the Church treated you, the way they treated Sean? You've still got your dignity, don't you, Felix? Your pride? Neither of those is worth sacrificing, certainly not for those three little words. *Ego te absolvō.*"

"Shut up." I gripped my head. "You're not real! You're a hallucination!"

"Or maybe I'm the subconscious projection of your own guilt. Maybe I'm the shred of demonic presence that's left from ten years ago, slowly whittling away your resolve. You don't really know, do you?"

"No." I shook my head. "You were cast out."

My double's eyebrows rose. "Was I? How, then, do you account for your strange powers? Your ability to see what no man should see? Did you think that happened by chance?" He shot forward, tracing the flat of the knife along my jaw. "*I* gave you that gift, boy, and you've squandered it! Wasted it on mewling kittens and party tricks. Do you think that's why I gave it to you? So you could hide it away? Fuck that, and fuck you."

My jaw trembled. "What do you want from me?"

He withdrew the knife and shrank back to squat over the opossum's corpse, his eyes flashing red as his face spread into a wide grin. "Thus sayeth the Lord: 'Let My people go.'" With a cackle that bounced off the trees, he disappeared into a cloud of sulfuric smoke. The smell left me heaving into the tiny space in front of me.

Even if the roots were the best hiding place in the world, I couldn't remain, not with the rotten egg stink of the demon, the reek of my vomit, and the rotting smell of an opossum carcass there. I stumbled out of the roots and fell to my knees, gasping for purer air. The roar of a mountain lion was nearby. It'd caught my scent already, and I was too tired to run, but I had to do something.

I staggered to my feet and limped forward, throwing my exhausted body from tree trunk to tree trunk. My limbs ached. The cuts along my palms and sides burned. My feet were so bruised I knew they should hurt, but they were just numb from the cold. Still, I limped along, moving away from the sounds of the mountain lions moving around in the brush.

I left the small depression and found myself in a valley where no trees grew. Moss carpeted the forest and vines fell from the canopy overhead. A small stream trickled through the center of the valley with smooth stones at the bottom. I paused at the stream.

Several robed figures stepped out from behind the trees ahead of me. I turned to go back the way I'd come and found the same. They didn't attack me, didn't shout, or say anything. They just stood there int heir hooded robes, hands folded, staring down at me.

The moon crawled out from behind the clouds just in time to illuminate Laura as she found her way to the edge of the drop off in front of me. Two mountain lions stalked alongside her. A dark smile played on her lips, but she, too, said nothing.

The only sound was the voice of my double in my head. "You're going to die here, Felix."

I turned and ran up the creek bed, parallel to the robed figures on either side of me. At least, I tried to run. In my condition, it was all I could do to limp forward.

Laura kept pace with me on the ridge, her shotgun ready to shoulder. She could end this at any moment with a single shot. I was a slow-moving target. Easy prey, even in the dark. Yet she let me stumble on, watching from above with glee sparkling in her eyes.

The end of the valley loomed ahead, terminating in the yawning mouth of a cave. Surely, Laura would follow me into it, but the thought barely crossed my mind. I was so tired, so cold, so dizzy and lost, the rational parts of my brain had long ago stopped working. In full fight or flight mode, the only thing that mattered was survival. The cave would be safe. She wouldn't find me in the cave.

I ran for it.

Cool air flowed out of the cave like the breath of an ice giant. My bare feet splashed through chilly water and over slippery stone. It was too dark in the cave to see my hand in front of my face, let alone if I was headed toward a deadly drop.

I reached out and ran my fingers over the cool, rocky surface. It was impossible to run in pure darkness, so I shuffled along, inch by inch, feeling my way as I went. My breathing echoed back on me, tricking my ears. Were there footsteps behind me or was I only hearing my echo? There was no way to tell, and no turning back. The only way was forward.

I limped along until my throat was tight with panic. What if there was no end to this cave? There had to be hundreds of miles of caves in Kentucky. The state was famous for it. This one could go as far south as

Tennessee and I'd never know it. Maybe I should turn around and go back. Yet turning around meant removing my hand from the wall, something I wasn't willing to do. Laura and her people were also waiting back at the entrance for me. They had to know there'd be no escape.

"I'm fucked," I whispered.

"Fucked, fucked, fucked!" My whisper echoed back in agreement.

As I came around a curve—or at least what felt like a curve in the cave wall—I paused. There was a faint light ahead, a dim blue flickering. An exit? Oh, thank God.

At the end of the cave was a gate. It was all that stood between me and a set of crumbling stone stairs. A rusted padlock held the gate closed, but I broke it with a rock. It nearly crumbled in my hands.

I practically crawled up the stairs and through a wooden trap door into a locked room. The air was stuffy, thick, and smelled of iron, urine, and feces. A dull glow of light and warmth radiated from some coals in an old fireplace. I rushed to sit near them, coaxing the fire back to life with shaky breaths.

"Come on, you damn thing. Light!"

Something shuffled in the dark behind me.

I spun around. "Hello? Who's there?" As soon as I said it, I felt like an idiot. Isn't that what stupid people called out right before they got stabbed to death in slasher flicks? It was probably just a rat or some other wildlife. I was still way out in the middle of nowhere.

I returned to the fire, slowly bringing it back to life. Nothing was ever quite so comforting as that first bit of warmth after the cold, painful trek through the woods.

Whatever was in the room with me shuffled around again. I turned and got my first look at the horrible chamber.

It was huge, at least as large as the whole bottom floor of the Hemlock mansion. The walls were simple cement and the floor sloped toward a central point where a drain waited. Dark stains colored the cement near the drain. I tried to convince myself they were just rust and not something more horrific.

Wire cages lined the far wall, each one bedded with newspaper or straw. Only one was occupied. The other three stood empty, their doors wide open. Whatever was in that one cage was the source of the shuffling sound I'd been hearing. I stepped away from the fire and stopped. A large, wooden table stood nearby, and on it were various tools. There were saws, knives, needles, pliers…everything one would need to torture a human. Behind the table stood two X-shaped pillars of wood stained with the same suspicious rust color near the drain. The metallic cuffs on each of the four ends told me they weren't there for decoration either.

In the center of the room, built over the drain like a bench, was a stone slab with strange symbols carved into it. Some I recognized from my books on demonology and the occult. Others were foreign to me. I stood over the bench, examining the marks in the flickering firelight, trying to determine their purpose.

Chains rattled and another naked man sat up in the cage. He squinted at the light as if it'd been quite a while since he'd seen it. It had been a while since he'd seen soap or a razor. A month at least. His hair and beard were matted and full of bugs.

Thin fingers wrapped around the bars of the cage. "Who's there?"

It wasn't until I studied the corners of his eyes that I recognized him. When it hit me who I was looking at, I almost fell over. "Senator Hemlock?"

CHAPTER TWENTY-FIVE

Senator Hemlock stared at me, wild-eyed, jaw trembling. "You shouldn't have come here."

The words sent an icy shiver down my aching spine.

"Didn't you hear me?" He gripped the bars more desperately. "Go on! Get! Get out of here before she eats you alive!" The pleading warning transformed into a fit of mad laughter as he collapsed against the bars, ripping out his hair in chunks. Senator John Hemlock wasn't dead, or sick, or in Washington. He wasn't anywhere sane anymore.

I started for the cage, determined to set him free, but paused when I saw it wasn't just his hair he was ripping out. The senator had dropped to his knees and dug his fingernails into dirty flesh. Blood welled to the surface, running over his knuckles and splashing to the floor in large drops.

"Don't!" I called out and raised a hand.

John didn't stop. He raked his fingers through his flesh, ripping it off. It came away like melting wax, liquefied and dripping in thick, bloody strands.

Underneath, his body boiled. Bubbles rose beneath the bare bloody muscle, pushing out his nose, shoulders, and spine. John screamed in agony and doubled over while the flesh melted off his hands. He lifted one, still screaming at it, and watched as the melting skin reformed itself into webbed bastardizations of their former self. Fingerbones extended, curling into claws. His jaw dislocated, bent and distorted. He spat blood and teeth to the floor four or five at a time while new ones grew in larger, sharper. Light yellow fur grew rapidly into place.

A mountain lion. So this was why she'd hidden him away. This was what had happened to Senator John Hemlock.

I fled the room and found a set of wooden stairs, pulling myself up them as quickly as I could go. My legs were stiff and sore, but I would rest them when I was safely away from Laura. While I didn't know where the stairs led, it had to be somewhere safer than her private torture room.

At the top of the stairs, a wooden trapdoor waited. It was locked but the wood was weak. I smashed a fist through it and easily unlocked it on the other side. I climbed into a small room, no bigger than a closet. I didn't think I'd ever been in there, but something about the space struck me as familiar. Whatever it was, I could figure it out later.

With a grunt, I pulled myself through the broken trap door and turned the knob on the closet door. I expected to find it locked. Why not? Everything else had been. Yet this door wasn't.

It creaked open, and I stuck my head out.

All the tentative hope I'd let swell to the surface deflated like a balloon at the sight of a familiar hallway in a familiar house. The door was the one Willa had stopped me from opening the afternoon before.

Laura stood in the hallway, hands folded in front of her, and flanked on either side by men in dark robes. She smiled. "Welcome back to Hemlock House, Felix."

"No…" I sank to my knees in the doorway, too exhausted to go any further. All this time, I thought I was running to safety, they'd been herding me back to the house. There was no escape. No hope. No reason to fight. Laura had finally won.

Laura squatted in front of me and took my chin in her hand. Her manicured fingernails dug into my skin. "Oh, don't look so sad. You did well. Better than I expected for a city boy. It wasn't always going to be this way. You were supposed to take longer to help Raina like all the others. I could've taken what I needed from you slowly and you'd never have known." She pushed my face to the side and stood. "Instead, you succeeded, and as if that wasn't enough, you had to go poking around, putting your nose where it doesn't belong. This is *my* house, Felix Cross. My family. And you will soon learn never to come between a mother and her plans for her daughter."

She gestured to the robed figures behind her. They came forward and scooped me up to drag me back down the stairs. I didn't resist. What was the point? Even if I somehow managed to free myself, where would I go? We were miles from the nearest neighbor, and even further out from any real help. Laura and her people would just catch me. The best I could hope for at this point was that she would kill me quickly and get it over with.

John paced around in his cage, now fully

transformed into a mountain lion. He let out a growl as Laura walked by, but she didn't pay him any attention. I expected her goons to walk me to the cage next to him and throw me inside, but we marched right past the cages, heading for the wooden crosses.

While they closed my wrists and ankles in the uncomfortable metal cuffs, Laura opened a fridge tucked into a corner and lifted a plastic bag full of some unidentifiable meat. "I see you met my husband." She chucked the meat into the cage with John.

I winced as John tore open the bag and eagerly gobbled up the meat.

"Is everyone like him?" I asked.

"Everyone?" Her hair flared out like a cobra's neck as she turned around quickly. "You mean Jacob and his family. I'm sure he told you about the curse."

The man strapping me into place pulled back his hood, revealing he was Jacob.

Laura smiled and placed a hand on Jacob's shoulder. "This isn't all Jacob's fault. Don't blame him. It's mine. I should never have rented out that cottage, but John insisted. He has a good heart, John. But you know what happens to bleeding hearts in the Senate. They get trampled all over. Why, he never would've been reelected without my help. A progressive senator in Kentucky? Please!"

"You know you can't keep this up forever," I said. "He's a senator. Someone's going to miss him."

"Don't you worry about him," Laura said and let go of Jacob. "I'll deal with that in time. Right now, he's learning what happens to weak men. Until he can prove he's a real man, he'll stay right where he is, mewling like the pussy he is. Nice and tight, Jacob."

"Yes, ma'am." Jacob reached to tighten my

restraints.

Laura looked me over with an exaggerated frown. "You know, I thought you'd be different when you first showed up. You came into my home like a storm, ordering me around with your little shopping list. It'd been a long time since a man made me feel that hot and bothered." She leaned in, sniffing my hair.

I turned my head away and tried not to be sick again. "If you're planning on torturing me, you should know I spent two years living with a dominatrix. You're going to have to try real hard."

Laura wrinkled her nose and stepped back. "And then I learned what sort of man you *really* are, Felix Cross. A pervert. Sexual deviant! Sodomite!"

"Is that what this is about? You want to punish me for my sin?" I threw my head back and laughed. "Oh, that's a good one. You've got it so wrong, you don't even know what you're talking about."

"It's not me that judges you," Laura spat. "It's your God that judges you, Felix. Who sent you to me. You can curse His name when I hurt you. Call for Him to come and save you. Go on, do it, man of faith." She put a hand to her ear waiting for a moment, then smiled. "Looks like He's abandoned you. In that case, it's up to me, isn't it?"

"Should I get the others, ma'am?" Jacob interrupted.

Laura turned her head to address him. "Not yet. This will take time."

"We can draw his blood now. Let's just take it and be done."

"Blood is easy enough." Laura reached to caress my cheek. "It's the tears that will be difficult with this one. Those eyes have already seen hardship. We'll have to extract both the old-fashioned way."

She walked over to the table filled with instruments of torture.

"You're going to torture me? Slice me open, pull off my fingernails? You think that'll make me cry?"

"Yes, actually," Laura said, running her hands over the tools. "Eventually, it makes everyone cry. But not today. Not now. I don't want to get blood on these shoes, and I've got a campaign meeting in half an hour." She glanced over at her husband pacing in his cage. "Someone's got to make sure my idiot husband stays elected." Laura's smile faded as she turned back to Jacob. "Well? What are you waiting for? Get the hose hooked up so we can leave."

Leave? New panic sped my heart to a painful pace. "Wait, Laura. You can't just *leave* me here!"

She blinked rapidly and laughed. "I can do whatever I please. This is my home, and you are my prisoner."

Jacob dragged out a lawn sprinkler and hooked it up to a hose he ran through the hole in the cross between my legs. Laura waited for him to finish before moving to the fire I'd stoked back to life.

"Jacob, man, you don't have to do this." I swallowed. "I know people who can help you with this curse. Good people."

"Jacob!" Laura folded her arms and tapped her foot impatiently.

He refused to look me in the eye. "I'm sorry, man. I really am. I'm so fucking sorry, but I don't have no choice." Tears glistened in his eyes as he finished his work. Jacob hesitated a moment, but quickly started walking again, this time faster. He took the stairs up. I flinched at the echo of the closet door slamming shut.

Laura smirked at me. "You know the real kicker is,

I have no intention of lifting the curse I put on his family. He needs to know his place." She turned over a few coals before grabbing a nearby bucket of water and dousing the flame completely and heading for the stairs without another word.

A moment later, the lights went out.

I hung in silence and complete darkness for a long moment of disbelief. This wasn't real. It couldn't be. All the things I'd been through, all the pain and the horror, and this was where it took me? To die alone in the dark?

I didn't have long to contemplate my situation. The water sprinkler turned on, dousing me with icy water. I gasped and tried to draw in air, but it was as if my lungs had frozen, unresponsive. My body tried to curl up, but the restraints kept me from being able to move. I could twist and flinch, but no matter what I did, I couldn't avoid the spray of water. It came out as a constant stream at first, and then a pulsating arc that struck my stomach and chest. Then the water sprayed me head to toe, toe to head, before going back to a pulse. Head to toe, pulse, steady…there was no pattern. No way to predict how the water would strike me next. No way to escape. As long as the water hit me, I couldn't even think. It was so cold, it should've been ice.

At first, I promised myself I wouldn't scream, but when the shivering became so intense that every twitch of muscle ached, screaming was the only thing I could do to remind myself I was still alive.

I don't know how long I hung in the dark, pelted by icy water. Time loses meaning during torture. Without access to the sun or any light at all, I had no way to judge if hours or days passed. Pain gnawed at my insides, the after-effects of the hallucinogenic tea. I held my bowels as long as I could. At least when they let go, I knew there'd be water to spray me off, even if it didn't get everything.

The screaming turned to silence, which turned into mad laughter at the irony of it all. Maybe I was just losing my damn mind. Torture someone long enough, and that's what happens.

It was about that time the water sprinkler shut off without warning. At first, I was glad it'd stopped, but then the silence settled in. I could hear John breathing and making big cat sounds somewhere off to my right, which was a comfort in the first few hours. It was good to know I wasn't alone at least. Yet even he fell silent after a time. I thought he'd just gone to sleep, or maybe the toll was too much on his body and he'd died. I could be in the room with a corpse and not even know it.

"John?" I called out.

No answer.

"John!" This time, louder.

Still no answer from the senator.

Maybe I should sleep too, I thought. There was no telling what sort of torture Laura would think up next, or when I'd get another chance. It wasn't exactly comfortable up on those wooden beams, and I was far from warm with the icy water still drying on my skin, but at least the shivering had stopped. That was probably a bad sign.

Still, I was so tired. So damn tired…

I closed my eyes.

Loud rap music suddenly blasted into the darkness. I flinched at the sound and John immediately woke up and roared. If my hands had been free, I'd have covered my ears. Since they were restrained, however, I had to hang there and listen. Not only was it bad rap music—which I wasn't a fan of—but it was bad Christian rap music. Whoever the artist was, they were off-key, off-tempo, and didn't understand that Christ didn't rhyme with nice. As the song faded out, I breathed a small sigh of relief that it was over…until it started *again*.

That particular song played only twice, followed by the theme song to some children's show and a hymn set to modern rock music. It got so bad, I tried to distract myself by counting the words. Then my count got all screwed up by a fast rapper.

When the first song came back on, I found myself missing the water sprinkler. I reared my head back and laughed into the darkness.

Over time, we cycled through things in a random order. The music would end and the spraying cold water would begin, or I'd get both at once. That was the worst, when the music and the water came together. The silence was almost worse the few times it was allowed to extend between water and music. I knew one or the other would be coming and spent the quiet time just waiting to be hit with cold water or awful screaming at a painful volume.

Laura was right about one thing. This torture was far more effective than pulling out fingernails and breaking bones. I would've done or said anything to make it stop.

After a particularly long period of silence, the lights came back on. I had to snap my eyes closed because the light was just too intense after so much darkness. The door above squeaked open and Laura descended. She'd changed out of her hunting clothes and donned a plain white dress. Her hair hung in a loose style around her shoulders.

She came down the stairs with Willa and someone else in another hooded robe. It wasn't Jacob. At least, I didn't think it was. He had a different walk, or maybe that was just my imagination.

Laura walked up to me, studying my face. "You poor dear."

I flinched away when she reached to touch my face, but there was no avoiding being touched. After suffering through her torture for hours—or days, maybe—I had no defenses left. I couldn't shut out the feeling she fed me through her skin. A shadowy darkness emanated from Laura, a hatred so thick and heavy it took my breath away. And the hunger! Not for food, or drink, or sex, but something even more seductive: power. She craved it like I'd been craving cigarettes, needed it like I needed my next breath. Such a strong need to be worshipped, to be wanted, to be *needed*…it was no wonder she'd traded her daughter. No price was too high to pay.

Yet even as I lived through Laura's hunger and hatred firsthand, I couldn't bring myself to pull away. Her hand was the first warmth and comfort I'd felt in days.

She held her other hand out to Willa who placed a slice of bread in her palm. "Hungry, Felix? It's been quite a while since you've had anything proper to eat. I bet that's gnawing at your insides, isn't it?"

My stomach groaned. My mouth watered at the sight of it. Just how long had I been down there?

Laura ran the bread over her tongue and offered it to me again. "How about now?"

I didn't care.

She moved the bread within reach and I surged forward to try and grab a bite.

Laura pulled it away, laughing. "Oh, you didn't think it would be that easy, did you? If you want it, you'll have to do something for me." She stepped in so close my nose burned with the scent of her perfume. Laura grabbed either side of my face and pressed her lips to mine, frowning after a moment. "Come on now. Do you want the bread or not?"

I broke and wept, not because of the pain in my aching cold limbs, not because I was facing more torture and death, but because Laura had somehow managed to make me need her as much as she needed power. God help me, I kissed her like I meant it, hoping stupidly it would make everything stop.

She stepped back with a smile. "That's the way!"

A new, icy pain struck my side. My head lulled forward and I held back vomiting bile. Something red dripped from a new hole in my stomach. When did that get there?

"Bless your heart," said Laura, holding up a tiny fruit knife. "You actually thought I'd feed you. Willa?"

Willa practically skipped forward, holding yet another one of those blasted vials. She held it up to my cheek, collecting the tears I'd just shed. When the bottle was half full, she passed it to Laura and got out yet another bottle to collect my blood.

"What is all this even for?" I asked.

"A spell, of course." Laura shook the vial of tears. "To bind Belial back to Raina, of course. I'd use John's fluids, but we used those the first time. Obviously, it didn't hold. I think yours will. You're much younger than he was, and touched by power."

"You're going to put the demon back into her?" I

shook my head. "Why?"

"Because all power comes at a price. This is the price he demands."

"She's your daughter!"

Laura shrugged. "You know, everyone always says that. As if that's supposed to mean something. As if the little brats just pop right out of you deserving love. Well, Raina certainly didn't. She screamed nonstop. She got pneumonia as a baby and almost died. Did you know that? I was relieved when I thought she'd die. When she survived, it was all I could do to keep her entertained and away from me most days. Always wanting snacks and to show me her terrible drawings. Honestly, if Belial helped her in any way, he improved her art. It was awful before."

I stared at the madwoman in front of me, unable to think of any other reason she shouldn't continue, so I just repeated what I'd said before. "Raina is your daughter, Laura. Even if you didn't want her, why this? Why go this far? Surely there were easier ways to win a Senate seat."

She let out a doubtful chuckle. "You wouldn't be saying that if you'd ever talked to my husband. He's cute, but that only takes you so far in politics. The man had some funny ideas about progressive politics and bringing Kentucky into the twenty-first century. *Kentucky*, Felix! Imagine if I'd let him go on about shutting down coal production, transitioning to clean energy like solar and hydro-power. This is a state born from coal. We are born breathing the dust and die exhaling it. The blood of Kentuckians is black with coal, Felix. You can't go around this state and campaign against coal and expect to win."

The door opened and another robed figure entered,

dragging Raina by the hair. Raina was wearing a nightgown and struggling against him with everything she had, but she was still weak. Still small. She was no match for a full-grown man.

"Momma!" she cried when she saw Laura and reached for her. "Save me, Momma!"

The man dragged her right past Laura, close enough that Raina was able to grab onto Laura's ankles. Laura kicked Raina's hands away and stepped back, out of reach. I'll never forget the look of betrayal in Raina's eyes. The move crushed her. All the fight left her and she started sobbing.

Seeing Raina lit a new fire in my chest. I fought against the restraints, knowing it'd do me no good. "Stop it, Laura! You want to put that demon in somebody, leave her out of it. Take me instead!"

Laura laughed. "You poor, broken thing. Why would he want you when he could have her?"

"No! Hey, don't walk away from me! God damn you, Laura Hemlock! Damn you!" My curses meant nothing to her and did nothing for me, but I had to speak them just the same.

Laura smirked. "It's time for phase three. Release him."

The restraints holding me in place suddenly released, letting me fall to the ground. I tried to rise, intent on tackling Laura and punching her until her face caved in, but I was too weak. Hands curled around my arms and dragged me away from her.

Only Willa came with me, skipping alongside me and giggling.

"What's happening?" I asked her.

She smiled widely and did a little turn. "You'll see. It's a surprise just for you!"

I twisted my neck to see where they were taking me. We hadn't moved far, only to one of the other three X-shaped crosses. Three hooded figures were dragging me to the far one. They lifted me to it and forced my hands above my head. Instead of binding me there, however, they pressed a twelve-inch spike into my palm.

It finally hit me what was about to happen. "No! No, stop! I gave you what you wanted!"

Pain exploded with the first strike of the hammer. I opened my mouth to scream, but it came out as a neutered whimper choked by a sob. Another started on the other hand before they'd even finished the first. Each crash of the hammer against nails was a lightning flash of red and white agony. When they were done with the hands, they hammered into place a board at my feet and placed them one over the other, driving another spike through them into the board.

The whole thing took only minutes, but it was more painful than all the collective misery of my life in one.

Willa smiled up at me, shifting a hammer over her shoulder. I wouldn't have thought such a small woman had the strength to drive the nails home, and yet she'd done it with glee. She saw me looking at her and winked. "If you thought that was fun, watch what happens next!"

CHAPTER TWENTY-SIX

They placed Raina on the stone altar and tied her down with rope. She was so broken by her mother's betrayal that she didn't even fight.

After Raina was secured, the robed figures—Willa included—formed a circle around the altar and knelt. Laura paced through the circle. A serving cart had been wheeled in from somewhere, on it the vials of bodily fluid that Laura had collected earlier, as well as a glass and pitcher.

Laura unbuttoned her white dress and let it fall to the floor. She stood over the cart naked and lifted the pitcher full of red wine high a moment before pouring some of it into the glass. "Brothers and sisters, we have gathered here in this sacred place to call forth the demon Belial and bind him once again to the chosen lamb." She lifted the first vial. "The seed of a holy man!"

"The seed of a holy man," chanted back the small crowd in a murmur.

Laura mixed the contents of the vial into the wine

before continuing. "The saliva of a blasphemer!'"

"The saliva of a blasphemer."

"Blood of the consecrated! Tears of the sacred!" With each declaration, she added a vial of my bodily fluid to the wine and stirred it in. Laura raised the glass high. "Drink now and prepare for his coming!" She gripped the back of Raina's head with one hand, raising it and pressing the glass to her daughter's lips.

"No!" Raina turned her head and spat.

It was Willa that rose to help Laura, pinching Raina's nose closed until she had no choice but to open her mouth to breathe. Then the two of them poured the whole glass down her throat. They dropped Raina's head and left her sobbing and gagging on her vomit.

"And now, let us worship," Laura said.

One by one, the gathered people disrobed, each a naked white body under the thick black robes they kicked to the floor. Though most of their heads were to the back of me, I recognized some of their faces. Among the cultists were men whose faces I'd seen in photos hanging on the walls, photos where they'd been shaking Senator Hemlock's hand or posing, all smiles, with both the Hemlocks. Most, though, I didn't recognize, nor did I try. They'd all fallen into groups of three or four, sometimes more, engaged in a mindless orgy. And Laura had called me a deviant.

At least they weren't looking at or paying any attention to me, which meant I had a chance.

I tried with shaky breaths to move my fingers. It was agony. The nails in my palms had caused the middle and ring fingers on either hand to curl inward. Even trying to move them was like having lightning coursing through my hands. Strangely enough, those two fingers were the only ones that felt anything.

Either due to adrenaline or the placement of the nail, the rest of my hands were numb.

My feet hurt worse because of how I had to strain to exhale, lifting my body slightly each time to do it. Every time I moved, it opened the wounds a little more, ripping and tearing flesh and muscle. If I'd had anything in my stomach, I would've vomited from the pain alone.

I have to get free. It was the only thought in my mind. I had to get out of there. It no longer mattered that there was nowhere for me to go. Survival instinct had kicked in, leaving me with two options: fight or run, neither of which I could do while hanging on a cross.

I took a breath in, held it, and tried to pull my left palm forward. There wasn't a word in any of the languages I knew for the excruciating pain that throbbed through my palm and shot up my arm. I gritted my teeth, closed my eyes, and tried again, each time achieving only millimeters of movement. Yet the tiniest bit of progress was still progress, and eventually it would work, right?

I'd just have to try harder. Willa had put the nail in there pretty good.

I can't. I stopped trying and let my head hang until I remembered I needed to breathe out. Warm blood trickled down from my palm and pooled on the concrete floor next to where Willa had dropped her hammer.

I stared at it. A weapon. It was right in front of me. All I had to do was get down and take it.

Raina's sobbing broke through the moans and groans coming from the orgy. "Please, mother! Please!"

Laura had brought out one of Raina's paintbrushes and painted symbols on the girl's body in blood. Where she'd gotten the blood, I didn't know, but she held it in a small plastic dish and hummed as she worked.

"Why?" Raina demanded, still crying. "What did I do wrong?"

Laura paused in her task and took her daughter by the face, peering down into her eyes, mocking a loving gesture. "Nothing, child. Nothing but be born to a higher purpose. This is your purpose, child. To serve and obey."

Fuck that. Maybe I didn't like kids, and I was never a fan of the wealthy or politicians, but Raina didn't deserve what was happening to her. She'd done nothing wrong but be born to a selfish bitch like Laura Hemlock.

With shaky fingers, I forced my left hand into a fist and yanked it forward with all my strength. It came away from the wood, bringing the nail with it. I let out a gasp as the pain overrode my rage for just a moment before I chose to harness the anger, use it as fuel.

My right hand came away easier than the left.

Freeing my feet was more difficult. I couldn't bend over without feeling dizzy, and if I fell over, I would tear my feet so bad I'd never be able to walk on them. I didn't know how I was supposed to cross the room or pick up the hammer, yet I was determined to do both. To loosen the nail driven through my feet, I had to lift both my feet at once in a hopping motion. Each time I did, the nail moved the tiniest bit, but the pain worsened.

I finally pulled free and fell face-first to the floor where I lay for a long moment, trying to remember how to breathe. My feet still hurt like hell. I didn't realize why until I sat up and looked down at them. The nail might've come free from the wooden block, but it was still through both my feet. There was no choice but to pull it out by hand.

Four times I tried easing it out, and four times I thought I would either throw up or lose consciousness because it hurt so damn bad. Maybe it would be better if I just pulled it out in one movement. I pawed around on the floor, searching for something to put between my teeth. I settled on the hammer because it was the only thing close by.

Breathing evenly, I placed the wooden handle between my teeth and bit down hard enough to leave indentations. I gripped the nail between my thumb and forefinger and pulled as hard as I could. Even with all that effort, it slid out in inches, pulling bits of meat along with it. Blood pulsed from the hole, pooling on the ground around me and the world tilted. Still, I pulled, hands trembling, forehead dripping with sweat, stomach aching.

When it finally came out, I collapsed, lying in silent tears on the cool, damp concrete floor. *Get ahold of yourself, Felix. This isn't the time to lie around.* But I couldn't move. I could barely breathe or think.

"Get up." It was Sean talking to me now. He stood over me, frowning down at me.

I rolled over onto my back. "I can't."

"Yes, you can. You've survived a broken back, Felix. What are a few holes in your hands and feet? Christ himself suffered far more than you ever will."

"It's not a fucking competition, Sean." I closed my eyes and tried to breathe steadily. Every time I took a breath, the pain throbbed worse.

"She needs you, Felix."

"I know, but what the fuck am I supposed to do?"

The hammer was suddenly in my hand. I stared at it.

"You know," said Sean, just out of my frame of vision. "You know what you have to do."

I sat up and he was gone. Well, not gone. He'd never really been there in the first place, had he? Maybe I'd lost my mind from the torture, or the pain, but I was still lucid enough to know that my grip on sanity was fleeting. Did that make me insane? Did crazy people know they were crazy? It didn't matter now. For now, I had a job to do.

Slowly, silently, I stood. It didn't hurt as bad as I expected it would.

Before me, the nameless members of Laura's cult were all lost in their pleasures, paying no attention to me. Even Laura had left Raina alone and gone to join in, but only after smearing her arms and chest with the rest of the blood. Willa and some white-haired old man were busy licking it off of her.

I staggered toward them, the hammer loose in my grip. Even as I walked between two piles of writhing, thrusting bodies, no one looked up. No one saw me. It was as if I had become the figment. I was unreal now, gone from their plane of existence to one of my own where only pain and anger lived.

I looked at them, all of them, curled around each other like knots of vipers, studying faces. There were powerful people in that room. Not just senators, but personalities with a presence on television, on social media, people who led others in their chosen medium. I knew their faces, had seen them on screens and posters. I'd read their slogans printed on t-shirts, mugs, billboards, and bumper stickers. They were giants and

I was a gnat.

Except now, the tables had turned. They weren't so powerful now. Now, they were just naked bodies, helpless and blind. I was the one with the hammer.

My hand was numb, the wooden handle slick, but the weight of my hammer was perfect. I could swing it with ease. Whatever pain came from clenching the handle in my mutilated palm, I could bear it. But who should I strike?

The world around me rumbled, voices rising, the movement of vipers quickening toward climax after climax. Power buzzed in the air like static electricity. It moved over the surface of everything, prickling skin, making hair stand on end. Laura's ritual was working, and the demon Belial was about to answer her call.

And there I stood among the liars, the hypocrites, and the people drunk on power and the blood of innocents, a hammer in my hand.

I could end this with a single strike to Raina's skull. She would die, and the demon would have no host. The ritual would fall apart. There was no telling what might happen then. Belial might be angered at being called forth without the required sacrifice. He could kill everyone there. Or maybe he wouldn't come at all. Either way, it would be over and Raina would never have to live with the pain of knowing her mother had betrayed her. Thinking about it like that, killing her was a kindness. A girl like Raina wouldn't know how to live in the world on her own. At best, she was traumatized. At worst, she'd need severe psychiatric intervention regularly for the rest of her life. With one blow, I could end her suffering.

Or I could turn the hammer on the others. I could crush skulls and mash eye sockets. Raina could go free.

She would survive this, even if it meant a lifetime of suffering. Yet if I killed the cultists and broke apart Laura's band of worshippers, the results would ripple through time and cyberspace. I could dismantle empires built on the backs of people like Raina, like me, like Sean, like Jade. Regular people who just wanted to live. Good people.

With my hammer, I could topple giants.

I raised the hammer and picked a victim at random, an old white man whose bald head was turned away. The hammer cracked against his skull and he went down in a single blow to the back of his head. The people beneath him never stopped moving, never stopped fucking. Whatever trance they were in, it would take more than the death of one to break it.

I struck another in the side of the face, and another in the shoulder. Bones cracked. Skulls caved in and eye sockets shattered. Blood and teeth flowed to the floor like water. I kicked bodies off of bodies and broke noses with the hammer before breaking the whole face.

I killed them all as they slept in Laura's trance, dead to the hideous thing they were doing.

As more bodies became still, the power in the room reached a crescendo. I held up my hammer to strike and red lightning danced over the steel head. Despite my efforts, I had come too late. Laura had all the power she needed now to complete the summoning.

I pushed away the last body and stormed for where she lay among the dead, dying, and living. It made no difference to her. A body was a body, and all of them were willing. I pulled a man away and smashed his face. Then I grabbed the woman.

She turned around. It was only as she looked at me with terror in her eyes that I realized I had my hands on Willa. The memory of her smile, her utter glee, at crucifying me flooded my brain at breakneck speed.

Her eyes widened at the sight of the hammer. "No, please!"

I grabbed her by the hair, hauling her from between Laura's legs to shove her against the altar.

Her hands gripped the stone altar and she stared at my bloody body as I advanced, shifting my grip on the hammer. "I was only doing what I was told!"

"If you thought that was fun," I spat, "wait until you see what happens next." I brought the hammer down diagonally, hitting her first in the right temple. The second upward swing crushed her jaw and left it hanging loosely. The third smashed into the side of her left eye. Willa's eyeball exploded into blood, the eye itself drooping uselessly like a particularly thick glob of snot. She brought her hands up, but it wasn't enough to save her.

When I was done, I dropped the hammer, and looked at her bloodied, lifeless body on the ground, panting.

"Oh my God!" Raina whispered. "You killed her! You killed them all!"

I swayed on my feet and, for the first time, got a good look around me at the destruction I had caused. Not everyone was dead yet. Some were still dying, slowly, painfully, limbs jerking and choking on their vomit. But they'd all be dead soon.

A gun clicked behind me. "You see, Raina? Do you see what sort of man he is?" asked Laura. "Your man of God is a monster."

I turned around slowly. Laura had risen from the ground and found her gun somewhere—I didn't know where. This one wasn't a shotgun, but a small ivory-colored handgun with gold trim. It was a pretty gun, but what it would do to me when she fired it would be anything but beautiful. It would be like what I'd done to all the people dead and dying around me, and I would deserve it.

I spread my arms wide. "You want to kill me, Laura? So be it."

Her jaw shook. She shifted the gun.

I closed my eyes.

Soon, it would all be over, one way or another.

CHAPTER TWENTY-SEVEN

The gun shook in Laura's hand. I wondered if she'd ever had the guts to take a life herself before, or if it was something she'd always let other people do for her, like everything else. She'd never earned anything she had the hard way. No, she'd lied, cheated, and stolen it.

Well, too fucking bad. She would have to dirty her hands herself if she wanted me dead. Everyone else was already gone.

Raina continued crying behind me, begging for us to stop. Poor girl didn't realize we'd already passed the point of no return. There was no stopping what was about to happen.

Laura's bloodstained body trembled. "You ruined everything! And you want to call me a monster. Look at what you've done. The blood on your hands! You've killed more people than anyone else in this room."

I looked down at the throbbing holes in my hands. In time, they would heal. That was if I survived this.

"I know what I'll do." Laura lowered the gun. "I'll

call the police, that's what. Yes, and show them what you've done. I'll call up the sheriff directly and—" She cut off her sentence abruptly as a huge, black shadow settled over her.

Power swelled inside the circle she and her cultists had activated, dancing between the edges and the altar at the center. It crawled like static over my skin, pulling flecks of blood away as if they were metal drawn to a magnet.

The dead cultists twitched and jerked as the blood was drawn from the wounds in their heads and faces. Those still unlucky enough to be alive let out frantic screams as the force of the unfinished spell Laura had worked drained the blood from their bodies.

Crimson flew in ribbons toward the swelling shadow from the cultists, binding to its surface, forming a thin skin.

I looked down at the holes in my hands, expecting the thing to drain my blood as well, but I was left untouched. I hadn't been involved in this part of their ritual. Laura, too, remained untouched, but only because she wasn't bleeding from anywhere…yet.

Storm winds rose in the underground chamber, rising like a torrent to carry more blood to the monster born of Laura's ritual. The howling grew so loud, it blocked out the screams of the dying.

Laura raised her arm to shield her face and stepped back from the blood shadow. "Look what you've done! You've killed us all!" She turned to run for the stairs, but a dripping tentacle whipped out of the blood shadow and wrapped around Laura's ankle. It jerked her from her feet. Her chin bounced on the cement floor, stunning her only a moment. That was all it took for the thing to drag her several feet over the concrete floor toward the pulsating bloody mass.

She screamed and rolled onto her back, kicking to try and free herself. When that didn't work, she fired six shots into the blood shadow's tentacle. It absorbed them all without being bothered.

I turned away and began furiously stripping the bindings from Raina's body. "Don't look at it!"

Raina couldn't help but stare, wide-eyed at whatever the demon was doing to her screaming, pleading mother behind me.

I pushed away the last of the ropes and lifted the tiny girl into my arms, forcing her face against my chest so she couldn't see. "Don't look!"

I closed my eyes tight and put my hands out, searching for something, anything to guide me. All I found was air and so I staggered forward, knocking aside bodies as I shuffled painfully over the floor in search of a wall.

Behind me, Laura's screaming ceased to be any human sound, devolving into the terrified screeches and cries of a wounded animal being devoured alive. There was the sound of claws ripping apart meat. Wet squelching sounds followed, accompanied by the unmistakable snapping of bones.

I held Raina's face against my chest with one hand and reached into the nothing with the other, a desperate prayer on my lips. Lord, deliver us from evil! If not me, then her. The girl's done nothing wrong. She deserves the chance to live. Take my life if you must, but let the girl live!

My palm pressed against the smooth surface of wood, and I knew I'd found the stairs. I dared to open my eyes. All that was left of Laura was her beautiful, pale face. Empty eyes stared at me as her head and exposed spine slid across the floor into the hungry hands of the blood demon. The rest of her was splattered in strings and chunks all over the floor. A fire had sparked somehow, and the flames were busy devouring her bloody robes.

"Help me!" Senator Hemlock gripped the bars of his cage and rattled them as the fire crept nearer. "For God's sake, help me!"

I looked down at Raina, who was trembling in my arms. If I went back for him, I would have to put her down. She wouldn't be able to get out on her own, not in the state she was in. To even get to him, I'd have to somehow make it past the rampaging demon and walk through fire.

I swallowed and shook my head, turning away. "I'm sorry. I can't."

"Help me!" He reached through the bars.

The movement only served to draw the demon's attention. It gave up chewing on Laura's bones and whipped out a new set of tentacles to grab him from his cage. Senator Hemlock screamed and pulled his arms free, but the flesh and muscle from the forearm down stayed in the blood demon's grasp. He lifted the naked bones of his hands and arms, screaming in horror. The demon thrust the wads of bloody skin into its mouth and reached again for the senator, dragging him toward the cage bars. It didn't seem to understand that a human couldn't break apart and fit through the bars. Or maybe it didn't care. Either way, it wasn't going to stop until it had dragged him out of there piece by piece.

Flames licked at my heels, prompting me to run the rest of the way up the stairs. I found the trap door and shifted Raina over my shoulder to push it open. I had to put her down because I wasn't strong enough to climb up the ladder with her. My back was screaming in pain.

Raina let out several panicked gasps and tried to claw her way back onto my shoulder. "No, no, no!"

I grabbed her by the shoulders and shook her. "Raina! You have to climb the ladder!"

"I can't! I *can't!*" She sniffled and wiped tears from her eyes with the back of her hand.

The floor was getting warm. Smoke poured into the small space, thick and foul. Soon, we'd burn up with everything below us if we didn't get the hell out of that house. I didn't know what else to do to get through to her so I shook her again. "Do you want to die, Raina?"

She sniffled and coughed. "No."

"Then get your ass up that ladder or I swear I'm leaving you here to die!"

Raina blinked at me as if she weren't sure at first. Then she slowly turned and gripped the ladder. She went up slowly, like an inferno wasn't about to burn through the floor and feed us to an unhappy demon.

I pushed her the last few inches and climbed as fast as I could, pulling the trap door closed behind me. It wouldn't slow the spread of the fire much, but even a few seconds might buy us long enough to get out of there.

Walking out of the closet and into the hallway was a shock. After days or hours of torture, suddenly being surrounded by finery was almost too much to handle. We wandered through the hall, both of us seemingly lost, though we must've known our way around. When we came to the small closet by the front door, I yanked it open and pulled several coats and hats down from where they hung. Raina slipped on a worn pair of her mother's heels we found at the back of the closet and I found a mismatched pair of rain boots that weren't too small. One of Laura's coats had a pair of woolen gloves. I pulled them on.

The whole house had flooded with smoke by then, setting off the fire alarms. I wrapped a gloved hand around Raina's and we left Hemlock House.

It was dark outside, but edging toward dawn. Having been underground for so long, I didn't know what day it was, but the air was warmer than before. It smelled less of death and decay and more like flowers waking from their buds.

As usual, no cars waited in the driveway. The Hemlock family's limo would be parked over at Jacob's house. It was probably the closest transportation, but I couldn't bring myself to trek through the woods to fetch it. Getting to the neighbors' house on foot was preferable.

We stumbled down the stairs and out onto the circular driveway where Raina pulled away from my grasp.

"Raina," I said. "We have to go."

The fire had finally escaped the basement and crawled into the main house. I could see it dancing in the windows. Soon, the whole house would be aflame and someone would see it. They'd call the fire department. Once authorities got involved, there would be a lot of explaining to do. Explaining I didn't want to be around for.

"No," she said, finally calm again. She crossed her arms and turned around. "I want to watch."

I'd like to say I understood why she wanted to watch her family home burn down. That I knew how she must feel, betrayed by the people who were supposed to love and protect her, but I didn't. I'd been lucky enough to grow up with parents that loved me, even when it was difficult. I couldn't imagine the pain Raina must've been in the moment she realized her mother sold her into torture for her profit. Whatever pain I felt in my hands, feet, and the cut in my side, it was nothing compared to what she'd felt. I could stand in the dawn firelight of her burning home for that.

And so, we stood together but apart, Raina and I, each in our separate worlds of pain and regret with all the world stretched out before us. Ash fell like snow, and in it, a child was born again, free from the tyranny of her mother.

CHAPTER TWENTY-EIGHT

We walked nearly two miles to the nearest neighbor's house. The elderly lady who answered the door nearly fainted at the sight of two naked and blood-soaked strangers. She called the police. Afterward, I called Bishop X.

The bishop showed up first. Surprising, since I thought I'd left him in Chicago. He came with a whole motorcade of people, including a sweet little lady who put Raina in a warm robe and ushered her into one of the cars with the promise of taking care of her.

"What's going to happen to her?" I asked, nodding to Raina.

Bishop X offered me a cigarette, then struck a lighter for me. "She'll need a lot of counseling, I expect."

I leaned the cigarette into the flame and puffed until it was alight. That first rush of nicotine tickled the inside of my chest, forcing my heart to skip a beat. I exhaled relief. "Girl like that doesn't belong in a world like this, X. She might look like she's in her twenties, but she's still just a kid. Someone'll have to take care of her."

"I agree." X nodded and folded his arms over his bulky chest. "I sent someone to the house. It's still burning, you know. Or what's left of it. Mostly, the Hemlock mansion is just a smoldering hole in the Earth."

I frowned and thought of Jacob. What he'd done to me was wrong, but he'd done it for a good reason. He was a family man, thinking of his kids. I couldn't blame him, and I certainly didn't want him dead. "What about survivors? Anyone?"

X shrugged. "No survivors. Not even any bodies. They tell me the senator and his wife are missing. Should I even ask?"

I pulled the cigarette from between my lips, pausing as my gaze lingered on the bloody gauze wrapped around my hand. "She traded Raina to Belial, X. Payment for her husband winning his stupid election. Fucking politics." My fingers shook as I took a long drag. I forced them to stop by making a fist. "I pulled the demon out and the bitch tried to put it back in because his poll numbers were shit."

"Then you'll love this." He reached into the car to fetch a folded newspaper.

I took it, unfolded it, and almost threw up when I saw the senator's approval rating was suddenly through the roof. I was glad I'd left him down in that cage. Maybe he didn't sacrifice his daughter, but he'd benefited from it. At some point, he must've suspected something was wrong, and he chose to do nothing. That made him complicit.

I wadded up the newspaper and threw it back into the car. "Fucking politics. I don't know why I'm surprised."

A white truck with the state wildlife enforcement agency emblem on the side slowed on the road, coming from the direction of the Hemlock house. It pulled into the neighbor's driveway. Gravel crunched loudly under the tires and the brakes squealed slightly as it pulled to a stop. The driver's side door opened and a man in a green police uniform climbed out.

"Fish and Wildlife is here?" I looked to X for an explanation.

He adjusted his jacket. "This should be good." With a raised voice and a forced smile, he approached the officer and extended his hand. "Hello, there. I'm Bishop Xavier. This is my associate, Mr. Cross."

"Officer Galloway," grunted the other man, taking X's hand. He just nodded to me. "Mr. Cross."

I nodded back. In the time it'd taken him to show up, X had been kind enough to give me wipes to clean the blood off, and I'd donned some cheap but respectable clothing. Unless the officer did a strip search, he wouldn't find much amiss just by looking at me.

Officer Galloway tucked his thumbs into his gun belt. "I just heard over the scanner there was a disturbance out here and thought I'd respond since I was in the area."

The front door of the little old lady's cottage opened. She waved a hand. "My mistake, Officer. These nice young men surprised me is all. I wasn't expecting visitors and well…out here in the middle of nowhere, living by myself? You never know."

He wrinkled his nose and grunted, skeptical, before turning back to us. "You fellas mind if I ask what you're doing out here?"

"Outreach and mission work," X replied and adjusted his white collar to draw attention to it.

"God's work," I added, not without a note of sarcasm. I gestured to the cloud of black smoke in the sky. "Say, you know anything about what's happening down the road?"

X shot me a warning glare. He would've elbowed me were he standing closer.

Officer Galloway removed his hat and ran a hand over his bald spot. "Senator Hemlock's estate is down that-a-way. Burned to the ground, they said. 'Course, I'm not involved in that. I didn't get called down here cause of that. I was further down the road a ways, responding to a call about a cougar in the area. You believe it? A cougar all the way down here? Haven't been any cougars spotted this far south in thirty years."

My heart slowed almost to a stop. I pinched the cigarette and held it away from my face. "A cougar you said? Just one?"

"Here. Have a look." He gestured for us to come with him.

I followed him to the bed of the truck where he pulled back a blue tarp, revealing the still body of an adult male mountain lion, a single bloody hole in the big cat's skull. But not just any mountain lion. This one was a replica of one of the lions that had been chasing me through the woods, I was sure of it. I turned away. It was all I could do to put my hand over my mouth to keep from being sick.

"Yeah, big fella." Galloway put his hands on his hips and thrust out his chest. The bastard was proud of what he'd done. "He came charging at me. I had no choice put to put him down."

I finally managed to collect myself enough to speak.

"What about the others?"

"Others?" He shook his head. "No other cougars in the area that I'm aware of. It's not uncommon, or so dispatch tells me. Males get pushed out of their territory by deforestation. Housing developments and such. They go a-wandering. Boone National Forest is prime territory. They just don't normally come down this way. He probably didn't know me from a deer. To him, I was just food, and he looked awful hungry. Guess that's the real horror of the situation, ain't it? It's not his fault, but the poor bastard still had to die. The only thing he was guilty of was being in the wrong place at the wrong time." He stared at the dead mountain lion for a moment before grabbing the tarp and pulling it back over the bed of the truck. "Welp, I better get his body up the road to the crematorium. You folks be safe now." He tugged his hat down, climbed back into his truck, and left.

I watched the white truck amble down the gravel driveway, a cloud of dust in its wake. The dead mountain lion was Jacob. I knew it as sure as I knew I was alive, and yet…I hoped it wasn't. I hoped killing Laura had lifted his curse, and he was far gone from this place with his wife and kids.

"Is there something you're not telling me, Felix?" X asked. "You seemed rather stunned to see that big cat."

"Nothing," I lied and tapped the ash from the end of my cigarette.

"What about Mr. Yeats?" X asked.

I shook my head. "Dead end. The girl had never actually been to Hell."

"Then where was she for fifteen years?"

That was the one lingering question, wasn't it? If Raina hadn't gone to Hell, then I had to believe what she'd said under hypnosis. "While under hypnosis, Raina described a facility where she was taken and held in a cell. Apparently, she was tortured. She claimed the torture was supposed to make the demon inside of her surface. It left her with the power of clairvoyance, X. She can see shit before it happens. Paints it too. Wickedly accurate."

He raised an eyebrow and eyed me askance. "Do you think there's any truth to it?"

I choked on the next mouthful of smoke. "You mean do I think there's some incredibly powerful organization out there that's kidnapping the possessed and torturing them to give them psychic powers?" I shrugged. "After what I just saw, it's tough to say I don't believe in anything."

"You should listen to the girl," said Sean on the other side of me. "She's got no reason to lie."

"She didn't lie about anything else," I agreed. "But she's just a kid. Maybe she's confused."

"Under hypnosis?"

I grunted. "Good point."

X glanced up and down the driveway. "Felix? Are you feeling all right?"

I looked at him, tilted my head back, and laughed. All right? Who the fuck would be all right after what I'd just gone through? In the last ten years, I must've had thousands of encounters with demons and the possessed, but none even came close to the evil I had just escaped. I still wasn't sure which evil it was I was referring to whenever I thought that. Did I mean the wealthy senator's wife who had tried to seduce me to help her sell her daughter to a demon? Or the demon himself? There just weren't words for how messed up the situation had been.

And yet we'd lived. Raina and I had survived and walked away, even if we were both irrevocably changed by the encounter. She'd been left without a family. I was left without a hiding place. No longer could I crawl into myself and ignore what I knew to be true: evil was all around us, invading the lives of the innocent. I had the power to stop it. Not just the power, but the responsibility. Call it a gift, call it a curse, call it whatever I liked. It was there and it wasn't going away anytime soon. Hell knew my name. That had to mean something.

I had wasted the last ten years of my life chasing shadows. No doorway to Hell would allow me to walk through and collect Sean. Even if there was, the soul I brought back wouldn't be the sweet and innocent soul I had known before. Sean Yeats, the seminary student full of faith and fire, was gone. Dead, even if his soul and body disagreed. I would never get him back either.

"Then who am I?" asked Sean's phantom next to me.

"A figment," I replied. "A piece of madness left over from when I wasn't myself. A fiction I tell myself so I don't have to admit it's my fault you're gone."

Bishop X frowned and gripped my shoulder tightly. "I think you could do with some rest."

"I'd settle for a steak dinner," I mumbled.

As he led me toward the SUV, I cast a glance over my shoulder to where Sean had been standing, but he was gone, like always.

Though he was gone, there was still a part of me that wanted to believe some piece of him was out there still, watching over me as only Sean could.

CHAPTER TWENTY-NINE

SEAN

"Wake up, sunshine!"

Ice cold water splashed me in the face. I gasped awake only to choke on it as it followed into my mouth and nose. My head throbbed and my feet were still numb. I was still upside down. My shoulders ached from carrying the weight of my entire body and being stretched to their limit out to either side. I found the strength to turn my head and cough, spitting out the filthy water.

Someone ripped the blindfold away from my eyes and shined a stinging light at me. I closed my eyes against the pain of the light, but that didn't help. They just pried my eyelids open.

I fought the pain to stare at the grunt with his fingers all over me. He wore the fatigues of a soldier, but even at my lowest, I couldn't believe the people doing this to me were really who they seemed to be. If I did, I might lose my grip on reality and all faith in humanity.

"Any change?"

"No, sir." The grunt stepped aside.

The face that hovered close next was one I knew well and had known since long before I came to the facility. He had a grandfatherly look about him, the sort of face that belonged to an old man average people trusted. Glasses, silver hair...anyone passing him on the street would look him over and never consider him a threat. They'd see the little square of white about his collar, smile, and nod. A priest was a good man, a Godly man, deserving of respect, even among atheists.

They'd all be wrong. Father Leon was the most dangerous person they'd ever meet.

He smiled at me, a deceptively warm smile. "What about you? How are you today, Sean?"

I clenched my teeth and tried to suppress a shiver. The water had suddenly reminded me how cold it was in the facility. Of course, my definition of cold had changed several times since they brought me here, shifting ever lower.

What the facility was, I didn't know, or where, only that it was there and I was in it. Every room in the facility held a new and inventive way to cause pain or misery without the hope of death. The facility had a whole staff of expert doctors, trauma nurses, and surgeons on staff day and night to keep their prisoners alive. There was no escape from the facility, not even in death.

I thought of all manner of awful things to say to Father Leon. I had trusted him, believed in him, followed all of his advice when he was my advisor at seminary. He was the one I had called and confided in when Felix was facing possession. And yet he had betrayed me, betrayed us all. That wasn't the crux of my grievance against Father Leon, however. He had betrayed God and showed no remorse.

His bushy eyebrows rose. "Nothing to say today? Well, then maybe your Lord of the Flies has something more interesting to share. Let's talk to him now, shall we?" He gestured to someone I couldn't see standing off in the darkness.

I closed my eyes. "Our Father, who art in Heaven, hallowed be thy name…"

They spun the cross and all the blood rushed too fast from my head to my feet. I gagged on bile. There was nothing else to vomit. Ropes tightened around my wrists and ankles. My breathing quickened. I couldn't help it. Though I knew what was coming, I was still human enough to feel fear and pain. "Thy kingdom come…"

"Gag him," Leon instructed.

They slipped the same strip of cloth that had been over my eyes into my mouth and shoved it to the back of my tongue. Still, I continued my recitation of the Lord's prayer. It was our ritual. They would pull my arms and legs until they almost came away from my body. They'd cut pieces of me off, poke holes into parts of me that should never have holes. They'd hold matches to the soles of my feet, to my eyes, to the palms of my hands, hoping to break me.

And I would pray.

"Don't take it personally." Father Leon ran his knuckles over the side of my face almost tenderly. "This isn't about you. You know that, don't you? Just tell your demon to cooperate. Demonstrate for us the awesome powers he's gifted you, and we will make this all stop."

Inside, the demon that's been hiding there for years

uncurled and stretched. Soon, it will be his turn to play their game. He was better at it than me. He liked the pain, liked how broken he thought it made me. Even he didn't understand the truth.

Ten years in some underground facility, tortured, possessed, fed only stagnant water and moldy food…they had hurt me. They'd made my body sick and scarred me, body and soul. In time, they had stripped everything from me. My sanity, my dignity, my freedom, and maybe even my life. The one thing they'd never take from me was my faith.

Just as the ropes began to pull tight, a new door opened and light flooded the dim chamber. I flinched away from it.

"Father Leon?" The male voice was uncertain.

"This had better be good," Leon snapped. "What is it?"

"This just came for you on a coded channel." He held out a phone.

Leon took the phone and glanced over it, his pale face blanching an extra shade. He tugged on his collar and swallowed. "My God. He's done it. The crazy bastard survived it."

"Sir?" asked the grunt. "Who?"

He lowered the phone. His lip twitched as he looked at me. "Felix fucking Cross, that's who."

For the first time in years, my heart jumped, and not because of particularly gruesome torture. Felix was alive, and he was out there, on their radar. Did I dare hope he was looking for me? Maybe even working to find this place and shut it down?

He shoved the phone back at the messenger. "It would seem we have a mole in our operation, gentlemen. Very well. He wants a war, we'll give it to him. Gentlemen, it's finally time to move to phase three. Pull him down and get him cleaned up. And for God's sake, somebody get me Bishop Xavier on the phone! If anyone knows how to deal with Felix, it'll be him."

They untied my wrists and ankles. New pain flooded into the previously numb appendages, but I didn't care. Felix was alive, and they were worried he was coming for them.

I lowered my head in thanks. *Thy will be done…Amen.*

AUTHOR NOTES

It's pretty wild how a book's concept can change from start to finish. When I first thought up the title and plot of *Shadows over Hemlock*, it was about a haunted house outside a secluded mining town. The big bad of the story was supposed to be the spirit of a witch that inhabited a tree. Yes, Felix was supposed to face off against a possessed tree at the end.

And then Coronavirus happened, we all got quarantined, and I sat down to watch *Tiger King*.

If you've seen this Netflix documentary series—one that only could've gained popularity in a year like 2020—then you'll probably see where I'm going with this. An evil tree is cool and all, but what about a truly evil cat lady? It began as a joke and then grew into Laura Hemlock. The whole book's concept changed as I began to realize my tree antagonist just wasn't the story I wanted to tell.

Even as the story unfolded during writing, it wasn't immediately clear to me how personal this book would turn out to be.

Horror first began to resonate with me when I saw the 1976 adaptation of Stephen King's *Carrie*. I grew up in a restrictively religious environment. My mother wasn't as awful as Carrie's mother was to her, and thankfully I had more friends than Carrie (and no psychic powers), but I saw myself in the title character. I felt her rage at being picked on for not knowing what all the other girls knew. I understood her fear, confusion, and anxiety around sexual maturity. I knew Carrie because she was like me in a lot of ways, and did what I could only dream of. She destroyed the school bullies and her abusive mother. For me, Carrie is as empowering as she is terrifying.

While I was writing this, my abusive adoptive mother made several attempts to reach out to me. As the days marched on, and I was faced with Mother's Day and the anniversary of my birth mother's death, as well as my abusive adoptive mother's unwanted contact, I was in a very dark place. Some of those feelings were written into this book.

This book has been therapy for me in a way. It's also a love letter to the books and classic movies I love like *The Exorcist* and *Carrie*. There are demons in this book, but the true evil isn't the supernatural. It's the familial. And, of course, there's a bit of *Tiger King* in there too because it's impossible not to be influenced by the media we consume.

Maybe one day I'll write the book about the evil tree. I'd still love to. But this story—the story of a mother, her daughter, and the man of God between them—is the one I had to tell first. It was my story. Now that it's written down, the fears and worries that gave me nightmares and left me tortured in my own way are dead and gone. Like Raina, I've realized I don't have to dwell in the house my mother built. I am my own person, free and alive and living every day the best I can.

If the horror genre is about one thing, it's about hope, specifically the hope that we can overcome impossible odds and survive terrible things. Maybe that's why so many people are drawn to scary movies, books, and media. We see ourselves in the monsters sometimes, yes, but also in those who survive.

Felix is nothing if not a survivor. His adventure is just getting started though. We're going to grapple with mental illness, divided family, discrimination, and more in the coming books. Oh, and probably the Illuminati or something like it because it wouldn't be an E.A. Copen book series without a larger conspiracy, right?

Anyway, I hope this book was a valuable distraction to you when you needed it most.

Please wear your masks, wash your hands, and we'll get through this together.

Until next time, dear reader!

BOOKS IN THIS SERIES

Shadows over Hemlock
Whispers in the Walls
Blood of the Lamb

OTHER BOOKS BY THIS AUTHOR

The Hellbent Halo series
Fractured Souls
Smoke and Mirrors
Devil's Due
Flesh and Blood
Hell to Pay

The Lazarus Codex
Death Rites
Organ Grind
Shallow Grave
Knight Shift
Death Match
Death's Door
Night Terror
Dark Revel
Dark Horse
Casting Shadows
Lost Soul
Until Death

The Silver Bullet Chronicles
Cold Spell
Fool's Gold

Other Books
Beasts of Babylon
Broken Empire: Aftermath
Parallel Worlds: The Heroes Within (anthology)

ABOUT THE AUTHOR

E.A. Copen is a coffee addict living in southern Kentucky with her cats and books. When she's not writing, she enjoys cooking and watching just about everything but romantic comedies (unless there are zombies in them).

She's been a film school dropout, a professional puppeteer, and retail rebel, all of which allowed her to develop a cynical sense of humor. She is also an unapologetic nerd and occasional enjoyer of comic books and anime.

She is a prolific writer of inclusive, action-oriented urban fantasy, horror, and science fiction with several Amazon bestselling novels.